David Prete is a writer, actor, director, teacher and native New
Yorker. His critically-acclaimed first book, *Say That to My
Face*, was published in 2003.  His writing has appeared
in *Narrative*, *Ground* and *People's Stories*. He currently
lives in Chicago and is subject to MFA Directing program at
Northwestern.

Also by David Prete

Say That to My Face

DAVID PRETE

August and then some

FOURTH ESTATE • *London*

First published in Great Britain in 2011 by
Fourth Estate
An imprint of HarperCollins*Publishers*
77–85 Fulham Palace Road
London W6 8JB
www.4thestate.co.uk

Visit our authors' blog: www.fifthestate.co.uk

1

Lines from 'The Waste Land' by T.S. Eliot reproduced with permission of Faber and Faber Ltd

A CIP catalogue record for this book is available from the British Library

ISBN 978-0-00-718300-5

Set in Sabon by Palimpsest Book Production Limited, Falkirk, Stirlingshire
Printed in Great Britain by
Clays Ltd, St Ives plc

Mixed Sources
Product group from well-managed
forests and other controlled sources
www.fsc.org Cert no. SW-COC-001806
© 1996 Forest Stewardship Council

FSC is a non-profit international organisation established to promote the responsible
management of the world's forests. Products carrying the FSC label are independently
certified to assure consumers that they come from forests that are managed to meet
the social, economic and ecological needs of present and future generations.

Find out more about HarperCollins and the environment at
www.harpercollins.co.uk/green

Datta: What have we given?
My friend, blood shaking my heart
The awful daring of a moment's surrender
Which an age of prudence can never retract
By this, and this only, we have existed

T. S. Eliot

Vengeance and hate, well, they're both very bad emotions.

Kurt Vonnegut

June 28

Jake Terri Savage is awkward, I know. Mostly they call me JT—
skips off the tongue right. No one calls me Terri. That was my
grandmother. But right now an old lady's name fits me because
I'm hurtin like one. Even with this dolly there's no easy way to
lug an eighty-pound slab of slate down seventy blocks. I feel like
a father lifting his deadweight kid out of bed, and with every step
the kid's insistence to sleep gets heavier. I got a system though. I
hold the slate between my palms, balance it on the dolly, and take
short steps until it starts falling to one side and the dolly kicks
out. Then I stop, straighten it out, and start from scratch. That's
it—that's the whole system. But hey, it's getting me through the
rush hour hoard of Upper East Side commuter motherfuckers.
And even though this thing has the weight of an unearthed
tombstone, I should make it to the East Village before dusk.

But this summer heat, man. After eight hours of working
outside I'm glazed in the kind of New York summer sweat an
air-conditioned store would turn to rock candy. I've been on a
demolition job the past month breaking up an old lady's Upper
East Side patio. They would have hauled this piece away with
the rest of the broken slate and concrete, but I swiped it for

1

free furniture. Chipped edges aside, all four feet by four feet of it held up under construction. I got milk crates (whose misuse can lead to my prosecution) waiting on the floor of my studio. I'll lay this on top and voilà: table. What my fine home decor lacks in price it makes up for in weight. I'm not gonna say this for the entire seventy blocks, but this thing is a pain in the dick to maneuver.

At 68th and Lex near Hunter College, summer students line up at a smoking halal meat truck for curried shish kebab. Flies zigzag around the garbage next to them casing grease-stained paper plates. Across the street, suits, slackers, and in-betweens file down the stairs of 6 Train entrance. They squint at the five-thirty something sun until they dip below the sun line into the station's darkness, and their faces relax. Nobody, not even a fly, notices the gloveless guy rolling a huge chunk of slate down the street. But hey, invisible works for this cat. Shit—I can't clench my hands. My fingers feel sculpted to this slate. I guess I could make it down those stairs without this stone slipping away from me and landing on an innocent New Yorker. But fuck it. I'm walking. For possibly twisted reasons, wheeling this thing home is now a quest.

What sucks about the city are things like this neon sign on 64th Street blinking about shoe repair. They come at me too fast to defend, and instead of 'gum up your sole' my head sees the dashboard in Nokey's '91 Volkswagen GTI—the burnt red glow of his dashboard. My sister in the back seat. I whiplash my head away from the neon sign to find a nice ass or something better.

Lex and 42nd, Grand Central. My shoulders and back burn, and thousands of people loop from their suburban homes, to their city jobs, from their city jobs to their suburban homes, a daily cycle that equals some of their life. I wonder what ordinary feels like. Or if it's real.

In a coffee shop on 23rd and 2nd a woman looks out the window. I stop. Balance my slate on the dolly. She lifts a cup to her expressionless face, too deep in her head to notice me or the passing crowd, and stares through us like we're water. Seems she's picking through thoughts she's yet to share over a table of friends and martinis. Thoughts she's afraid will make her sound desperate or just weird. My sister Danielle's face imposes itself over hers. Slit-like eyes seemingly impossible to see out of, pouty lips, and a potent sadness pinning down her smile. But these moments have the life expectancy of a flame in a bottle. Someone bumps this woman's chair and startles her out of her head. She smiles at their apology then turns away. Now she sneaks a look around to see if anyone noticed the haze she was in. No. She's safe. She fondles the button on her cuff, checks her watch, and takes another sip.

In Tompkins Square Park guys in billowy white clothes and dreads to their waists sit under the shade of trees in a drum circle, their bongos and djembes echoing through the whole park. You can't help but feel like your legs are moving to their rhythm when you walk by. Next to them some guys practice Capoeira and make it look more like a dance than martial art. In a fenced-off area dogs headlock each other, and skid out on pee-soaked wood chips. A few NYU or FIT students sit on the ground balancing sketchpads on their knees trying to do the trees justice with charcoal and newsprint. On the north side guys play street hockey. In the playground little kids with sagging bathing suits run around under sprinklers. The last mustard sun rays of the day give everything more meaning and take away my ability to grasp it.

Me and my slate leave the park on Avenue B and turn down 9th Street. The only lot without a building is the community garden next to my apartment, which looks as woefully out of place as a shiny piano in a junkyard. I get a few doors down from my stoop and hear, "Don't be calling me bitch. You think you my father?"

"How could I be your father, my shit ain't in jail?"

These two. The lonely looking girl and the hybrid geek/thug boyfriend. I've seen them around the building, sitting on the stoop, her hands between his knees, smoking on the fire escape, his hand up the back of her shirt.

He goes, "You actin like I'm trying to make bank off you. I'm askin for like a couple dollars. Damn." He lowers his voice. "You know your uncle got it."

"No he don't."

He wears a tank under a Sammy Sosa Cubs jersey open so you can see the thick chains around his neck. "Ah-ight, forget it then. I ain't asking you for nothin no more, ah-ight?"

"See why you gotta be actin like I don't do shit for you?" she says.

"You don't."

"I sleep at your place when you want me to and I don't when you don't want me to." He shrugs with no retort. "I got no money. You hearin me? No cuartos, papi."

One time I saw her throw her sneaker off the third-floor fire escape and nail him right in the chest. He picked it up and started walking off. She climbed back in her window and a few seconds later busted through the front door and chased him down the block—not like he was running. She yanked the back of his sweatshirt then he flipped around and lifted all of maybe ninety pounds of her by her waist onto the hood of a parked car. She

4

pounded on his shoulders with half-clenched fists until he grabbed them. Then she stared into him like the only thing that would calm her down was locked in his mouth, and he opened it for her.

Now he says, "I'm outta here. Like that I'm outta here." He spreads his arms, raises his shoulders and backpedals. "You watching me go? Cause I'm going."

She's like, "Uh huh, uh huh."

"Ah-ight," he says as a final warning. "I'm out."

He passes by me. "Fuck you lookin at?"

"I live here."

"Then go live." He keeps walking.

She yells, "It's like that?" as more a threat than a question. "It's like that?" He doesn't stop. "Ah-ight go head. Go head." And with every *go head* she seems to be asking him to come back. Until he's around the corner and she stops yelling for him.

Now it's just me, her, and my table. She sits on the steps to our apartment trying to shrink away from the scene she just caused: head almost between her legs, arms crossed at her stomach. I stand on the sidewalk making like I didn't really hear anything and when it feels time I push my table over to the stoop, and lift it off the dolly that I kick near the garbage cans. I heave the slate up a stair at a time. She doesn't move. When I get close enough I feel a sadness coming off her like heat. It's wrapped its hands around her neck and pulls her whole body down toward the stoop. I ask her if she's OK.

She takes her time deciding to answer me. Without lifting her head or eyes, she says, "You ever get tired?" I would not have put money on hearing that line.

I say, "It's pretty much how I go through life."

"That's how I am. Fuckin tired." She's dropping most of the tough girl act she laid on her boyfriend; her melancholy now seeps through the cracks in her voice.

I lean the slate against the door, wipe a chalky hand on the thigh of my pants, then once across my chest. I hold it out above her head. She sees it coming out the corner of her eye and doesn't flinch, so I lower it the rest of the way. Her hair is slicked back in an off-center part that breaks her head into two uneven sections. The surface is shiny black, and hard like plastic. When I touch her her eyelids beat fast time for a second then close. She drops her head further, tightens her arms around her stomach, and presses her knees together like she's trying to suffocate something. I run my palm back to her ponytail then let go. I grab my table again and ask if she'll be all right.

She makes a hissing sound through the corner of her lips telling me I'm stupid for thinking she'll be otherwise.

I tell her I'll see her around and lift my slate.

"What you doin with that thing?" she says, still looking down at the stoop.

At risk of cutting our strange connection short I say, "Long story."

"Ah-ight," she tells me, accepting that as the entire answer.

"I'm JT."

"Wus up."

That's all we offer each other.

She keeps looking at the steps, I keep looking at the top of her head.

"Who are you?"

"Stephanie."

I nod. "By the way, the Cubs suck."

She forces a laugh through her nose.

I lift the keys from my pocket, balance the slab with one hand, and unlock the door with the other. I slide into the lobby as the door slams behind me and wipes out the last moment of this scrunched-up girl.

6

Now I got five flights above me. This might be the hard part. First floor I go step by step: eighty pounds, eighty pounds, and eighty pounds to the top. In the second floor hall I hear a woman in her apartment talking to her dogs like they can hold a conversation in perfect English. "No, Jasper. I don't know why he hung up on her. Why can't you let the show happen in its own time? Look at your sister, she's not making a racket. I'm not trying to compare you to her, but she knows how to behave." I wonder if her dogs understand the concept of borderline personalities.

I look up the third-floor staircase, testosterone myself up, lift the slate maybe a foot off the ground, and run up about ten, twelve stairs without stopping. I crash it on the top step and my momentum tips it over. It smacks against the wall and echoes through the entire building. I should probably go back to the one-step-at-a-time method.

Ralphie, the super—and the guy Stephanie lives with who I'm pretty sure is her uncle—opens his door to see what's up. "What you do?"

"Sorry Ralphie, I'm just getting this to my apartment."

"Whas dat?"

"It's, uh . . . it's gonna be a table?"

He squints in confusion. "Ah ha." Ralphie's all of five-foot nothing, but muscularly compact, energetic, with eyes as playful and vicious as a terrier's. He shoots Spanish/English blend out of his mouth like a Chinese waiter yelling short orders to a cook. He's the reason I even have this apartment.

It went like this: I moved down to Manhattan from Yonkers—more like trickled down here intending to be homeless. I'd just got the job working for the landscaping company by using a fake address—easy enough since they don't mail our checks, we pick them up at the office. I'd been sleeping in Tompkins Square Park, showering after work with the hose behind the company's office. I wasn't in the best of shape, but at least

I wasn't shooting heroin. So, one night, mid-autumn, this guy I knew from the park—nineteen, from Philly, discs in his earlobes, we used to shave each other's heads—was walking with this other guy who was nodding out on his own feet. The Philly guy was telling him to fight through it, to use his will, but the guy's will gave out and he collapsed. Philly called me over and asked if I would help carry the guy to the hospital. After a few blocks of hauling the guy I realized I smelled as much like a dog run as both of them, and that I had zero desire to someday be the one getting carried to a hospital. I helped Philly get the guy close enough to the emergency room door then let him do the rest. On my walk back to the park I thought, *winter's coming, my hair looks like shit, I own two shirts—this whole thing isn't really me.* So I started looking for a place to live. One day after combing the streets for *for rent* signs I wound up resting on Ralphie's stoop. I jumped when he opened the door behind me with a broom in his hand. "You no sit here," he said. I got up and apologized. He started sweeping.

"You don't have any apartments in there, do you?"

"No," he said. "We got nothing here."

"I have a job," I said, in case that was the issue.

"Good," was all he said.

"I don't have a place to stay yet, you know? I just moved here, you know?"

"I know."

"So I'm looking, if you know anything."

"Where you live before?"

"My parents."

He nodded his head and kept sweeping.

"I used to be an auto mechanic. So maybe, you know, I could help you out around the apartment."

"Nobody has cars." Which made a lot of sense.

"But now I'm a landscaper."

That one we both laughed at, realizing there were as many shrubs around the building as there were cars.

Because he took in Stephanie who was probably living in some shit family situation, because desperation was probably shooting out of my voice in every direction, and because Ralphie is a good guy, he decided to tell me an apartment was opening up soon.

". . . this guy, he miss his rent for seven times. He leave here this month. You go down to the office, and fill the application. The guys: you tell them you know Ralphie. And then you see."

"That would be so great. Where's the office?"

Turns out that deadbeat's lease wasn't up for another year-and-change, and they didn't have plans to renovate. So between the letter from my boss, Frank—who I fuckin love for being cool enough to say I made a lot more money than I actually did—and Ralphie's recommendation, I got in.

I think Ralphie likes me; he sees me leave for work every morning and knows I wasn't lying about the job, but I understand why he's keeping an eye on me. I'm still a shaved-headed wildcard kid who dresses like a derelict.

Now he watches me closely as I lift the slate from the wall and stand it upright. It starts to fall toward me; I brace it. Ralphie pulls off his baseball cap, which has probably been on his head for a decade now, and with his palm, smoothes back his already matted gray hair.

"You need help?"

"No, it's OK, I got it."

Two little kids pop their heads out of the door behind him. A girl with her finger in her mouth and a miniature boy version of Ralphie, hat and all. All three of them watch as I pick up the slate and lay it on my foot. In unison they all cringe.

"You want no help?" Ralphie asks again.

"No, I'm good."

"You loco, you know? Crazy."

"Yeah, I'm starting to see the full-sized picture."

"Be careful, OK? Don't hurt nothing."

"I won't."

He turns to the kids, "Ivamos." They scurry back inside.

My studio is part of a railroad apartment that was broken into smaller spaces. It has exposed brick on one wall, and a curtain— not a door—separating the bathroom from the rest. I get a laugh out of the wood floors. Lay a marble anywhere and in ten seconds it rolls to the south-east corner. There's more paint on this radiator than there was in my mother's Yonkers apartment. So many coats on the walls I think the place has lost a few square feet since it was built. A futon lies against the side wall. No frame, just a mattress with a sheet that's got little holes worn through it where my toenails rub while I'm on my stomach. Next to the bed are two cardboard boxes. One's got my clothes in it and the other is filled with books and paperwork—things I'm using to get my GED. There's also an alarm clock I never have to use.

All by itself on the floor is a black spiral notebook. I write in it sometimes about things that I'd rather not get started on right now.

The milk crates are waiting for me. I guide the slate down onto them and step back for a better look. It's . . . it's a table. Dark. About a foot off the ground, covering more of the apartment than it felt like it would. I sit on the floor facing it and cross my legs. It's perfect eating height that way. I stand up and look at it like it's supposed to do something.

I'm hungry.

10

Out the front door Stephanie's gone from the stoop. I walk across Tompkins Square Park. Low sunlight stretches tree shadows over benches and heavily pierced and tattooed squatters who set up beds in the grass. With dreads past their shoulders, they huddle behind a cardboard sign that says they need money for their dog, who also has dreads.

I sit on a bench hoping to get tired. I say no to people who ask me if I got a light. Make split-second eye contact with a few dozen people who walk by then watch them go their way. I stay put until streetlights come on, and memories of living here creep back in. My apartment isn't great shakes, but it beats this park, and this park, as a transition to sanctuary, beat the shit out of Yonkers.

A guy and girl who may or may not have another place to sleep tonight walk by me with their arms latched like the safety pins that hold their pants together. I see Nokey putting his hand on my sister. I wonder if he hadn't done that would anything else have even happened. I get off the bench, head to my apartment, and try to leave that thought in the park.

Rain

Yonkers is bookended by two strips of water—the Hudson River and the Bronx River—and if you stay in the middle of the city long enough, which I definitely did, you can actually feel them pulling you from both sides, wanting to take you down south past the boroughs of New York City into the Atlantic. The waters start to feel like tarmac, runways for take-off. And if you give over to the pull, let the river take you, you get a ticket to Europe and beyond. I've seen this done. Somebody's brother or sister from the neighborhood just took off downstream and we never heard from them again. In some places, to gain legend status, all you have to do is leave.

The Hudson River, the bigger of the two, belongs to the downtown crowd. From their apartment windows they see the sun dip behind it, watch cargo ships and sail boats leave wakes in it, and hear trains run parallel to it before it dumps commuters onto their front lawns farther up-county.

The Bronx River, which is two blocks from my dad's house—which until last summer was also my house—belongs to the city's northerners. We rode our bikes on the footpath next to it when we were little and drank beer on its banks when we were a little bigger. Some nights, Nokey and me used to lay down on the damp dirt that lines it, tell stunningly and embarrassingly stupid teenage jokes, and look for faces in the stars. At night if we drank enough beer and the breeze hit just right, the tree branches looked like they were rotating, cutting spirals upward into the dotted sky. So we stayed put, let our backs get muddy wet, and fell into the sky with the help of nature and alcohol.

After a few days of rain the water would get higher, faster, and the ripples louder—I could hear them two blocks and two stories away from inside my dad's house. And let me tell you straight up: that was a tempting sound to hear trying to fall asleep in a house I had every desire to leave.

If you wanna get away from Yonkers by riding the Hudson River it's pretty much a straight run to the Atlantic. But if you're taking the Bronx River you'll have to be a strong swimmer.

You gotta cross the Westchester County line into The Bronx and swim past Hunt's Point and the Bronx Terminal Market, where they plunk the rotten produce in the water. Past that the Bronx River becomes the Harlem or East River where if you catch a stray current you can crash into Riker's Island or get sucked into Flushing Bay and spend the rest of your days lapping at the shore near LaGuardia Airport. But if you drift west a bit, you wind up kissing Manhattan at East Harlem which, like some first kisses, feels smooth, promising and lasts for about ten minutes, then you slide down to Hell Gate somewhere near 96th Street. Clear that and you still might get snagged by Brooklyn's Red Hook, a piece of land that sticks out like a dockworker's tool; it can keep you flapping there like a soggy piece of toilet paper. After the Hook you're at the place where the East and Hudson Rivers become one. There you have to dodge the anchors of the Verrazano Bridge and make sure you don't get thrown into the dead end of Jamaica Bay.

Understand—we didn't swim in the Bronx River. The geese didn't even go for a dip. They only came to shit. Sometimes you couldn't tell if it was a big piece of water with a little shit in it or a big piece of shit with a little water in it. But there was a highlight. About a half mile south of my dad's house the river stretches fifty feet wide, and a wooden footbridge connects the banks. Fifteen feet below the bridge is a waterfall—if we can call it a waterfall. The water crashes from about a foot and a half up. And give me a break, this is Yonkers I'm talking about, not Canada or South America, we run a deficit in the claim-to-fame department, so I'm calling the little shittin thing a falls. Thank you.

In the hot season the sun stayed around longer and the clothes came off quicker. I don't think the girls in the neighborhood knew they'd been helping me mark time by stripping down to their bathing suits. Their bodies differentiated the identical school years. Between sixth and seventh grade Colleen Burke grew boobs and Lanie Raniolo started shaving her legs. Between ninth and tenth grade Katie Ryan's thighs got big and Julie DiMatteo started lifting weights.

Below the footbridge, just past the base of the falls, rocks scatter like grey turtle shells spaced so that someone with long enough legs, like my sister, could step from bank to bank without getting their feet wet. But Dani didn't usually cross the river. Mostly she hopped herself to the middle, sat down and hugged her knees to her chest while the rest of us got drunk and loud, while couples sat with their legs dangled over the side of the bridge, backs to chests. The water split apart at the back of Dani's stone island and came together again at her toes, swirling up a little force field around her.

Dani had been on the swim team since she was small. It was weird looking at her surrounded by all that unswimmable water—like an actor in an empty theater—you'd think she'd have wanted to go in, but she was a quiet kid, you know? And quiet people, it's hard to know what's in their head.

———

We were hanging out on the bridge over the falls—the whole crew of us—we tied our six-packs to the bridge on a rope long enough to reach the river, to keep them cold and out of view. That day on the footbridge, Nokey was scoping Dani's just-turned-thirteen-year-old chest and body that really did look like a woman's. Being my younger sister or being someone Nokey's known since before birth didn't mean she was out of the game.

(Nokey's not his real name, by the way. It's short for Gnocchi, which still isn't his real name. It's Eugene Cervella. But since the third grade, people have been calling him Gnocchi Cervella—in English it roughly translates to Potato Head. He hates the name, but he always acts like he's got something else in his head besides brains, so he can't shake it.)

He went up to my sister and started with: "Listen, Danielle. I don't want to be a rock in your shoe . . ." and followed with a hand on her shoulder.

Whether he's hitting on girls or not, he's always working his hands. They're big and heavy enough to separate at the wrists. His pinky is the only finger thin enough to fit in the neck of a beer bottle, and his nails are too thick to bite through—he has to use a scissor. His hands are smart, and make him a good mechanic. His father only had to show him how a torque wrench worked once like three years ago and it stuck—he never stripped a thread. It's like his fingers memorize things on contact. When we worked at his father's garage together, he'd handle customers and in the prints of his fingers record where and how they could be touched. This practice made repeats

15

out of first-time customers and kept the regulars revolving. Some guys he'd give the one-hand shake with a matching slap on the shoulder. Or the classic two-hand shake, grabbing their entire hand—or just tapping the tips of his fingers on the back of theirs. For the ladies it's a hand on the back when he'd lead her to the office to pay her bill. With the older ladies, he would link his right arm with their left and lay his free hand on their wrist.

He wore his mechanic's coveralls cut off at the shoulders and below the knees, so all the married rich chicks could get a good look at his arms and cobra-tattooed-calf busting through the ragged edges. He was good for his dad's garage business and swears that's why his dad bought him the weight set. And this kid is a great wide receiver; he catches long passes like his palms are made of flypaper. He might even be scholarship worthy if he'd join the friggin football team already, but he has no time for organized anything; he'd rather set records hardly anyone will ever hear about.

Two summers ago he decided to jump in the river from the footbridge, which nobody ever did before because at about fifteen feet high and with no running start it looks like you could never clear the rocks to the water—which is maybe five feet deep on rainy days. Well, he *almost* cleared the rocks. He fucked up his ankle pretty good, bruised his back and got seven stitches on his ass. You would think that might have been a sign, but he didn't see it that way. When the cast came off his ankle and the stitches out his ass, he tried again. This time he didn't do it on a whim. He told people he was gonna do it on a particular day so we could all see him jump off the bridge again and possibly bust his head or slice his butt open. Thankfully, that time, he cleared the rocks. He came out of the river wet wearing only a pair of cut-off denim shorts with not so much as a scratch or a hair out of place. Everyone applauded. See, that's the tricky thing about Nokey—just when you're convinced all he's got in his head are potatoes, he makes you believe he can do anything.

Me, because I've known him so long, I look at him do his thing and it's like watching a third-grader in a teenager's body. I half expect him to call me from the back seat of his GTI after he's just finished with a girl and ask me if I want to go put quarters on the railroad tracks like when we were eight.

For as long I've hung around the cheeky fuck, it's been easy for me to love him. Except that day on the bridge when he said, "Listen, Danielle, I don't want to be a rock in your shoe, but I must say you're looking very cute these days." If he had stopped there, with the lame fuckin line, I might have been cool with it. But the goddamn hand on the shoulder bit. Maybe that's the curse of knowing what someone's capable of. Knowing how skillfully they can disguise their agenda in charm.

Danielle didn't look as bent as I was. She deadpanned him right in his face and said, "I'm not wearing shoes."

Now, from where I was standing, Noke should have backed up—made light out of the rejection. But the fucking guy kept coming.

"Yeah, I can see you're barefoot. *Rock in the shoe* is just an expression. It means a pain in the ass. Like I don't want to be bothering you. Be annoying like, you know, like how having a rock in your shoe would be annoying."

Dani stayed quiet and let his joke sprawl flat on its back. This was flag number two signifying a dead end. But that didn't matter to Nokey Cervella.

He said, "I don't mean a real shoe. I mean a make-believe shoe. A hypothetical shoe."

"I don't have any hypothetical shoes."

17

That may have given me the first laugh of the whole thing if I wasn't feeling so ready to pounce.

He said, "You're not gettin me," and his smart-ass hand ran down her arm and landed on her wrist that was covered with a dozen silver bangles. Dani flinched, and pulled her wrist away. "No, Nokey, you're not getting me."

Finally he was ready to lay off. He held his hand out in front of him like a stop sign and said, "I'm getting another beer now." He turned around and walked to where I was standing, grabbed the rope and lifted the six-pack from the water. "What the fuck?" he said. "Was I not being nice? I thought I was being nice. JT, what was I being?"

And Dani, who had been standing still watching him the whole time, finally climbed down beneath the bridge, hopped to her favorite rock and sat down.

Noke goes, "That's a weird chick, man. I mean I know she's your sister and all, but don't you think she's gettin a little weird?"

"Now she's weird cause she's not into you?"

"What's wrong with me?"

"You want the short list?"

"Fuck off."

"Hey, take a walk with me."

"I'm good here. You go for a walk."

I had to get serious and loud: "Fuck knuckle. Take a walk with me."

We walked on the path next to the river, moving away from everyone.

"I hardly even touched her. And I'm a good guy. Like you don't know I'm a good guy? Aren't I a good guy?"

"Listen, maybe it's better you don't hang out here for a while. Let's say we split the river for a while? I mean we work together, we gotta spend every day?"

"We were getting laid at her age and now you don't want her

18

to because why? She's a girl? Does the term 'psycho brother' mean anything to you?"

"It ain't that."

"Oh, come off it. You haven't been able to bullshit me since kindergarten, so stop it. Your stubborn wop's starting to show."

"It ain't that."

"Then it's your stubborn mick."

I looked back to see if we were out of shouting distance from the rest of them yet. Not quite, so I lowered my voice and picked up the pace. "She's thirteen."

"Thirteen's not a disease."

"You're seventeen, that doesn't bother you?"

"Should it?"

It's hard to reason with ignorance. "I don't like guys messing with her," I said.

"Look, she gave me the brush off. So I consider myself brushed. I'm off the case. But here's some news tough guy, I'm not the only one who's gonna try to wet my luck with her so get used to it."

"I don't want guys messing with her."

"Yeah, I heard you."

"I don't want it," I repeated. Every smart piece of me said to keep it all to myself, because this guy could bad judge a situation to death and the last person I was gonna let him do that with was my sister. But another part of me wanted to tell him everything, and that's why I kept repeating myself, hoping he would read my whole mind, and finally everything would be out without me actually having to say it. If we didn't know each other so well, he probably would have thought I was autistic, but he caught on that there was something else I was getting at. His voice got real deep, like it does when he's getting serious with you.

"JT, what the fuck?"

19

"I don't like it." I picked up my pace even more and looked over my shoulder.

"You're freakin me out, man."

"I just don't like it."

He stepped in front of me, put one of his heavy hands right under my throat and stopped me from walking. I could have cut off his hand and ate it. "Quit saying that. Stand the fuck still and tell me what you're talking about?" I was trying to speak but I couldn't. "Come on, it's me for Christ's sake. Tell me."

"NO." I slapped his hand away.

He slapped mine back.

I grabbed him in a headlock.

We both fell to the ground.

I wanted him to fight back so the talking would be over, but he wasn't throwing any punches cause he knew I wasn't really fighting him. And we both knew if it was a real fight his punches would have been the first and hardest to land. He let me roll him onto his stomach and hold him down. "Just get the fuck out," I yelled.

"It's not your fuckin river. Get off me."

"No."

"Let me up."

"Will you leave if I let you up?"

"No."

"Then forget it."

"You gonna keep me here till you get hungry, idiot?"

"Till you leave."

"JT, let me up and tell me what the hell is going on."

"Fuck that. I tell you something and it's like telling everyone we know, you bucket of shit spud brain."

For that, he bit my hand.

I let go of his neck and squeezed my right hand with my left.

"Oww you motherfucker." I shook out my fingers. "Did you

just fuckin bite me?" I looked at my right knuckles that now had red teeth marks. "You *bit* me."

"If you really want me to, I will fuck you up."

"I want you to stop asking me questions."

Noke walked up to me real slow, his arms up in the peace position, showing me his huge palms. "Did I break the skin?"

"No."

"Talk to me. Now."

If there was a way to get out of it then I didn't see it. He would have been on my ass for months. And I supposed I did owe him an answer for why I threw a choke hold on him. "Noke, you have to make me a deal."

"Done."

"You cannot open your mouth to a single soul."

"I won't."

Even though he sounded sincere I said, "How do I know that?"

"Because it's me."

June 28

From Tompkins Square, I walk back to my apartment, lay on a futon mattress that takes up a quarter chunk of the floor. From the fifth floor all the lovers' quarrels, music, bed moaning, garbage and food smells—everything people let escape—pass through me on their way out the roof of the building. I'm the conduit for everything coming out of this building, a lightning rod in reverse. But not tonight. Tonight it's quiet. And definitely not the same quiet as laying on a riverbed in Yonkers with Nokey, taking a slow ride on the Earth, moving on the same rhythm as all the other passengers. This is a throbbing quiet, like an ear infection. I see that woman in the coffee shop. My sister's face under another girl's skin. My sister standing on the footbridge over the river. Nokey looking at her. Noticing her. My heart starts tripping. And I'd put cash on the Dalai Lama not being able to slow that shit down.

Fuck. Here comes the panic. It shoots up the back of my neck, dries out my mouth and paralyzes my tongue. My heart flaps around my chest like a fish on a line. Every fucking night, the constant ringing and thinking will not stop—yelling at me that I should start drinking heavily close to the edge of a rooftop.

I try to laugh it all off until the early signs of blue light start to seep in the windows, that's usually when I get my hour and a half of sleep. I heard that resting is just as good as sleeping, which doesn't help me, because I can't stay still enough to rest. I clasp my hands under the back of my head. I can feel my hair growing back in. I've kept shaving it since I left the park. Don't know why. I find all kinds of twisted positions to lie in, but eventually I stand up. Look out the window, open the refrigerator and see if anything has changed since last I looked. I pee. I grab a pretzel out of a bag from the counter. I drink some water. I try jerking off, and I can barely feel anything—I haven't done the one-gun salute in months. I'm numb in a lot of places and it terrifies me, OK? It terrifies me like sleeping, like my own thoughts, like money, like death, like listening to my heartbeat, like thinking about my breathing, like feeling like this forever, like being alone, like being with someone, like jail. My eyes spin around this apartment looking for the right woman's face, the cure, the quietest thing, but I find brick, wood, paint. A book. I scan a page in this Gabriel García Márquez book that I'm supposed to be reading for a GED class and can't follow for shit. Tomorrow at work I'll fight to stay awake while hauling a thirty-pound bag of rocks in each hand—when sleep isn't safe. Or possible. No one is looking for me. See, this is what I don't fucking want—a quiet building. I want kids running across wood floors, I want muffled music or domestic squabbles shaking the walls. I throw the sheet off, stand up. Look out the window, come back to the mattress, put my back to the wall and tap my right knuckles into my left palm for noise. Tap, tap, tap, tap, tap . . . Faster, faster, faster. Louder. Keep going. Keep a rhythm. Go, go, go, go, go. All right, I gotta stop that shit. Now my hand hurts. Great. No way man, I can't have the buzz in my ears be the only thing to listen to. I pace. Somebody give me a little neighborly help goddamn it, I need to hear some noise. OK stop. Breathe deep. This night will be over just like the rest of them. Breathe again. Why do they tell you to do that, it just makes it worse. This is like free-falling upward. SON OF A BITCH. I rock back and forth on my feet. Please. Everything is OK here. It's way too early to touch that notebook, let it stay on the table. OK, sing Bob Marley: *Everything's gonna be all right. Everything's gonna be all right.* I need a stereo in here. "Danielle." *Everything's gonna be all right.* Yeah, right. "Table. Rocks. Patio." Sometimes I say words out loud to drown the silence. "Neighbor, neighbor." Sometimes it works. "Patio. Table. Hey. Hey-yo. Hey. Shit. Stephanie. Ste-phan-ie."

July 5

"Five at-bats," Brian says as we lift bags of rocks off the pile. "Did I say that already? *Five at-bats* and I couldn't get a hit. I mean this is the playoffs, pal. This is when I shine. Down by two, I got runners on the corners and I fly to fucking center."

Brian's got this kind of muscular wisdom passed down from his Irish ancestors who survived the potato famine and cursed a lot. Now combine that with a witty ability to sneak attack you with an Oscar Wilde quote, a smile that can sell dirt, and—this may be the most devastating of all—a charm that could let him fuck six different women a week and not make it seem cheap. He wears his smarts like a pair of jeans faded and frayed in all the right places to fit only him. I've felt off balance around him since day one. He's so cool it pisses me off.

"You think I would've cut down my swing and popped one over the shortstop's head. No I fly deep to center. End of inning, end of game." Unlike me, Brian is never tired.

We're on East 82nd Street. In front of us are thirty-pound bags of gravel piled five feet high on wooden flats. Our job for the moment is to move every bag from the street, through the brownstone behind us, and into its backyard. Each sack is cinched with a metal clip at the opening, so we grab them by the few inches of excess bag on top, like brown bag lunches. With one bag in each hand, me and Brian walk from the sidewalk through a side gate that lets us into the bottom floor of the brownstone. Oak and leather furniture, wood-framed paintings, and stained-glass lamps are weatherproofed against dirt and dust with plastic tarps. We go through this room, up eight more stairs, and into the courtyard where we lay the sacks on a cleared quarter acre of dirt that in a few months will be a new patio. We stand the bags upright in rows that remind me of the candles we lined the sidewalks of my old neighborhood with on Christmas Eve—spidering out from the church, lighting paths to God's house.

The last ten days were demolition. We got rid of all the old slate and concrete except for the piece I carried home. Most of our next few weeks will be spent carrying the layers of this new patio bag by bag. The layers go like this: Gravel to level the land. Black tarp to stop plants from using the sunlight to eat, grow. Sand to level and cushion the slate. Concrete to fill the cracks between the new pieces of slate.

We go down the stairs and into the bottom floor of the brownstone. "I sat on the bench literally hiding my face," Brian says. "I haven't lost it on the field like that since I was young enough to crap my jock. I'm such a pansy. And I give you shit about how much moving rocks hurts."

"Balls don't fall where they should. It's all so unjust."

He looks at me with a twisted face. We climb eight stairs and into the backyard, drop off the bags. "That was pretty non-sequiturial of you, Wedgie." (A nickname I hate.) "But since you brought it up, yeah, you're damn right it is. For as long as anyone can remember this whole life is unjust."

First week on this job together we broke for lunch at a deli on Lexington. At the counter, I ordered a turkey wedge, lettuce, tomato, mayonnaise and Brian said, "You from Westchester?"

Soon as I heard that word I felt like a porcupine folded inside out. I said, "What?" to stall for time. And he said, "That's what they call heroes up there. I got cousins in Yonkers. In the City we call em heroes, up there they say wedge."

It was all kinds of wrong. Yonkers was never a word he was supposed to say, let alone know someone from. I breathed into a closing throat, knowing I needed to work out an alternate past immediately. Before Brian mentioned Yonkers he had been helping me wipe away my grease spot of an adolescence. Our system was that we saw each other Monday through Friday and didn't have to know anything more than what was on the daily schedule. "No, I'm from Staten Island. I told you that."

"No you didn't."

"Why wouldn't I have?"

"Fuck should I know? Then why'd you call it a wedge?"

"That's not allowed?"

"Hey, I mean no personal disparagement about how you choose to order your lunch, but you sound like you're from Westchester. That's all, Wedgie boy."

The guy behind the counter said, "Six seventy-five," so I reached into my pocket with my dirty hand and the semantics argument was over.

But the nickname stuck.

We go back down eight stairs, into the brownstone. "Not to break your stones too hard, Wedgie, but discovering life is unjust is not an original find."

"It's senseless too. I mean, we've spent the last month hauling bags of rocks down the stairs, up the stairs, and out the back of this woman's house, so we can build her a deck. She's in a wheelchair, she can't even walk on it. And by the time we finish it she'll probably be dead. So why even build the damn thing?"

"To get a paycheck, friend." Up eight stairs, onto the street, pick up more sacks. "Think of it like this, even if she dies before we finish—and I'm not saying she won't, the sweet rich old bag—the broad left you part of her fortune. If you wanna know why, go ahead, figure it out. Whether you get your answer or not you're still gonna be hungry the next day. Better question is what you're gonna do while you're being fed."

Down eight stairs, into the brownstone. Up eight stairs, into the backyard, drop the bags. "You get where I'm coming from?" Brian wants to know. Down eight stairs, into the brownstone.

"Maybe," I tell him, trying to shrug off the subject. Up eight stairs, onto the sidewalk.

A woman hot enough to make men nosedive in the street walks by us. Brian says, "Hello ma'am." And she smiles at him. "If you're feeling as pretty as you look the world must seem right today." She keeps walking and smiling.

"Dude, where do you get this stuff?"

We lean against the pile of rocks. "Same place we all do. It starts here," he points to his crotch, "and if you've got half a brain it goes to here," he points to his mouth. "When you been rejected as much as I have you start to use it more freely. It's counter-intuitive, I know, but I'm living proof." We pick up our next round of bags. "Ninety-eight out of a hundred women on the street think I'm repulsive. The other two are willing to look through the repulsion right to the charm. Respect the odds, play the odds."

Down eight stairs into the brownstone. "When I first got this job," Brian says, "my father told me, 'At least you're not in a mine where you can get black lung, or a factory in Mexico where someone will cut your throat for forty-five cents.' You can argue with the guy, or you can get comfortable on your side of the scale." Up eight stairs into the backyard. "Me? I got no problem taking this rich broad's money. It's clean. Better than wearin a tie for some real estate company." He motions to an empty section that has no bags. "Let's fill that gap." We drop the bags.

"How's it better?"

"Cause real estate is inherently an ass-fuck business. Everyone knows it. And I'd rather not fuck people in the ass for a living." He stands still, pulls his gloves off and wipes his forehead with the back of his hand. "My family's owned two houses in Jackson Heights for seventy years. My grandfather and his brother built them. We don't pay rent to no one. *That's* justice."

"You all live there together?"

"Yeah."

"How is that possible?"

"We have four bedrooms."

"That's not what I mean, but go ahead."

"We'd rather not be landlords. Landlords are legally allowed to turn tricks for money. I'd rather steal someone's money on the street at gunpoint than draw blood from their neck with a pen. It's more out in the open that way." He slaps me in the shoulder with his gloves. "See now you got me on tangents. I hate tangents." He puts his gloves on. "You spend way too much time in your head and you got me going there. The bottom line is you build this thing, you get to eat. That's the justice you get, Wedgie."

"I wish you'd stop calling me that."

"I know. Let's keep moving."

Down eight stairs, into the brownstone. Brian lowers his voice. "Listen, do I think it's fucked that there's a fifty-thousand-dollar vase sitting in some highfalutin jerk off's living room when it can feed some people I know for ten years? Yes. Is it mind boggling and unjust? Yes. Can I do anything about it? No."

"Why not?"

"Cause even if I go home tonight and figure out a way to tip the scales, I'd still have to come here tomorrow and carry rocks.

29

It don't change nothin. What's the expression? 'Fair is fair and foul is foul'?"

"Something like that." Up eight stairs, onto the sidewalk.

"Point is . . . I don't know what that means. Look, I don't know why you're so bent to figure out what's just—not my business—but put it this way: on a softball field you got a white line that separates fair from foul, and out here there's no lines. None. We don't have line one. And if we did we'd all be moving it for our own good. Now stop asking me about this shit, you're making my day longer. What can I tell you? Life's disappointing. Get a hooker." We pick up more rocks.

Me and Brian high-five each other after making it through the eight hours.

"Why you work half days on Friday again?" he asks me.

"Because I'm special?"

He laughs. "Mr Mystery. I'll see you tomorrow."

I walk through Central Park on my way home, which makes me feel like I'm missing out on owning a dog, having a picnic, a girl, a pair of shorts and a bike. I like poets' row though. All these statues of these guys, most I never heard of, under an arc of elms. They sit permanently carved in their best moment. Not in their mediocrity when they had broccoli in their teeth or got drunk and accidentally pissed on the cat. And good for them. I lie on my back on a bench, looking up through the twisted branches, waiting for the blue background to turn black.

In the East Village I buy a six-pack at the deli and bring it up the stairs of my building. On the sixth floor I see someone has propped open the roof door with a brick. This is supposed to

30

be an emergency exit only, and a red warning sticker on the door says an alarm will sound if opened, but I seriously doubt this alarm has ever worked. From the roof I see strips of orange and red fading at the horizon; the summer tar smell stings my nose. I take a few steps and hear a slow slapping noise and out-of-breath breathing coming from the front of the building. I walk toward it and under the water tower Stephanie and her boyfriend are going at it. He's behind her with his shirt draped over her ass and pants halfway down his thighs, one hand grabbing a chunk of her hip, the other holding a fistful of her ponytail. Stephanie's jeans are attached only to her right ankle, a light blue pair of underwear tangled in them. She's kneeling on her shirt to protect her knees from the roof's baked-in heat. Now that I see more of her skin I realize how dark it is. And she's skinny. I'm maybe twenty feet away and can count her ribs. She's humming in between breaths. "Um hum. Um hum." I backpedal quietly and leave them to it.

I walk to the other side of the building with my six-pack of Corona, sit on the short brick wall at the back of the roof, and look at downtown Manhattan and drink.

Three beers into it I hear the roof door slam behind me and tiny pieces of rubble get crushed under someone's feet. I turn around; Stephanie is walking to the edge of this roof about ten feet to my left. Her arms folded over her chest. She stops at the edge and we catch each other's eyes for a second.

I say, "What's up."

"What's up."

I look behind her for the boyfriend. No sign. I look back to her and she shrugs like she don't care he's gone. She sits down, takes the elastic out of her ponytail, puts it in her mouth, reaches back, re-gathers her hair, then ties it back again. She sniffles, wipes her finger under her nose then on her jeans, folds her arms over her stomach, leans her chest close to her knees. She's got

31

a nervous twitch, more like a twist—the ball of her right foot twists on the top of the roof like she's repeatedly grinding out a cigarette.

We sit for a good few minutes, her twisting foot making the only sound.

Without eye contact she says, "I saw you see us."

My jaw freezes. What do you say to someone who calls you on watching them get fucked from behind? "Sorry. I didn't know anyone was up here." I take a long swig.

She shrugs, looks at me, her foot stops. "It's OK." It feels weird and comfortable staring at her. She turns her face away and her foot goes back to doing its thing.

We both look at the skyline against its now black background. The city breaks itself down from neighborhoods to blocks to buildings to rooms—millions of tiny pieces—and offers nothing for keeps; it just doles out the same-sized impermanence to everyone. Beautiful selfish city. It makes us eat, sleep, and fuck right on top of one another, makes us breathe the backwash of each other's breath, daring us to survive a lonely life lived so close to so many people.

The sun's leftover heat still seeps out of the black roof. Stephanie's foot keeps twisting out the perpetual fire beneath it. We sit under the arc of airplanes taking off and landing in Queens as two virtual strangers this city has thrown together for the night, wondering if this place might sometime feel like a home.

July 6

Grand Central Terminal. Hundreds of people move under the green ceiling of constellations that hear every voice. I walk to the main concourse; the heartbeat in my head reminds me how much I drank last night. I squint at the departures board. *12:07 Hudson Line local to Poughkeepsie departing from track 32, making stops at 125th Street, Morris Heights, University Heights, Marble Hill, Spuyten Duyvil, Riverdale, Ludlow, Yonkers* . . . I could recite that shit in my sleep, if I slept.

Coke in hand, turkey hero with mayonnaise in mid-bite, I flip around toward my track, and crash lunch-first into a woman hustling to get her train. She glances back and throws me a "Sorry," with an I'm-too-late-to-be-too-worried face. I wipe the mayonnaise off my mouth . . . Oh, shit. I vaguely remember walking down Avenue A last night crashing into another woman. Did we crash? No, I think I grabbed her. Probably grabbed her. Maybe she smacked me. Did I get smacked? Yeah. I think I did.

On the train I take my last bite, crumple the wax paper, put it back in the brown bag, and lay it on the seat next to me so no one sits

33

there. I lean my head against the window and try to get comfortable in the seat that was designed by an idiot. My face feels ten degrees hotter than it needs to be. *Beer*, my head keeps telling me with every heartbeat, *beer, beer* . . . I touch my cheekbone. Yeah, I think I did get smacked last night. The details aren't clear. Probably wasn't as bad as a couple weeks ago when I was walking down Avenue A, saw this girl coming at me, and decided to grab both of her shoulders. I stopped her in mid-stride and her boyfriend asked me if I had a fucking problem. I told him the last time someone asked me that they were in the third grade and still sleeping with their mother. When he tried to shove me I was quick enough to grab him by his wrists and yanked him off the curb smack into a parked car. But I was too sloshed to stop his fist when he came back at me. He only got off one punch because girlfriend was yelling at him to stop. With my ass on the street I told him that he just proved the opposite of what he was trying to prove. It sounded like a good line at the time. It made him turn back around, made his girlfriend grab his arm and yell at him to stop already. Which he finally did. I just wanted to gum up the works of their relationship, separate them for a second, see how they handle drunken scrutiny. Yeah, I'm guessing last night was a milder version of that.

Me and Stephanie didn't say much beyond *what's up* last night. We sat up there invisible to the rest of the neighborhood until my first six-pack ran out and I went to the deli for more. I asked her if she wanted one, but she said no. Sad girl.

After 125th Street the train crosses the East River, hugs the banks of the South Bronx, and shoots up the Hudson. I see signs fly by with the word Yonkers on them. My heart rate speeds up and my insides try to make a B-line out my ass. This stop always comes too soon. I think about staying on. Taking this train as far as it goes then hitching a one-way ride north, which is stupid because people don't hitchhike anymore.

I step onto the platform and my t-shirt gets blown in the trail-wind of the train. I watch the train go up the tracks and get smaller until I can't see or hear it.

The river is about a mile wide here and seems to separate nature from nurture. I stand on the nurture side with the new apartment buildings and cafés. Cliffs inhabited only by trees stand on the New Jersey side and look down perpetually forgiving the Yonkers side.

I pass a café lined with bay windows that has a new co-op building above it. Right now it's past lunchtime and the place is practically empty. A few waitresses lean on the bar and pick at their fingernails while the television over their heads plays last night's Yankees highlights. A few tables are taken by people sitting across from each other, talking to someone else on their cell phones. This café's valet wears a white shirt and a bowtie, and sits on a stool in a chained-off parking lot that can hold maybe ten cars. He stares at the water and fingers the stack of unused parking stubs.

I walk three blocks away from the water on a street lined with tall brick housing projects. Cages cover the first floor windows, graffiti covers front doors, and smashed lights hang above entrances. The buildings resemble the hospital where my mom worked: flat, only the essentials. Summer-school kids walk by them, dip their hands into bags of Bugles and Doritos. They laugh and talk loud enough that I can hear them over the four lanes of traffic between us. They've hung backpacks from their elbows and attitudes on their faces that explain they can do anything they want, no permission needed. It's like watching me and Nokey a year ago.

A few blocks past that stand City Hall and the Yonkers court-house buildings. The courthouse clock says I have five

35

minutes to get into the Integrated Domestic Violence building.

My charges have been read. Probable cause and intent to steal and sell have all been established. The trial date is set for two months from now. But I'm being good. I have sought and maintained employment, enrolled in an educational program in pursuit of a GED, am complying with periodic check-ins with the authorities, refraining from possessing firearms, undergoing family psychological treatment, and failing to see where the justice is in all this relentless bullshit.

Family psychological treatment works like this: we all sit in a white, cinderblock-walled room and stare in opposite directions. We pick at the arms of our padded metal chairs as our appointed counselor asks us questions about how we feel and why. My mother cries in that quiet dab-your-nose kind of way and my dad says absolutely nothing.

Today is no different. Our counselor says, "What's going on today?" She's got this low, one-note tone that makes everything she says sound like it's in parentheses.

After she asks what's going on there's a real long silence.

I say: I think I got punched last night.

COUNSELOR: You think you got punched?

ME: Yeah. Not sure.

MOM: (Looks at me, concern in her eyes.)

COUNSELOR: Why do you think you did? And why aren't you sure?

ME: I'm not sure. And I don't know.

COUNSELOR: Did you get into a fight?

ME: Probably not exactly.

COUNSELOR: Where were you?

ME: Hard to say exactly.

COUNSELOR: Were you out somewhere?

ME: Yeah. I think so.

COUNSELOR: Who were you with?

ME: Well if I did get hit, I guess the person who hit me was
    there. Other than that—
MOM: Jake, please stop.
COUNSELOR: No, it's OK.
MOM: Why do you constantly badger this woman?
ME: I'm not—
MOM: She's trying to help.
ME: OK.
COUNSELOR: It's OK, Mrs Savage.
MOM: *Miss.*
COUNSELOR: (Cringing.) I'm sorry.
DAD: (Inhaling deeply, letting it out as protest.)
MOM: Just call me Francine already. (Head falling into hands.)
COUNSELOR: Francine, you all get to talk about whatever
    you want to talk about. Anything that's on your mind.

Silence.

COUNSELOR: Anything.

More silence.

Mom wipes nose.

Counselor looks from face to face, encouraging and waiting
    for the next word.

Dad picks at chair.

Silence.

ME: I'm OK.

Short silence.

COUNSELOR: What do you mean, Jake?
ME: If I was hit—
MOM: Jake . . .
ME: I'm saying that if I was *hit*, and I might have *been*, I'm *O-K*.
COUNSELOR: Well, Jake, according to your psychiatrist's evaluation you're not really OK.
ME: He's not my psychiatrist. I don't *have* a psychiatrist. I only went to one because they told me to.
COUNSELOR: He's a medical doctor whose diagnosis for you was "severe depression".
ME: I maintain my right to refuse medication, because *I'm not depressed*. How many times do I have to say this? If he wanted to give me something to knock me out at night, then fine. But apparently he didn't think sleep was so worthy, so forget him. I'm OK. All right? I'm A-OK. Not that anyone was worried.
COUNSELOR: Is anyone worried about Jake?

Short silence.

DAD: (Staring at the floor, expression hidden.) I am.
EVERYONE: (Silence.)

———

She yells my name as I trot down the courthouse stairs, her voice a perpetual panic attack. I turn mid-step and with my eyes ask what she wants. She settles on the stair above me, a forced sliver of a smile poking through her puffy face.
"You gave our counselor a hard time in there."
"We all get them."

If I know my mom, she's now using the obvious as a segue into what she really wants to say.

"Jake." She preps herself with a deliberate inhalation. "I want you to know you can come home."

Do I know my mom?

"Home?" I say like she's joking.

"Yes."

"Where's that?"

"With me."

"Not an option, Mom."

She nods her head and purses her lips as if she was expecting a response like that. She reaches up to touch my peach-fuzz hair. "You don't look very good."

I duck away from her hand. "Me? Look at the eyes on you."

"That all you've been doing?" Now she looks me back in the eye and I notice a familiar distant gaze, a clear film covering the emotions in her eyes. I recognise it from when she's gotten one of her doctor friends to prescribe her sleeping pills. "Little Xanax too?"

She lets out a sigh so distinctly defeated that I'm sure I'll be able to reproduce it on my deathbed. "How any other way can I sleep?"

"Lot of Xanax. You got any for me."

"I'll get fired."

"Oh, please. I gotta get to my train."

I'm able to take one step down before she says, "Wait."

"I'm late. Whudda you want?"

She reaches into her shoulder bag and pulls out an envelope.

"I don't need that."

"But Jake, look at you. Your shoulder bones are sticking out. You can't be eating."

"I eat great. Thank you."

"Then take it to go to the dentist or something." She emphatically extends it in my direction. "I mean what if something happens to you and you have to go to the doctor? Or the hospital? Take it."

39

"I'll take some Xanax."

"I insist you take it."

"I insist you put it away."

She drops her arm, still holding the envelope at her side. "You can't do whatever it is you think you're doing by yourself. Our counselor won't say that, but we all know it. You can't take this one alone."

"I've taken many things alone."

She shakes her head like she pities me. "Look. You tried something, Jake. OK? And I know it's almost more than I can say for myself. It wasn't the smartest thing, but I get it OK? You wanted to fix things."

I point directly at her chest and say, "Someone had to."

For this she slaps my face. Which stuns us both for a few seconds.

"Jesus, this is like the family habit. We don't smoke, but we can backhand with the best of em. I wonder if the courthouse security cameras caught that one." I do jumping jacks on the stairs. "Hey, coppers. Judges. You getting this?"

And for this I get three slaps in the mouth. Then she vices my face between her palms. "Goddamn you. Stop the fucking sarcasm." She lets go of me. "Get real. There's things we're not going to say in there. We both know that. But don't you get it? I'm forgiving you."

"YOU'RE forgiving ME?"

"Yes. And neither one of us can afford for you to not accept that."

"Why's that?"

"Because we're already family; we don't need to be enemies on top of that."

I take my time backing off her and taking the steps down again. Behind me she says, "You could stop hating him."

"I don't."

"Yes you do. You're afraid of him. He's got a way of scaring people for good. Trust me."

"I'll take some Xanax."

40

Purple dress, red painting

Me and Dad would crouch down on the linoleum kitchen floor, only five of his two hundred seventy pounds rolling over his belt. He'd shake the dice in his fist, blow on them and say, "Multiplication," then I'd call out how many pennies I'd want to bet. I'd put up my change, he'd roll the dice, they'd clink against the wall and stop. "Quick: five times four," he'd say, then swipe them up.

"Twenty."

"Right." And he'd give me my payout.

Again, he'd shake the dice, blow on them and say, "Subtraction." I always bet five cents on subtraction, it was my strength. He'd roll . . . a six and a four would come up, I'd say, "Two," and make an easy score. He'd shake the dice again, blow on them, say, "Multiplication," I'd bet, he'd roll . . . "One times one."

"One."

"Right. But the house takes your money, because snake eyes means you crapped out," he'd yell.

"Shhh. You're gonna wake Mom up."

"I'm a screamer in the tradition of . . . you know, those people

41

who scream. The Irish ones. Banshees," he says. "Nothing to be done about it."

This was homework.

But often—and it took me a while to figure out why—I winced at his affectionate slaps on the back. At the dinner table I stuck a fork in my palm to dull the gucky sound of him chewing pasta. And I had visions. Him walking into fire. Face cracking. Drowning in shallow water. Me, pissing a poison arc in his direction that would dissolve him on contact.

It was just another purple dress with a little gold trim around the neck and hem. But for my five-year-old sister Dani, it was a fairy costume. My mom got her this magic wand to go with it—a little plastic one that lit up and everything. In what Dani called her fairy dance, she'd get up on her tiptoes and take these little ballet-looking steps from one side of the living room to the other. It was like watching Tinker Bell run track. She'd ballet over to you, circle her wand three times over your head and say, "I'm the purple fairy and I grant you a magic purple wish," then crack you in the head and run away laughing. She'd hit you no matter what you were doing; watching TV, eating, talking on the phone . . . she'd come into the bathroom and smack me with that thing when I was on the bowl. Cute as she was, she definitely had a little wise ass thing going on.

You couldn't get her into bed unless you turned it into a game. And the game was always some version of this: we'd all be sitting downstairs in front of the TV until our nine-thirty bedtime rolled around and Mom announced it was time to hit the sheets. Dani would say, "You have to find me first," then run up the stairs into my room and crawl under my covers. Mom and I would walk up the stairs expressing our impossible tiredness and how we couldn't go to sleep unless we found Dani. We'd open the door to her room and yell, "Dani are you in here?" When no answer would come we'd call for her in Mom's room then the bathroom. Yawning with the crushing weight of slumber we'd say, "Oh well, I guess we lost her. Might as well go to sleep." I'd sit on my bed right on top of her and jump up like I was startled. "Whoa, Mom, there's something in my bed." I'd pull the sheets back and say, "Look—a foot." I'd pull them back a little more. "And there's a leg attached to it." Dani'd giggle from underneath. Mom would say, "Must be a laugh box attached to that leg." I'd pull the sheets all the way off. "Oh my god, there's a girl attached to it." Dani would try to run away, and Mom would grab her, bundle the sheet around her like a sack of laundry, and sling her over her shoulder. From inside the bundle, you'd hear, "You still didn't find me." Mom would unload Dani onto her own bed and tickle her for about five minutes. Then maybe she'd go to sleep. And if she did it definitely wasn't a full night's sleep.

That's why we developed the knock system.

Our rooms were right next to each other and the headboards of our bed were on opposite sides of the same wall, so you could hear a knock go right through it even if it came from the soft fist of a five-year-old. The system worked like this:

One knock: *Come in.*

Two knocks: *Goodnight.*

Three knocks: *What's up?* (This one you used if the other person had accidentally hit the wall when they were getting into bed or something or were making some other kind of unidentifiable noise.)

Four knocks: *All clear.* (This one was usually used right after the *What's-up?* combination.)

If she sent me the one *Come-in* knock, mostly it wasn't really because she had to tell me things. She just wanted to play tent.

When the single knock came, I'd get out this little flashlight

I had on my night table, put it between my teeth, then crawl on my stomach like I was in a combat zone through the hallway and into Dani's room and climb under her sheet.

I remember how big her eyes looked under those sheets, like brown cue balls with lashes like paintbrushes. With the sheet over our heads I'd shine the light on her book and read out loud. God forbid I'd read without doing the voices. No way she'd let me get away with that. Whatever the characters in the book were, a fox, a dog, I'd have to sound like one. This one time I was reading her a story about a rabbit and she said, "A rabbit doesn't sound like that."

"How do you know? You talk to rabbits?"

"Yeah. Don't you?"

"Maybe," I said. "What's your rabbit sound like?"

She made this squealing high-pitched voice that woke up our mom. Mom came in the room and said, "Do you know what time it is?" Dani popped her head out from behind the sheet and said, "It's no-parents time." Then pulled it back over our heads.

Mom said, "Come on, it's after midnight."

Dani popped her head out again and said, "No parents allowed."

"This parent's allowed."

"No," Dani said, "you can't come in if you don't give the secret knock."

"I'll give you a secret knock. Now, go to sleep."

"No knock, no coming in. It's the rules."

Then Mom pulled the cover off our heads. "The rules are gonna change real fast if your father wakes up."

That's what it took for Dani to give in. That's always what it took for Dani to give in—the threat of Dad doing something. She looked at me and said, "Put the secret reading light back in the secret place."

———

I don't know exactly when it started, but sometime around age seven or eight she got real quiet. Hardly ever talked around the house or even at school. And if she did you could barely hear her. Her voice dissolved into this permanent kind of whisper and you didn't know if she was talking to herself or to you. You had to get real close to hear anything. And I noticed she stopped touching people; wouldn't do it with her magic wand or her own hands. Wasn't like we were running the most affectionate household. Dad's affections always came as some kind of open-handed slap to the ass or to the back of the neck—trying to get other kinds of affection from him was like hugging a gravestone. Mom would throw an arm-lock around us sometimes, but Dani wasn't having it; she started squirming away from hugs, turning her cheek away from kisses and stopped sitting on people's laps. And her eyes—I swear they shrunk. The lids laid at half-mast like a camel's.

One night—I was about eleven, Dani was seven—I woke up to this bizarre scratching noise coming from her side of the wall. It wasn't knocking, it was scratching. And in my barely awake state, it felt like something was coming after me. When I realized it was coming from the other side of the wall, I knocked the three times: *What's up?* And the scratching stopped. I waited for the four *All-clear* knocks. But they didn't come. So I gave three knocks again: *What's up?* Nothing. Just quiet. I let it go. Figured she was OK, and went back to sleep. A few nights later I heard the same scratching again. This time I knocked once: *Come in.* The scratching noise stopped and she gave me the four *All-clear* knocks. But something about it felt off. So in the morning I said, "Dani, what was going on with the scratching last night?"

She said, "I wasn't scratching anything."

"Then what was the noise?"

45

"The noise was scratching, but it wasn't *me* scratching."

"Then who was it?"

"Men." She whispered this like it was her big secret.

"What men?"

"Invisible men."

"If they're invisible how do you know they're men?"

"Only I can see them."

"What do they look like?"

"They have knives."

That's when this fast chill ran up the back of me. "What do they do with them?"

"They scratch."

"What do they scratch?"

"You know . . . My bed."

"Do they scratch you?"

"No."

"Let me know if they scratch your bed again. OK?"

"OK."

I'm guessing all kids do and say things that seem a little, you know—out there. And everyone lets it go because they're kids. But Dani wasn't being normal-kid kind of weird.

It was a finger painting. Different shades of thick red lines smeared over one another. I could see how you might think it was a horizon line at sunset. Before it was dry, Dani took something sharp, maybe the point of her pencil, and scratched lines through the paint. Now, I don't know much about painting, but when a seven-year-old is already going for different textures, you gotta think she's got talent. Or something to say. Or both. Mom hung what she thought was a cute little sunset picture on the refrigerator. It was her habit to

46

display things that signified normal happiness. But about this sunset, she was way off.

We were eating dinner in the dining room and Dad told me to get him another beer. OK. I go into the kitchen and open the refrigerator where this painting hung. It'd been there for a few months probably. And you know, things hang around long enough (like the Sears bullshit portraits of me wearing argyle and crooked teeth that Mom displayed on the living-room end tables) and you stop noticing them. So I grabbed the beer, shut the door, and there was this goddamn painting staring me in the face, stopping me.

My mother hung it horizontally, but Dani's name was written sideways, going up the page. I moved the magnets that were holding it up, put my fingers on it and spun it around vertical, so her name was at the bottom, right ways up. And that's definitely the way it was supposed to go, man.

You never know when you're going to understand a little more of what's going on inside someone. Looking at it vertically there wasn't any sun in that picture at all, no horizon. But hundreds of unmistakable long red streaks of blood. Dani ran her finger up and down that paper with as many different shades of red as the Board of Education supplied a first-grader. Then she scratched lines into those streaks.

I don't know what made me run upstairs and into my sister's room, but I stood next to her bed, my father's beer in hand, and just looked around. Nothing was strange, nothing out of place. I didn't know what I was looking for, when I pulled the blankets off her bed.

Carved into the wood of her headboard, down near the mattress, were pictures of tiny girls' bodies. Skinny legs and arms poking out of triangle dresses. Little floating stick figures without heads or faces.

Yeah, Dani was seven, but what the fuck? I was only eleven.

I went back down to the dining room, put the beer on the table in front of my dad, and he said, "You grow the wheat yourself?" He looked at me, and I fuckin looked at him, my vocal cords feeling like stone columns.

I might have been fifty percent of one parent and fifty percent of the other one, but seeing the faces of these people I was supposed to love—and worse, answer to—I couldn't recognize one crease, curve or color of resemblance. And those visions of Dad hurting and burning came back. *You son of a bitch. If God really is your manufacturer then I'm gonna sue the bastard for faulty design.*

"Don't you say thank you to your son?" my mother asked.

Dad lifted his can. "Here's to us, Jake. There's few what's like us, and they're all dead."

I said nothing. How could I? I had no idea what was really going on. So I stayed put and pushed food around my plate.

And Danielle. Her face was pointed down at her dish. She was trying to cut her salad with a butter knife that kept slipping out of her hand.

For the record here's a couple other things about my hate. I've tried to kill it, but that's like trying to punch out a fly—the damn thing just bounces off my knuckles and keeps buzzing around my head. And the other thing: it's burning out my own insides.

Frostbite

We were standing at the counter in the stationery store when my sister hauled off and punched my dad in the balls. Dad pulled a twenty out of his wallet to pay for his lottery ticket and outta nowhere . . . fist to the crotch. Dad folded over and held himself. Dani ran outside and the bell on the door clanged behind her. I thought, *Holy fuck, did she just do what it looked like she fuckin did?*

The dazed guy behind the counter goes, "Umm . . . Excuse me sir . . . I'm sorry, but . . . you have anything smaller?"

Dad said, "Keep the friggin change," and busted out of the store.

The guy held the twenty out to me and he said, "Tell your dad it's on me. I hope it's a winner."

I pocketed the bill and left.

Dani was standing next to the car. Just waiting. Not for our dad to yell at her or hit her back, just waiting calmly to be let inside. Dad unlocked the back door, she opened it and climbed in. I got in the front. Dad slid in the driver's seat, put his seat belt on, and turned the ignition. He sat with his hands on the wheel for a second, staring straight ahead. All three of us in silence.

In the back seat Dani folded her arms over her chest with an attitude like *don't even think about burning my ass on this one*. Dad tilted his head up to see her in the rearview, but she didn't look back. Then he looked at the dashboard and nodded. A nod that seemed to say he knew he had that punch coming and wasn't going to do anything about it. Nope. Not a damn thing. Not gonna retaliate, not gonna ask for an apology. Not even mention it. Just gonna put the car in reverse, pull out of the parking lot and drive home, twenty dollars in the hole.

———

A week after the lottery ticket incident—or the crotch-punching incident, or the twenty-dollar embezzlement incident, whichever way we're gonna look at it—I woke up to my mom yelling, "Go in the bathroom, wash your hands and face and brush your teeth!" Every school morning with the accuracy of an alarm clock my mother hurled these words from behind her bedroom door into our ears. You'd think after a few years she would have cut out the "Go in the bathroom" part. Like if she didn't specify, we would have climbed up to the attic to look for running water.

Mom's about five-one on a confident day, but has a set of pipes that can fill the house. She carries what little extra weight she's got below the waist like a slender bowling pin. She looks like someone who spends a few days a week in a gym, but she's never stepped foot in one. Her shape comes less from exercise than it does from anxiety and dread burning the extra calories. Her nervous energy keeps her hands constantly occupied, always moving things that don't need moving. In between bites of dinner she'll slide the salt shaker two inches to the left, then right, then back again like she's playing one-woman chess. When she's cooking she flutters around the kitchen from chair to stove to sink, a bird hopping from branch to branch, the whole time her head twitching in all directions like something's going to sneak up on her. She's so busy looking over her shoulder that a Chinese alphabet of burns scores her wrists from pulling pans out of the oven without pot holders.

Mom says my grandma Terri passed down recycling instincts. Terri taught her to clothes-pin used zip-lock bags to the kitchen faucet to dry out. I wonder if Terri's foot used to tap against the floor under the table during dinner like my mom's, like sending out Morse code. When her foot starts going up and down, my sister and I look at each other and smile because we know what's next. Our dad will hear it too and when he's had just about enough, he taps his heel really loud, and Mom jumps in embarrassment realizing what she's been doing. Then she says, "Sorry . . ." and me and Dani mouth the rest of the sentence with her: ". . . it just happens without me."

So that morning after washing and brushing, I came out of the bathroom and saw Dani's bed empty and unmade. Dad had gone to one of his construction sites at seven-thirty and Mom was getting cereal bowls out of the cabinet when I made it down to the kitchen.

1230 WFAS (Westchester's Talk Radio and Soft Favorites) played on the AM dial from Mom's old-time wooden kitchen radio—which was also a spice rack. The DJ came through the airwaves with a sing-songy voice so jolly and optimistic he sounded like he was trying to convince listeners—regardless of how much death and inflation he had to report—everything was so friggin dandy that no one in Westchester County ever really took a crap.

That morning it played to my mom twitching around the kitchen as she put cereal and bowls on the empty table.

"Mom, where's Danielle?"

She sighed then yelled to the ceiling, "Danielle, hurry up with your teeth, we have to leave in fifteen minutes."

51

"She's not upstairs."

"What do you mean?" She went to the refrigerator for milk.

"Remember how you told me everyone is always somewhere?"

"Yes."

"Well Dani's somewhere isn't the bathroom."

"Yes, it is."

"No, it's not."

She sighed, put the milk on the table, left the kitchen, and climbed the stairs. I followed her upstairs into the empty bathroom, then into Dani's room. She stopped when she saw her bed was empty. To me she mouthed the words, *is she hiding?* and I shrugged my shoulders. "Danielle, come on," she said, "we have to go." Then she stayed still listening for rustling sounds. None. "Was she in your room?"

"No." We checked my room anyway. Mom called out, "Danielle?" Nothing. This was getting weird. Dani was quiet, but a disappearing act was never in her repertoire. We went into my mom's room. "Danielle, come on, it's getting late." No Dani there either. In the bathroom Mom pulled back the shower curtain. Bathtub was dry. And just as Mom turned away from it she snapped into nurse mode. STAT. Fast as TV jumps to commercials I saw what she was like at work, calling out BP numbers, scrambling for sutures, wiping sweat off brows, keeping cool during life and death.

She went back into each room and opened the closets saying, "OK, game's over."

"You haven't seen her since you woke up?"

"Not uh. Maybe she's in the car."

Mom looked at me like I knew something she didn't. "Why would she be in the car?"

"Because everyone has to be somewhere. Right?" She had no time for her own piece of completely useless wisdom right then. She ran downstairs and into the kitchen, picked up the phone, started to dial, then hung it up, and thought for a second. "The car?"

I shrugged. "Maybe."

She swiped her car keys out of her pocketbook, and we hauled out the side door, down the stairs to the curb, where her car was parked and empty. She jangled her keys against her leg and her head twitched from left to right looking down the street. Neighbors were driving their kids to school and themselves to work. City commuters walked past our house to the train station while my mother stood on the sidewalk in her pleasant pastel nurse's uniform, took a big breath, and said, "I can't believe I can't find my daughter." She ran her hands through her hair and scratched her scalp with her mellow-long fingernails, her hands shaking. She wasn't the cool ER nurse anymore. Her panic made her too young for that. Thirty-five years peeled off her, and the stories she'd told me about her childhood showed in her eyes. She was nine, wearing her Sunday dress and wool coat in Rockefeller Center, separated from my grandma Terri, lost for hours in the huge crowd of people that came to look at the Christmas tree, shivering next to a cop when they found her. She was hiding in her closet, crying because her hand-me-down clothes were too big and made her look fat. She was seven, in the supermarket breaking a glass jar of artichoke hearts, then taking a slap in the mouth from Terri that made her lip bleed. She was thirteen, months after Terri died, coming home late from school in a panic that she wouldn't have dinner ready for my grandfather, then him being late. She was the interrupted kid, the misplaced care-taker of too many things. And then—because keeping it cool, keeping her feelings underneath where she thought they belonged was what she was best at—she somehow jolted out of it with a new plan: "Let's check the back. Jake, you go around the house that way and I'll go this way and we'll meet at the back door." We split up. Mom started off in a fast walk that turned into a run. That's when my head got loud with all the scary stuff that could have happened: stolen, kidnapped, beaten, killed, cut up for someone's pleasure. I guess it's a sign of the times when an eleven-year-old thinks these are actual possibilities. Any of those images alone were terrifying enough, but coupled with the idea that I might have to live in the house without her was a scenario beyond torture. The dinner table without her. The walls with no one knocking on them. I could predict the loneliness but I couldn't measure it. In that moment I remembered who I felt most connected to in the house. And it wasn't the people paying the bills.

Then I thought, *Idiot, you didn't check the porch yet,* and I made a deal with God. *God, if I get to the porch before Mom does, Dani will be standing there with her hands and face washed and her teeth brushed, in one piece ready to go to school.* I hoofed ass up the slope of the driveway and around the side of the house, racing my mom for my sister's life. "Be there," I kept saying. "Be there, be there." I did get to the porch before my mother did, but Dani wasn't standing there. She wasn't washed or brushed or ready for anything. She was lying on the wicker couch. Asleep. No blanket, no pillow. Just pajamas, socks and a red hooded sweatshirt pulled over her head. It's so like God to change the outcome of your prayers just enough so you can't quite tell if He personally handled your request.

Her sleeping hands had searched for heat and made their way to her mouth. Somehow she looked more vulnerable on the vinyl cushions of our ancient couch with its chipped white paint than she did in the images I'd conjured a few seconds before.

Mom came running up the porch steps. I turned to her and put my finger to my lips so she wouldn't wake her. I was proud to have been the one to find her. And for a second Mom listened to me; then she kneeled down to her and shook her a little. "Danielle." Dani's eyes snapped open and she let out a little scream. That made my mother scream. "What are you doing out here?" Mom asked.

"I was sleeping."

"Why?"

"I wanted to."

My mom looked back at me for a second, probably trying to see if I'd come up with my own answer. "Well I guess that's OK. But are you cold?"

"A little."

Mom grabbed her fingers and rubbed them fast between hers. Granted, the porch was on the side of our house surrounded by hedges and up enough of a slope that it couldn't be seen from the street, but that didn't seem reason enough for Mom to think Dani couldn't get swiped by some black-market psycho during the night. Maybe it was just me, but I expected a different reaction than: *Here, let me warm your fingers little girl and you'll be juuuust fine.*

"Go inside and get warm, Danielle."

"OK."

Dani stood up and walked through the side door. "And brush your teeth," Mom yelled. "We have to go to school now."

All that September, if Danielle wasn't in her bed in the morning, my mother would sigh and say to me, "Would you please go on the porch and wake your sister up." Seems a first-grade girl sleeping outside by herself regularly should have sent up a few more flags than it did. Dani started taking covers and pillows out with her, and that was enough because September was still bringing the kind of overnight weather a blanket could protect you from.

The night she came into my room, I mostly still feel like shit about. She tried to take the blanket off my bed and I think I said something like, *get your own and quit waking me up* or something stupid like that and yanked it out of her hands. But the thing was, it wasn't so much that she wanted my blanket as she wanted me to know she was out there. It sucks when it takes you a year to catch on to something any schmuck with a quarter of a brain could probably figure out in a half hour.

She stopped coming to me after that. So I started setting my alarm clock for 2 a.m. and kept it under my pillow so I could check on her and not wake up the rest of the house. Some nights she'd be asleep in her room, some nights she'd be outside and sometimes I'd take an extra blanket down to her. Other nights I'd say, fuck it, I'm not checking on her anymore. She's fine. And even if she's not, my parents will take care of it. Fuckin joke that was.

Then October came.

It was almost 2 a.m. by my clock. I knocked the one *Come-in* knock and got no response. I went into her bedroom and she was gone. I got a pair of gloves from my closet and went down after her.

She had the hood of her red sweatshirt pulled over her head, the string cinched up so tight it covered her nose, mouth, eyebrows; all you could see were eyes peeking out of the little hole like a pair of brown dice. She had two blankets: the one against her was fuzzy and plaid and the other was rust colored, so heavy and wooly you'd think it was issued by the Army. Somehow she got both the blankets around her body tight as plastic wrap, like she put them flat on the floor, laid down on one side and rolled herself up like a burrito. She looked up at me through her hood and I said, "Dani, it's freezing. You sure you wanna stay out here?"

She closed her eyes and nodded. How someone could be so soft spoken and so stubborn at the same time blows minds.

"OK, I got you these anyway." I laid the gloves on top of her and stood there for a second wondering what was going on in this kid's head. That's when she wiggled one arm out of the cocoon of blankets and knocked once on the wall behind her.

I said, "What?"

She knocked again.

"Whudda you want?"

She looked at me like *what the hell do you think I want*. Well, I didn't know so she knocked again.

"Stop, you're gonna wake them up."

She knocked again.

"Whudda you want already?"

One more knock.

I sat down on the couch next to her. "Tell me."

One slow knock.

"Dani, talk."

In her little whisper of a voice with her sweatshirt covering her mouth she said, "Mut's that mean?"

"The knock?"

"Uh huh."

"It means, 'come in' but I'm already here."

Then she rolled her eyes like I was being dense.

"Whaaat?"

"I mant you to come here."

"You *mant* me?"

She pulled the sweatshirt away from her mouth. "I *want* you to come here."

"I *am* here."

Then she wrestled her other arm from under the blankets and held them both out to me. "I mean *here*, here."

Then I understood.

It wasn't a simple goodnight hug she wanted. She asked for it the way people do when they have to go away for a while, or if they're about to do something they're scared of. It wasn't something she asked of me often. And I know it wasn't something I'd seen her ask of my parents in a long time. We held the hug longer than I think either of us expected. I wanted to keep it going but the air made my back cold. "I have to go inside now," I said with my face next to her ear. "Is that OK?"

She nodded her head and we let go.

I stood up and the heat of her disappeared from my chest in a second. She tied up her sweatshirt around her face again, made her arms disappear beneath the layers of her blankets and closed her eyes, not knowing the temperature would dip into the twenties overnight.

In the morning I heard Mom go into Dani's room and all exasperated and panicked say, "Jesus, Danielle," then run down the stairs. I threw my covers off and followed her to the porch. Dani was shivering and crying, balled up in the fetal position. Her hands tucked under her chin, my gloves lying on the floor. Mom tried to lift her up and yelled, "Are you crazy? Get inside." Dani just curled herself up even more. Mom pried one of Dani's hands free and said, "Danielle, squeeze my hand." She could barely move her fingers let alone make a fist, so Mom yanked her off the couch and pulled her into the kitchen. She ran the water, tested the temperature then put Dani's hands under it. As soon as her first finger touched it she let out a distorted scream, then squirmed away and fell on the floor. Mom tried to lift her up but Dani wasn't having it and rolled away. Mom yelled for her to stand up but she was thrashing around, yelling and impossible to get hold of.

"That's it. I'm taking you to the hospital."

Dani screamed, "NO," and stretched the word out for a good ten seconds, kicking the shit out of every snooze button in the neighborhood. She hated hospitals with a fear that seemed like it came from lifetimes ago. Wouldn't even go there with my mom for bring-your-kid-to-work-day. Indiana Jones had snakes, Superman had kryptonite, and Danielle Savage had hospitals. Why? Maybe she was scared of sickness or death. Maybe staying away from them convinced her she wouldn't turn into her mother. Maybe she just didn't like the slew of fading people laid out alone at a time when they shouldn't be. The kid's insides were a mystery to us all.

Mom tried to grab her again. "Danielle, get up."

Dani shook her head back and forth like she was shaking water out of her hair. Mom went into full force nurse mode; she wrestled Dani's hands out from under her arms and held her fingers right up to her face and said, "You see this?" Dani slammed her eyes shut and jerked her head away. "Look at this." Mom held her by her hair and made her look. "See that color around your nails? Your fingers are grey. You know what that means?" Dani tried to yank her head away again, Mom pulled it back. "It means they'll have to cut your fingers off if you don't get the circulation back. You need thermal pads and a tetanus shot and I don't have any of that here so you're going to the hospital. Now."

Dani said, "No."

Then Mom slapped her in the face, and that stopped the screaming.

"Get off this floor right now," Mom said, and schlepped Dani, now in a viciously quiet rage, to the car while I trailed them. Mom threw her in the front seat; I got in the back, still wearing my friggin pajamas. As soon as she pulled away from the curb Dani opened the door and jumped out. We had only got up to four miles an hour by that time so she didn't get hurt—just rolled over once on the street then got up and ran. Mom jammed on the brake, I slammed into the back of the front seat. We both jumped out and chased Dani down the block. Mom caught up and grabbed her by the hood of her sweatshirt so hard Dani's feet came off the ground mid-stride. Mom yelled, "ARE YOU TRYING TO KILL YOURSELF?" She slapped her in her ass a few times. "ARE YOU?" It got me wondering. Dani screamed again that she wasn't going to the hospital. Mom tucked her under her arm like a squirming football and carried her all the way to the car, which was stopped in the middle of the street. She opened the driver's-side door, threw her in and drove with one hand on the wheel, one on the hood of Dani's sweatshirt. At the hospital there was more screaming and wrestling from the car to the emergency entrance.

They got her circulation back and she didn't lose her fingers. But this is a hospital we're talking about—it seems like if a kid comes in there who has willingly given herself frostbite, a nurse or a doctor, or even a friggin orderly, might suspect something is messed up in their home or their head, and that they might try to hurt themselves again. But this was my mother's job and these were my mother's people. I don't know exactly what went down there—who decided to mind their own business and who justified what—all I know is no one in our house ever said anything about it again and Dad changed the locks on the door so we needed a key to get outside. Until then I thought it was cool that she slept outside—it was this quirky thing she did and made her . . . *her*. But when a quirky thing puts you in the emergency room it's not cool anymore.

July 12

I weave through the happy hour crowd of the East Village to my building. Stephanie and boyfriend are sitting on the front stoop. She's on the stair below him between his knees. He's whispering something in her ear that gives her an embarrassed laugh and takes a few years off her face.

When I get close me and Stephanie look at each other knowing we're beyond the point where we can't not say hello anymore. She says it first. I say it back. Boyfriend nudges her back with his chest probably wondering why she's so friendly with the new guy all of a sudden. Stephanie looks away from me to the step below. As I pass them on the stairs she looks back up and smiles at me. Boyfriend slaps her in the back of the head.

"What was that for?" she says.

"What was *that* for?" he says about our exchange.

His slap goes right through her head up my spine and out my mouth: "I said hi. You gonna make a deal outta that?"

Boyfriend looks at me slightly happy that I've started with him, but more mad than anything. "You gonna make it a deal?"

Stephanie says, "Nelson, stop."

"You stop," he tells her.

"She didn't do anything," I say. "Why you gotta hit her in the head?"

Nelson stands up. "Why you putting your business where it's not wanted?"

Now Stephanie stands up.

"I put it where I want to," I say.

"Keep it the fuck outta my face."

"Nelson, shut up."

"Oh, now you got his back," boyfriend says.

"I got nobody's back, I just don't want you fighting about stupid shit that ain't nothin."

"That's what we're doing?" I ask him. "We're fighting?"

"We ain't doing shit yet, but we can change that."

"Whenever you're ready."

He flies down the stairs to the street, spreads his arms out and shrugs his shoulders. "Ah-ight. Get off them stairs and we see."

"Nelson, stop that shit," Stephanie says. She jumps off the stairs to the street and on her way over to him does something weird. She pulls on her own ponytail. Pulls it so hard that she snaps her head back. It takes all of a half second, but it makes her face turn to something madder and older than it was before. She stands in front of him and puts her hands on his chest. "Nelson, forget it, forget it. This shit ain't worth it. He's just some guy lives in the building, knows my uncle, that's it. That's the whole story. You makin up the rest. Leave it the fuck alone or I'm history tonight."

"You wrong. I'm history tonight." He backs off like he's leaving. To me: "Watch your ass."

"Watch it for me."

Stephanie turns around pissed at me now. "Damn, just let him go. You stupid?"

Nelson says, "I am watching it." My final warning before he walks away.

"Why the fuck all you guys want to do is start throwing

62

down? Somebody look at you and you wanna throw. Fuck's wrong with you?"

"He started."

"No, you didn't just say that. You didn't just say 'he started it'."

"I meant he started with you."

"Oh, like I can't take care myself."

"No you can, I just—"

"Guys are stupid, yo."

"Only when a girl is involved," I say with little to no thought.

"Ain't no girl involved."

From above us we hear, "Estephanie, cómo estás?"

She and I both look up and see Ralphie standing on the fire escape. From three floors below I can see the face and hear the voice of the guy who has lived in this building way before this neighborhood was hip—when people were nodding out in his stairwells on a Tuesday, and when cops wrote it off as a wasteland. Standing on the fire escape is the guy who has kicked his share of derelicts off the stoop.

"Nada, tío Ralphie. We just talking. It's OK," Stephanie says. In her voice I can hear the shrewd innocence of a girl who has talked herself out of many kinds of trouble more than once—like she's got an arsenal of escape tones in the back of her throat. But this is light work so she only has to bring the innocent tone up to about a level two.

Me, I probably look guilty. I wave. "Hi, Ralphie." He gives us a nod that says he knows there was more going on besides talking. He looks down the block to see if boyfriend is still around. Nope. Ralphie shapes his face into a disapproving expression and makes sure Stephanie sees it before he ducks back in the window.

"I take it he doesn't like your boyfriend."

"Not really."

63

"Because he hits you?"

"He doesn't hit me." And that, from her arsenal, is a defensive and very convincing tone along the lines of, you-didn't-understand-what-you-saw-and-you-need-to-start-thinking-much-more-of-me-you-idiot.

"OK."

Stephanie feels the band at the back of her head that holds her ponytail. It's loose, so she separates and pulls a couple handfuls of hair to tighten it to her head.

"What you lookin at?"

"I'm just standing here."

"Me too." So we both do. Uncomfortably and for a while.

"Now what are you gonna do?" I ask.

"I'm not done standing here."

"It's Wednesday night and you got nothing to do?"

"You think I got nothing to do just because I got no man around?"

"I didn't mean it like that, I just figured your plans have changed and you might not have made new ones yet."

"So?"

"So?"

"So don't you got anything better to do?" she asks.

"I don't really like to make plans. They fuck me up."

"What's that mean?"

"Nothing. Long story."

We both just stand here for a little while brooding.

"Wanna go for a walk?" I finally ask.

She looks at me like I got problems. "A walk? Where?"

"I don't know. Around?"

"Around where?"

"Around New York."

"Are you wacked?" she says like she's asking me what time it is.

"No," I explain. Then I get skeptical of my answer. "Why?"

"You feel like you're a little off kinda."

"Look, I'm having a really bad year and your day doesn't seem to be any better, so I'm going to get a beer and take a walk, you're welcome to come or not come."

She looks at me like this makes no sense and therefore complete sense. "Ah-ight. I'ma go for a walk. Damn this guy is trippin."

<hr />

We've made our way into a vintage clothes shop on Avenue A. Stephanie liked a shirt in the window. I'm holding a beer in a bag and the saleswoman welcomed us in with a smile, but has been scoping me from behind the counter ever since.

"See now this can be all me." Stephanie checks herself out in a three-way mirror wearing a white billowy shirt.

"Then buy it."

"Naw, I don't just buy stuff."

"Why not?"

"If I want it, I leave it." She turns to get a side view. "I leave it for like two days then I come back just to make sure we still good together."

"Who's still good?"

"Me and the shirt. Yo, pay attention." She turns to face me. "Now, what you think?"

I crank up a little excitement and say, "I like it," then take a sip of my beer.

"I hate that word. Like. *I like it*," she says in a sarcastic high-pitched voice. And turns back to the mirror. "Don't you hate that word?"

"Not particularly."

"I mean I like food, but that's cause I got no choice but to eat.

If I get to pick something I'ma love it. Why I wanna waste my time on shit I only like? I don't gots a lot of clothes, but I love everything I wear."

"I guess I love pizza. But not with broccoli. Broccoli on pizza is a yuppie sacrilege."

"Yo, shut up, yo and tell me what you think of the shirt already."

"Why do you care what I think?"

"Cause your night sucks like mine."

"That's a good enough reason. Turn around." I take my time. "If we're talking about picking things cause we love them then get rid of that thing."

"Why," she says, all surprised and offended.

"Because it ain't for you. It looks good in some spots, you know like it's saying you look good right here . . ." I hold my hand in front of her boobs.

"But?" she says, leaning back.

"But at your waist it kind of puffs out and makes you look bigger than you are. And . . . let me see something." I lift the tag that hangs off the sleeve and read a handwritten $55. "It's costing you way too much to not be in love with every part of you. Hang that shit back up."

"Yo, don't you know shit? You not supposed to tell a girl she look fat."

"I didn't say you looked fat."

"Big, puffy, whatever you said, you ain't supposed to say it."

"OK, then tell me when else I'm supposed to lie and I might."

She turns profile in the mirror, pinches the shirt at her belly button and pulls it away from her waist far as it goes, checking out what that does to her. Then she lets it go and tries to flatten it against her stomach with her palm. "Damn."

"You gonna leave this one?"

"Yeah I'ma leave it. But maybe I'll come back in seven months."

"Why seven months?"

"Why you think?" she says and peeks back at me to make sure I understand.

"Is that why you're still with that guy?"

"Nelson," and she gives me a hard look.

"Sorry. Nelson. That why?"

"No."

"Then why?" She shrugs. "Are you cock clocked?"

"Fuck's that?"

"You heard of pussy whipped?"

I see it click in her head, and she smiles. "Ah-ight, I get it."

"That why you're with him?"

"Not uh."

"Then why?"

Stephanie computes my question—her eyebrows pinch together, form two lines between them, and her lips tighten. She doesn't answer this question with the aggressive clip I've been hearing so far. She wraps her lips around her answer and speaks it slowly. "Cause I like him."

Stephanie left the shirt. We stand on the street, I kill the last of my beer and throw it in a corner garbage can. "I wanna stop at that deli," I say pointing across the street.

"You drink a lot."

I shrug. "Probably."

We wait at the corner of Avenue A for the light to change, and some chick hustles across the street on a *Don't Walk* sign in front of two speeding cars. Every gorgeous part of her is coming right towards me and Stephanie. She's red in the lips, blonde in the hair, firm and soft in all the right places. Twenty-sixish? Her jeans worn perfectly at her crotch; she's got tits that someone somewhere lost an entire college fund trying to replicate. She can uncover a whole new layer of pretty by tucking her hair behind her ears, and probably hasn't paid for her own drink or lit her own cigarette since high school. Just before she reaches our side of the avenue, she literally stops traffic. The two cars slam on their brakes at the green light. Three guys poke their faces out their windows wrenching their necks in her direction, too stunned to scream or whistle. Some people laugh about how clinically insane those guys just went. This girl laughs too, feeling the familiar scene play out behind her. She's all grins as she steps onto the curb—loving the attention, walking like she's powerful and hot. And she is both. Stephanie's expression is all about envy—an envy that wants and hates this girl at the same time. She locks on this chick's face so carefully she could draw it. She keeps staring until this walking statue disappears into the Wednesday-night crowd.

Stephanie shakes her head, looks down the avenue. "You know what?" she says. "If you look at that girl's face, you can almost know for real what it's like to have anyone you want." Now she looks at me. "And no one you don't."

Two beers and two slices of pizza later we're calling it a night in the stairwell of our building. "Why were you carrying a piece of the sidewalk that day I seen you?"

"It was actually a piece of patio. I got it where I work. Now it's a table."

"What kind of table?"

"My only table."

"You eat from it?"

"Yeah. When I eat." Now we stop on her floor.

"You eat off an old sidewalk?"

"Patio. And I cleaned it."

"I wouldn't eat off no sidewalk."

"It's a patio already."

"Same thing."

"Not even close. If you wanna keep climbing I'll show you."

I open my door, flick on the light. "Welcome to the palace."

She looks blankly in every direction then down at the table. "That's it?"

"Try not to be so impressed."

"You put that thing on them crates and you call it a table?"

"You got a better name for it?"

"A big flat rock."

"It's slate."

"Big fat fuckin slate then."

"Well I like it."

"Boy is crazy. You're crazy." In a New York second Stephanie snaps into some kind of crime dog and cases the joint. She opens and closes all my cabinets, finds a couple glasses, a few boxes of pasta, and a half-used pint of white paint left by the old tenants. "No wonder you such a skinny ass." She opens the refrigerator: a plastic gallon of water, half a deli sandwich wrapped in paper, and a three-pack of Coors that used to be six. She closes the door with disgust.

"Can I see your search warrant, officer?"

She smiles, then pulls the bathroom curtain back. "No door?"

"Talk to your uncle."

She runs one hand on the counter, then runs the other over the table, holds her palms next to each other and to her surprise the table is cleaner than the counter. She gives me a suspicious look of approval, still not completely convinced the stone is worthy to eat from. Whirling around the room she says, "Damn you need some pictures or something. Does that stove even work?" She picks up my notebook from the table and cracks it open. I yank it out of her hand.

"Probably."

"Not that you got pots."

"Excuse me, but do you live here?"

"Fuck no."

I grab one of the two glasses out of the cabinet, fill it half with water from the fridge and excuse myself. In the bathroom I pop two Advil from their bottle, chew on them so they work faster—a trick my mom taught me—jerk my head back, then swallow.

I come out of the bathroom and Stephanie is looking at the futon mattress on the floor. "You got a mattress and a rock table on crates. That's it?"

"What else do you do in an apartment besides eat and sleep?"

"You *live* in it," she says like I forgot my own name.

"I live in this."

"Then you got a bare life. You don't even have curtains, yo. Cept the one over your bathroom door."

"I might get some."

"You think? Not even an answering machine on that phone. And where'd you get that shit from the nineteen seventies?"

"It's—"

"You must have a cell phone. You got a cell?"

"No."

"Why not?"

"Trust me. I'm better not easily found."

"What's in them boxes?"

"My clothes. And my books."

She gives me a look that questions my sanity. Then she takes a deep breath in and scopes the entire apartment and a quarter second before exhaling changes her whole attitude. "It's a nice place, though."

"Gee, thanks." She rocks around on her feet not knowing where to park herself. "So where you gonna live? You know, when you have your kid?"

"That's definitely the question." She keeps looking around the room like she's expecting to find something other than the mattress.

"Stay with your uncle?"

"Didn't ask him."

"Does he know?"

She walks to the open window and sits on the sill.

"I'll take that as a no." She gives me a look like she's impressed with my brilliance, then lifts a foot onto the sill, hugs her knee to her chest and looks down to the street. "What's up with your parents?" I ask. "I mean how old are you?"

"Which one you want me to answer?"

"Pick one."

"Sixteen."

"Parents?"

"Damn, you nosy."

"You're right. You don't have to tell me shit. Who the hell am I. You want something?" I make my way towards the fridge. "I got water. Like you might remember."

"I don't need anything."

"OK." I stop. We look at each other, I feel like I'm being sized up. I hold her eyes for a few not uncomfortable seconds, but then my hands don't know if they want to be on my hips, in my pockets, or just hanging down. They try all three.

She looks out the window again. "My mother's in jail."

My hands freeze mid-pocket. "What for?"

"Drugs."

"Selling?"

She nods. "And doing."

I take a few slow steps and stand next to her in front of the other window. "You visit her?"

"Maybe."

"How long's she been in jail?"

71

"Months, half year. I used to live with her uptown. Harlem. She went away and it was either my uncle or services. And fuck that."

We're leaving enough space between our sentences to dare the other person to keep talking.

"Ralphie seems like a good guy."

"Yeah, he's good."

"I seen a couple kids in your place the other day. Those your cousins?"

"Yeah."

"How many live in that apartment?"

"Counting me, five."

All night I've felt myself connecting to something about her, but I'm not sure what. There's something nonchalant about the way she talks about stuff, even the big stuff, letting her words out like cigarette smoke. But that's not what I'm connecting to.

"Why you looking at me like that?" she asks, the nonchalance upgrading to defense.

"I'm not looking at you like anything."

"Then what you doin?"

"I'm listening."

"You looking weird right now."

"This is my I'm-listening look. You just never seen me listen before."

"I ain't seen a lot of people listen."

She gets up and rubs her back where the window frame was digging into her. "I can't believe you live like this."

"You wanna ease up on my domicile."

"I mean, it's like . . . This ain't no home."

"Yes, it is."

"Your mother see you living like this?"

"Ha ha. No."

"What you mean 'ha ha'?"

"My mother was good at making our house look like people lived there. But really we all lived someplace else. You know what I mean?"

"You mean you don't like your family?"

"If I didn't answer that could we still keep talking?"

"Whatever." And she works her hand under her shirt and rubs her back again.

"You know you can sit on the mattress if you want. It's more comfortable than the windowsill. Plus it's all I got."

"Huh," she kind of laughs, and plops on the edge of it, now hugging both knees to her chest. "What's that?" she asks, looking at the book sprawled on the floor next to her.

"A book."

"You wish that was funny, right?"

"It's Gabriel García Márquez."

"Who he?"

"A great writer. Apparently."

"What's it about?"

"I have no clue. I'm reading it for a GED class, but I can't follow it for shit."

She nods, she's cool with that. "Might be better in Spanish."

"Can I ask about your dad?"

"Yeah. But you not gonna get a lot of answers."

"Whudda you mean?"

"I mean I ain't got nothin to say about him. I don't know where he is or what he does."

"When's the last time you saw him?"

"I don't remember." Whatever she can remember slows her rhythm down and puts her deep into her head. Even with me watching, she flips though memory files. Mostly to herself she says, "Stupid shit."

"What is?"

"My mother. I was like her gun. She took me to visit him a

73

couple times when I was young. She was fucked up about it. One time—I'm like five—she told me wear the clothes I had on yesterday. And no bath. I was like ah-ight, I didn't give a fuck, I hated baths anyway. And Moms, she usually took a bitch-bath in her perfume, but she didn't go near that shit that day. So we're walking there and she said, 'Lemme see your hands.' Ah-ight, here's my hands. She looked at them like she didn't like what she saw, then she take a chocolate bar out her purse, unwrapped it and tell me to scratch it. I was like, 'You crazy, Mom?' She say, 'Scratch it like it's got an itch.' I'm looking at her like she wants me to fuck a dog. She say, 'Just do it, do it now and you can eat it later.' So what do I know? She's my mom. I spend the rest of the day with chocolate bar under my fingernails. I didn't understand that shit then, but she was trying to play him like, *look at me and my poor dirty daughter*. Trying to make bank. Don't ask guys for shit. That's the only way you gonna get anything. She was twenty-whatever and she still didn't get it. He didn't say much. I do remember my mother askin him for money and him saying we should leave."

"She could have took him to court. Of course that don't always work out for the victim."

"Yo, I don't know why I'm telling you all this, and I definitely don't know why you askin."

"Me neither. But why does the why matter?"

She silently rips that question apart to see what's really in it, and her eyes squint into something that looks like an assault.

OK, now I see what I'm connecting to. It's a fight. Chick's got a constant fight going on. Her head is always slightly jutted forward like she's sniffing into the future for her next opponent. She's maybe five-two, maybe ninety and change. And she's squishy-cheek cute. Her whole physical package makes you want to pet her, but her attitude rests in something

74

more like an I-dare-you-muthfucka. I don't know if I should keep my gloves up or arms open. "Look, you wanna talk, then talk. You don't wanna talk then . . . I don't know, decorate my apartment."

"That was a little funny."

"Thanks."

She scoots back on the mattress, leans against the wall. Her eyes focus on something inside her. "I tried to go see him by myself when I got older. I was stressing. It's weird going to see your parents when you don't even know them. I went to the building. It was like hard just walking there. I felt like I was pulling a whole subway car behind me. His name wasn't on the mailbox no more and I asked a woman walking out the building if she knew him, she said no. So I left. And then when I left I felt like I got rid of my whole train." She laughs. "That train shit don't make no sense, I'm just tired." Now she slumps off the wall, lies back on the mattress, puts the pillow under her head, and keeps her feet on the floor, knees up. "It wasn't like draggin a train. It was like . . . I don't know, like being fat."

"That fucking sucks."

"You telling me?"

I shake my head. "You have any other family?"

"I got two aunts. Ralphie's sisters in Dominican Republic."

"I could hear your accent really strong just then."

"What accent?"

"Your, you know, Dominican accent."

"You didn't know I was Dominican before two seconds ago."

"No, I didn't."

"Where you think I was from?"

Very definitively I say, "Somewhere."

"White guys." She gives me a smile.

"What are their names, your aunts?"

"Lunie and Odalis. Valentine."

75

"Heard the accent again."

"Shut up, yo."

"No, no. I like it. And Valentine—I like that."

"Yeah."

"Ever been there?"

"Naw. They send letters to Ralphie. I read em sometimes. I got cousins there too."

"They your age?"

"Yup. Little younger."

She takes the stretchy tie out of her ponytail and closes her eyes. A few strings of hair break away from all the gel on her head. "Your hair ever move?"

"When I want it to."

She's slowing down now. All night she's been talking all kinds of fast and flashing faces at me, but not now. Her face is off duty and her voice is low.

"Shouldn't you be going out or something?"

"You kicking me out?" she asks without opening her eyes.

"No. I mean it's *Wednesday* night and all. Don't you usually go out?"

"And do what?"

"I don't know. Go to a club, get your swerve on."

Now her eyes open and her head pops up. "Damn you gettin more white as this night goes." She flops back down.

"I know it. Whudda you want me to tell you? My people don't swerve. They jig."

"No you do not know how to jig."

"I seen people do it at weddings."

"Oh, shit." She's cracking up. "That's some funny shit."

"Not that funny."

"Alls I can see now is you doing a jig. You wanna show me some?"

"Yeah, right." I take off my boots and lie on my back on

76

the mattress about a foot away from her. After a moment, she pushes her sneakers off with her feet then turns on her side. Her hands fall into a prayer position then sneak between her knees, like it's what they do every night.

Now we're quiet. And I don't know about her, but I'm not trying to think of things to say. I like it like this. It's a different kind of quiet than the middle of the night quiet I'm used to. I feel calm. I think by us not talking we're saying we're cool with each other. Cooler, in a way, than we were when we were talking.

"Sometimes I like not talking," I say.

"Um hum." More quiet.

Then some more.

Stephanie says, "I can hear you when you say serious stuff." She let that sentence out with a yawn.

"Huh?"

"Mostly when guys want to talk serious I can't really hear them. Like they mumble or they whisper."

"I only whisper when I'm trying to get laid."

She laughs. "You do that a lot?"

"Honestly, not really."

Our voices are so heavy and uncensored, like the end of this day is the end of a life and how much could it matter what we say right now.

"You don't stress me out." She sounds curious.

"That's good."

Quiet.

"Right? That's good?" I ask.

"Um hum." She snuggles her head deeper into the pillow.

Quiet again.

It's hard to tell if my tiredness is coming from her. I mean I can barely sleep with myself, so I just figured I couldn't sleep with anyone else, but now I'm thinking I can sleep with her. And I guess she's staying, although I don't want to ask.

I get up and make for the light. I turn it off and stand with my fingers on the switch making sure she's cool with that. Judging from her stillness, she seems to be. I take my fingers off it, go back to the mattress and shape the same position.

We lay here feeling out the new atmosphere.

"I don't want that shirt," she says through heavy lips.

"OK."

A few minutes later I flip on my side, my front inches from her back.

Noises jump five floors from the street through my window, so do the muddy yellow streetlights, and without curtains it's only dark as a rainy day in here.

Stephanie's breathing just got deeper. I look at her ribs under her shirt going up and down like a bow sliding on strings. Oh man. I really want there to be no other thought in my head, no other light in this room, no other sound, no other movement except her ribs. I stare, I mesmerize myself, but I don't see her ribs alone. Way too many memories of rivers and blood jerk around my brain. And not even this girl who trusts me enough to leave me alone with her breath can change that.

In spite of my head I put my arm over her waist trying not to disrupt anything. The only thing on her that moves is her arm—she lifts it from between her knees and slaps my hand fast and hard. I pull it back and keep my hands to myself.

My arms just twitched. My heart's doing its wee-hour drum solo. I must have fallen asleep for a bit. Stephanie is out cold. It's much quieter outside. Sounds like the bars are closed. But it's not getting light yet. Moving in slow motion, I sit up. Stephanie stretches into the empty space I filled a second ago. I wait for her to settle. I ease myself off the mattress, crouch next to her. My God she has beautiful lips. Her shirt rode up above her hip bone and I can see what looks like the top of a huge scar.

I pull the sheet over her. My knees crack when I stand up. Whoa, fucking headache. Dizzy. I put a hand on the wall for balance. In the kitchen I suck down two glasses of water, setting the glass onto the table with the least amount of noise I can. I sit on the floor in front of the table. Stare at the skinny black notebook for a while. And a while longer. A single car accelerates down 9th Street. I open the book. My handwriting is hard to decipher in some places, the words come in and out of focus, like the letters themselves are teetering between awake and asleep. My body feels like it could doze again, but I know better.

I hear Stephanie thrashing in the bed behind me. I flip around. She's pulled the sheet off herself. Now she rolls over onto her side. Then onto her stomach. She gets on her knees, folds her arm around her gut, and plants her face into the pillow. She stays there breathing heavy. Before I can say anything she scrambles up like there's a fire, heading straight for the bathroom. I get to my feet, "What the fuck?" She runs right past me, eyes still mostly closed, flings the bathroom curtain out of her way, drops to her knees, lifts the toilet seat, and throws up.

Oh. That's what the fuck.

After three long heaves and a lot of coughing she flushes. "Goddamn," she says through a scratched throat, then flicks on the light and turns on the tap. She slurps up water from her hand, swishes then spits. She does this three times. She comes out of the bathroom breathing a little heavy, wiping her lips with her fingers. Her face says the taste isn't out of her mouth yet, so she goes to the kitchen sink and spits one more time. Then runs the water over it. She holds herself up with the edge of the sink, breathing for a second. "Who's Dani?"

And my heart was just about to start slowing down.

"What did you just say?"

79

She turns around, wipes her mouth with the back of her hand and says, "I didn't see anything when I touched your book last night, or tonight, or whenever it was. But I seen *Dear Dani.* I didn't see any more of the letter." She sniffles. Swallows. "Who is she?"

There's quiet.

"Come on, I told you all kinds of shit." I still can't speak. "I write letters, too. To my aunts in Dominican Republic. I didn't tell you it last night, cause I didn't feel like it, but I do. Got a whole box of them in my uncle's apartment. Is Dani your girlfriend?"

"No."

Stephanie buttons the top of her pants that must have come undone in her sleep.

She struggles to focus her puffy eyes on me.

"You sure?"

"Positive."

"Then who?"

I pause. Close the notebook. "You sure you don't wanna go back to sleep?"

"Yeah."

"It's a long motherfuckin story," I say trying to brush it all off.

"That's OK with me." She nudges me with a nod.

Now we're in a mini staring contest. Her face waking up, already receiving whatever I might tell her. "All right." I put the notebook under the table. "You should probably sit down for this."

She looks around for a chair that doesn't exist.

Wherever they stood

When I turned twelve and my dad told me he needed to take me to his favorite bar and treat me to my first official game of pool as a teenager, I didn't tell him he was off by a year. I was all for him making me older than I was; I enjoyed feeling twelve months closer to leaving the house. It was better than my dad getting my age right. I would have killed to know what it was like to have a job. To own a set of keys to something. Be able to drive. To have my own place. To shave. To feel a naked lady. To shave a naked lady. To see how light it felt to have my parents off my back. So when he said *teenager* I thought, *cool, let's shoot some pool and kill a whole year while we're at it.*

After dinner, Mom, Dad, Dani and I ate ice-cream cake, I opened my new Nerf football with a plastic kicking tee, then my dad said, "Jake, go in the living room, to the lamp table next to the couch."

Mom said, "No, you don't."

"There's a little drawer under it."

"John, no."

"Frannie, yes. Open the drawer and get the keys out and bring them over here."

I did what he asked and from the living room I heard my mom say, "Where are you taking him?"

"He's my son. I'm taking him out for a ride. Now, that's enough."

Two shiny silver keys on a ring. He had soldered the separation on the ring so the keys were going nowhere. A medallion hung from it on a little silver chain, on one side it had a black cobra showing off its fangs, on the other my dad's initials. I have to admit, when I shook it around in my hand, heard the pieces clink together and felt its weight, I actually was older than twelve.

A 1965 Shelby Cobra. Two-seater, ragtop. Red with two thick white lines running over the hood and the trunk. So compact and low to the ground it looks like it can muscle its way underneath an eighteen-wheeler and throw it off its back. This thing is shinier than the counters at the Yonkers Raceway Diner and curvier than the waitresses. The way the story goes, Dad bought it the year I was born. What little refurbishing it needed, he and Noke's father, Ricky, did together. He would drive it a couple times a year, the first clear spring and fall days. That was about it. It sat in the garage as something I wasn't allowed to breathe on. I would stand on my toes at the window, press my face between my cupped hands and spy on it like it was a naked lady. But that night Dad pulled the garage door open, carefully slid the cover off it, folding it up as he went, and then, like a guy who knows how to wear the fuck out of a smile, said, "Get in."

If you put a car in neutral and keep your foot lightly on the brake, you can roll out of our garage, down the slope of our driveway, take a slight left and let the hill pull you the two blocks to the entrance of the Bronx River Parkway without having to hit the gas. And that's exactly what he did. Kept it in neutral as we crawled towards the entrance ramp and revved it a few times so I could hear the power and speed to come. We got to the parkway entrance and he said, "Hold on."

The wind blew my hair to one side; my dad grinned at me.

When we pulled up to the bar and got out of the car, heads turned and fingers pointed; people grinned at us like we had something they wanted, like we were famous.

He introduced me to the bartender as his "sidekick, Jake", and told him it was my birthday. "Happy birthday, son." I said thank you with the deepest voice I could manage. And he said, "You're welcome," in the same voice, which made me feel even farther from being a teenager than I was. Then my dad leaned close to him. "Smitty, we're just gonna shoot a game."

"Savage, I'd say something about if I thought anyone would care." My dad ordered a pint of Harp for himself and a soda for me that Smitty sank a skinny black straw in. Van Morrison's "Caravan" busted out of the jukebox like a birthday song and, feeling important, I followed my dad as he strolled to the pool table.

The place smelled like a cocktail of beer, smoke and lipstick. The windows were caked over in grime that the streetlights couldn't seep through. The only brightness came from the blue and red jukebox, one dim bulb over the pool table and neon Budweiser and Heineken signs. The barstools' vinyl seats were cracked and peeling from all the ass they'd had in the past twenty years. A woman in tight jeans, legs crossed, sat at the bar next to a guy who talked to her about something that had nothing to do with the fact that his hand was on her thigh. Past the bar were a few booths, one filled with four guys getting loud over a pitcher, another with a couple who tried to disappear in each other, which seemed like an easy thing to do in that place even if you didn't have someone to fold yourself into.

Two guys already had the pool table. My dad took me aside, sat me on a stool where we could see the game and said, "First thing we wanna do is watch these guys. See what they got and see if we can beat them. Understand?"

"Yeah." We watched them and they watched us watch them. After a few shots I asked, "What are we watching for?"

"Good question. Technique and confidence. Look at the guy in the white shirt, the one about to shoot. You can tell by the way he chalks up his cue he knows what he's doing. And see the way he looks at the table? He's scanning every ball. He's not just looking at the shot he's about to make, he's looking three shots ahead. And he doesn't crouch down and close one eye to line up his shots. Pool players from Omaha do that. Not that there's no good pool players in Omaha. But how would I know?"

Dad told me to take a few more sips of my soda. After I did he reached into his jacket, came out with a flask and poured something that looked like water into my Coke. That was the first time I smelled vodka and I swear I about got drunk off the fumes. I looked up at him as he screwed the cap back on the flask, and he hit me with one of his wink/smirk combos I'd seen him throw on my mom. It was a combination that stretched her bitter look into a smile and left her ready for surrender or compromise. She hated it, but was defenseless against it. You don't really see its magic until you're on the receiving end of it. In the quick of a light the room and your own thoughts disappear. The lines around his eyes spread into sun rays, as he admits, just between you and him: you're his favorite, the only one who really exists for him. And you believe every fractured second of it.

The white-shirt guy leaned over the table and set himself up for the shot. "He's gonna try and bank the green ball off that far cushion and get it in the close-left corner pocket. Watch." The ball hit off the far cushion and headed for the corner, but it hit the back of the pocket so fast it jumped right out. "Speed kills," my dad whispered to me. "He hit that way too hard. A little softer it would have stayed in. He's got good aim, but lousy control. He's jumpy. Guy like that can fly off the handle." Dad gave a knowing nod. "We wanna play this guy."

He walked to them and put four quarters on the side of the table. "We got next game, OK?"

The guy said, "Sure."

My dad came back and said, "Didn't wanna challenge him yet. Don't wanna seem anxious."

Eventually the guy in the white shirt sank the eight ball to end the game. He shook hands with his friend and called out to us, "You guys are up."

"Hey listen, you guys wanna play my son and me? It's his birthday and I told him we would win him twenty bucks at the table tonight. You in?"

"How old is he?"

"Old enough. You in?"

They looked at each other and laughed. "All right," the guy in the white shirt said. "We'll play you."

And that's when it got embarrassing, because even I knew I was being humored, that these guys were about to go for ten dollars each on a birthday present in the form of a thrown game. But my dad was having so much fun. He put the quarters into the slots, pushed the lever, the balls came out, he said, "Rack em, JT," and I thought, *What the hell, I'll play along.*

"Dad, why do you put chalk at the end?"

"So it doesn't slip off the cue ball. The white one."

"Got it."

Dad broke and pocketed two balls. He explained that we had to hit all the striped balls in and then the eight ball to win. "You try." And he handed me the stick, which was just a little shorter than me. "See the green one?"

"Yeah."

"You're gonna hit it into the left corner pocket."

"I am?"

"You are."

"How?"

"See where the light is reflecting off of it on the top right, that little speck of light?"

"Yeah."

"You're gonna hit the white ball so it hits that green ball right in that spot."

"Got it." I aimed my stick at the white ball.

"You gotta call it," my dad said.

"What?"

"You gotta say, 'Fourteen, corner.'"

I took a deep breath. "Fourteen, corner."

"Good. Don't hit it too hard. Just kiss it."

I had to lift one foot off the ground to take the shot. My hands were so sweaty the cue didn't slide through my fingers, it stuttered. I drew the stick back and hit the cue ball; where, I couldn't tell you, but apparently it was in the right spot because I actually sank the fourteen.

My dad let out a victory scream that wrenched necks. With hands that shook with excitement, but were steady with strength, he picked me up by the waist, lifting me over his head, making me the highest one in the bar. I held the cue over my head with both hands like my conquering weapon; he pumped me up and down and let out another scream that made everyone in the place—even our opponents—look up and toast me with a smile.

It felt good to be twelve.

Or thirteen.

Or whatever he thought I was.

That was, of course, the only ball I came remotely close to sinking. The rest of the time I'd hit one ball that would hit about six or seven other balls and four cushions with no results at all. Pop said, "Well at least you're playing a defensive game."

Every time my dad got up to take a shot he'd walk around the entire table and manage to bump into one if not both of the other guys. The room was small, no doubt, but I didn't see the strategy in turning pool into a contact sport.

After about the fourth intentional bump my dad turned around to the guy in the white shirt and said, "You trying to screw up my timing?"

"I'm trying to get out of your way, take it easy."

Dad looked at him long enough for it to be awkward. Guy said, "Take your shot."

"I will. Back off." Dad turned slowly and set himself for the shot. The guy made a face at his friend like, *what's this guy's problem?*

When it was the other guy's turn to shoot my dad bumped him from behind and screwed up his shot. "Doesn't feel so good, does it?"

"Listen, you got a big problem—that's obvious. But keep this shit up and you're gonna have another one."

Then the other guy jumped in. "Come on guys, take it easy, it's the kid's birthday."

"The kid's got nothing to do with this," my dad said. "It's your friend who's got his panties twisted."

"No panties under here, pal."

"Sorry. I meant diapers."

"How you want this birthday to go?"

"Just take your shot," Dad said.

"I will. Why don't you back up?"

"Sure." My dad did. The guy leaned over to take his shot and my dad said, "Asshole."

And that's what it took for the guy to turn around and get inches away from my dad's face, yell, "The fuck's your problem?"

We all knew that wasn't a real question. That it was just a preface to a punch. And the white-shirt guy would have been better off skipping that, because in the middle of his useless etiquette my dad raised his pool cue and slammed it in his balls. White-shirt guy folded in half like a switchblade and apparently understood that questions were no longer necessary, because from his bent position he drove his shoulder in my dad's gut, wrapped his arms around his waist and tackled him. Soon as my father's back hit the floor his neck snapped back and his head clapped against the tiled floor like a bowling ball. That scared me sick. The whole thing scared me, but that sound—the whiplash crack of it . . . even right now, playing it over in my ears, sends nausea through my stomach.

After that, the white-shirt guy landed his fist clear on the left side of Dad's face. He couldn't swing after that because his friend had grabbed his arms and pulled them behind his back and lifted him off Dad.

Maybe I was trying to drown out that sound I'd just heard, or maybe it was the couple sips of vodka, maybe because Dad finally felt like my teammate and teammates were supposed to back each other up, but I swung my cue. It skimmed it off the guy's white shirt. He didn't even notice. Then as hard as I could, I hit the table with it and it splintered like a bat off a fastball. I figured I was done. I had no more weapons and as a twelve-year-old kid I didn't need to go any further into the fight barehanded. So I just stood back and watched Smitty the bartender and three other guys pull everyone apart. The same eye that my dad had just winked sunlight out of was swollen and red. Smitty held my father in a full nelson and pushed him towards the door saying, "That's enough, Johnny. You gave em a good show." And Dad— as he was getting dragged out—smiled at me.

I looked back at the guy in the white shirt who, breathing heavy, and now released from his friend's grip, shook his head at me like something was a shame.

Outside Dad threw me the keys and said, "You drive."

"*I* drive?"

"Yeah, come on. We did real good in there, so we take the victory lap home."

I wasn't sure what doing real good in there meant to him. Starting a fight he had no chance of winning? Having his eye messed up? Getting thrown out by Smitty? We didn't even win the game.

"I'm not so good at driving, Dad."

"I'll show you."

Great. Just when I thought we were done with life lessons for the evening, I was about to learn how to drive the guy's prized possession. I had no First Holy Communion, no confirmation, no walkabout, no fire ceremony, not even a Briss—but my rite of passage was waiting for me in the parking lot of an old Irish pub.

Cars feel a lot bigger when you're behind the wheel. He folded up his jacket and put it under me so I could see over the steering wheel. When I came close to going off the road or veering too far into the other lane my dad—between checking out his swollen eye in the mirror—reached over, jerked the wheel and straightened me out. "You can't just hold the wheel straight, you gotta keep moving it. Roads are never straight even if they look it, so you gotta make little movements along the way."

"I'm trying."

"Get on the parkway."

"WHAT?"

"Make a left up here and get on the Bronx River. You can do it."

"No, no, no—"

"Hey just do what I tell you."

I got on and hugged the white line of the shoulder for my life.

After a few minutes Dad asked if I knew how fast I was going. I was too scared to take my eyes from the road to the speedometer, so I guessed. "Forty?"

"Try again."

"Forty-five?"

"Again."

"Forty-eight?"

"Son, you're doing *fifteen* miles an hour on the highway. You gotta pick it up. Give yourself a little more gas and get up to forty." I pushed on the pedal. My hands held so hard on that wheel you could have chiseled initials into my knuckles. "That's it. You're doin it. Remember: little movements. You always gotta adjust to your surroundings."

"Got it."

"If you see a deer, lean on the horn. They get stuck in light, but horns make them run."

"Since when do we have deer around here?"

"Never. I'm just telling you in case you drive someplace that does."

Apparently I got better at adjusting to my surroundings and we drove in silence for a little while.

Dad lit up a cigarette. "I know something about you, Jake."

"What's that?"

"You know how to back up your friends. You know how I know?"

"No."

"Because you swung the cue. If you'd just stood there and didn't do anything then no one would know if they could ever count on you for anything. Anyone who was watching you tonight knows that you back up your friends and fight when it's right to. And I was watching."

Yeah, it wasn't a game of pool and an illegal drink he gave me for my birthday. It was a test. And I was only driving home because I passed.

"When's it right to?"

"Decisions, decisions. They're a bitch."

Dani was asleep when we walked in, or at least she was in her room with the lights off. Mom was waiting in the kitchen for us

90

and when we came through the door Dad headed right for the refrigerator. "You should have seen your son. A natural on the table."

"What happened to your eye?"

Dad cracked open his beer and slurped the suds off the top. "Nothing. He was like a pro out there."

Mom looked at me. "You OK, Jake?"

"Yeah."

"Course he is," Dad said. "Kid had fun for once."

She threw him an accusing look then said to me, "Maybe you should go to sleep now." She came and gave me a hug and ran a hand over my whole head. It had a medical feel to it like she was searching for bumps. She said, "Happy birthday, Jake." Then she examined my face.

"Thanks."

Dad said, "Jake, we gotta do this again. You're a natural."

"Yeah."

"Maybe we get you your own stick next year."

"Sure. Night, Dad."

Climbing the stairs I heard the muffled voices of an unhappy and dejected wife and a father who more than anything just wanted her off his back.

———

I woke up that night having to pee real bad and stumbled down the hall with my eyes half open, guided by light seeping through the cracks of the bathroom door. Everything in our bathroom is white; the bathtub and bowl, the sink, the tiles and curtains. Only the floor is blue. The light from our ceiling fixture bounced off all that white and lit the room so hard that when I pushed the door open and walked in, my eyes got blown out for a second. Then my father came into focus. He was standing in front of the bowl, with his back to me, pants open like he was taking a leak. It took a second to register that my sister was sitting on the toilet bowl facing him. My father whipped around, zipping his pants and said, "Don't you know when to leave people alone?" My sister hustled past me and into her room. Dad said, "Get out, Jake." But I didn't move. He headed for the door and I moved out of his way. "Leave people alone," he said in my direction, his mouth smelling like a distillery. He moved down the stairs in the same dreamlike state I had just been in a few seconds ago. I followed.

In the living room we passed the couch he slept on when he and my mother were fighting, passed the tables with all the pretty framed pictures I could barely see—the house lit only by bleeding streetlights—but could feel looking at me. He stubbed his foot on a dining-room chair I'd spent so many dinners sitting on, listening to him chew.

He stopped in the kitchen and wrestled a bottle out of the cabinet. I saw his head in silhouette teetering back and forth on his neck like someone about to fall asleep at the wheel. I hit on the lights; his eyes squinted to a slit. The smile on his face turned to a deep frown, then back to a smile again. He opened his bottle, tilted his head back, poured a couple seconds' worth in his mouth, then swallowed and wiped his lips on his wrist. He kept his head pointed toward the ceiling and spread his arms wide like he was keeping balance on a tightrope or impersonating an airplane.

"What are you two doing awake?" My mother had come up behind me, stood in the doorway, and sussed that my dad was loaded. "Come on, Jake, leave him alone and go to bed." I thought, *what woke you up, Mom? Was it Dad? Or was it Danielle? Was it a tiny noise she made when she was trying hard not to make a sound because she was too scared? And have those sounds been waking you up for a long time now?*

Have you rolled over and fallen asleep on them? What are you trying to keep me from seeing by standing in the doorway of our kitchen in your nightgown?

Mom pulled at my pajama top to get me to start walking away. "Let's go Jake, let him sleep it off."

I kept my feet firm, looked in my dad's direction and said, "What did you do?" He fluttered his lips and specks of saliva spewed out between them.

My mother said, "He does all kinds of dumb stuff when he's drunk. Just go to bed. There's nothing you can do when he's like this."

Again I asked: "What did you do?"

"Trust me, he doesn't know what he's doing," my mother said like she was bored with him. "I've seen him get naked at parties when he was drunk. He can't even hear you."

Finally.

Watching my mother bury her head to what was going on and watching my father get away with it in his blackout, finally all the old anger and pictures of sunsets made sense.

My father turned to clay and crumbled down in front of me. I felt sane. I felt smart.

And I felt murderous.

I looked at the knife rack on the counter. Was he right? Could I be trusted to fight when I had to? And would I fight dirty? Sneak attack without a war council? I wanted to take that knife and cut out a chunk of his neck to make up for the fingers my sister almost lost to frostbite. A couple hours ago I smacked a pool cue over a guy's back. How much of a leap could it have been? And how could he have argued? He beat on a guy to commemorate a birthday. He must have agreed that the punishment for messing with my sister needed to be something more than that.

I walked to the knife rack, my eyes on him the whole time.

"Jake, just leave him alone before he starts swinging at

someone." She sounded a little more alarmed, and didn't want to get close to him.

It seemed logical to think that slicing him would be passing another one of his tests. It would mean a body and bloodstains on the floor. It would also mean charges piling up on me so high that the whole city, all its cops, lawyers and judges and everyone else would see it from wherever they stood. I'd be underneath that pile suffocating, my father standing on top of it.

Those images stopped my hand from taking the knife out of its holder. They made me want to be different than violent. Something worse maybe. Something he hated, that defied what he taught me to be, and was proud of me for being. I just didn't know exactly what that was.

Right now what I really want to be is a guy who can step into this scene and tell me to pick up the phone when everyone is asleep and call the cops. But options aren't retroactive.

"Will you just go to bed," my mother said again, all exasperated and shit. "Please."

And I did. I didn't go to my sister's room, or for the phone—I didn't call anyone out on anything, I asked no questions. I shut my mouth, walked out of that kitchen, left my parents alone and went to bed. Just like I did again and again for the next five years.

July 13

Odessa Diner, Avenue A, early morning. Stephanie and I sit in a window booth, me in my beat-up work jeans and t-shirt, Stephanie in yesterday's outfit. I'm wolfing down my breakfast, she moves her scrambled eggs around with a fork, mostly just looking at them. "Hard to eat in the morning?" I ask.

"Hard to do everything in the morning." She abandons the fork. "You always wake up this early?"

"I'm always up this early, but the waking up happens all night."

"Every night?"

"Every night since."

"That's like a year?"

"Just like a year, only longer."

"Damn, that sucks. I mean for real, that sucks."

"I agree. What time you got?"

She checks her watch, allowing me to change topics. "Seven forty-two. What time you go to work?"

"Eighty-thirty."

"Every day?"

"That's why they call it work. What time you have to be at school?"

"I don't."

"My bad, it's fuckin July."

"I'm done with school, anyways."

"You graduate early?"

"Nah, I'm just done."

She picks up her fork again and successfully takes a bite.

"Why?"

With a full mouth she says, "Being in school, not being in school, what's the difference?" A piece of egg flies from her mouth to my plate. We both look at it then look back to each other. "Sorry," she laughs, and puts a hand over her mouth, sweetly embarrassed.

"Difference is, if you go to school you can go to college."

"People in my family can't even pronounce college."

"Oh, and that means you shouldn't go?"

"With what?"

"With your brains and good looks."

"Boy is trippin."

"No I'm not, it's true. At least the brain part."

She leans back in the booth. "Excuse me?"

"I mean the brain part is what gets you into college."

She leans forward, forearms on table. "Let me tell you something about women."

"Oops."

Now she takes her fork in her fist and points it at my face. "Don't ever, ever let them think that you or anyone else might be thinking their looks ain't good."

"OK, I'm gonna backtrack just a little and say that no matter how good-looking you are, if you want to go to college—and I know you can—then you have to graduate high school first. Or at least get a GED, which is what I'm doing. It's easy, you should—"

"Um hum." She holds the fork in eating position again.

"And you are good-looking." No response. "Cute as fuck all."

She gives me a sarcastic squint. "Pretty as all get out." With food in my mouth: "Flowers are envious."

"Shut up."

"You can give a guy whiplash on a scantily clad day."

"Whoa, check out the big words on the college boy."

"Check out the beautiful girl on the other end of the table." We stare at each other. "Who is probably really smart."

"You gonna shut up now?"

"Yes."

I eat. She pushes eggs.

"So what do you do all day when you're not in school?"

"Babysit. Part-time."

"So what about when your kid comes?"

"Then I'll babysit full-time. Cept they call it mothering and you don't get paid."

I go back to eating. I feel her staring at me so I look up. "What?"

"Yo, what's up with ketchup *and* hot sauce on your eggs?"

"It's good. You should try it."

"I'm Dominican, not Mexican."

"I've noticed."

She looks out at the rush-hour crowd on their way to a normal workday. The scene glazes her eyes a bit. "You know, I don't sweat what you did." Then she turns to me and we hold a stare for a second.

"What did I do?"

"Trying to steal your dad's car. With your friend and everything—what was his name again?"

I take a deep breath to get it out. "They call him Nokey."

"Yeah that's whacked. Anyway, I heard more fucked up things." I have no trouble believing she has. And now I remember the scar on her hip and wonder if that's one of them.

"Well thanks for saying that."

She nods. "But how come they ain't putting your dad on trial too?"

"They might."

"Might?"

"Might, might not. It's complicated. Sometimes laws work in the wrong people's favor."

"I feel you."

"Hey, what happened to your hip?"

"What hip?" Her fight coming out again.

"Your left. What happened to it?"

She drops her head and pokes around her plate. "Nothing happened to it."

"It's a birthmark?"

"No."

"Then what?"

She sighs with a frustration that's older than she is. She drops her fork onto her plate, leans back in the booth, yanks her shirt up from her hip and pulls her pants far down enough so I can see it. "Here."

"The fuck is that?"

"What's it look like?"

"Umm, a tattoo of a Playboy Bunny with a blunt in its mouth?"

"Good for you." Now she yanks her pants down a little further. Underneath the smoking bunny spelled out in black medieval letters is *NELSON*.

"Please tell me you were drunk."

"I don't get drunk." She sits back up, grabs her fork, and looks out of the corner of her eyes to see who else saw that.

"Man. You didn't think of maybe getting it airbrushed onto a t-shirt or something."

"Look, I showed you, now shut up about it."

"OK." I stay quiet for a few seconds. "I only asked because I thought it was a scar."

"It might be. Look, I just want him to . . . Shit. You never did something to yourself thinking it might change someone else more than it be changing you?"

This pauses the shit out of me. "Maybe."

We keep eating.

"Yo, put your napkin on your lap," she tells me.

"What?"

"Your napkin. You supposed to put it on your lap. It's not doing you any good on the table."

"It's catching the stuff flying from your mouth."

"Now who's being cute?"

She dips her finger in her glass and flicks me with water.

"Wise ass," I tell her. She nods in agreement. "I think you're gonna be a great mom." And she smiles the kind of smile that replaces her fight with self-possession.

More eating.

"Hey, yesterday . . ." I ask.

"What about it?"

"When we were on the stairs with your boyfriend and you went after him . . . what was the deal with you pulling your hair? Why'd you do that?"

"I pulled my hair?"

"Yeah."

"You trippin again."

"You did."

"Why would I pull my own hair?"

"That's my question."

"Yo, you stupid, yo."

"Says the chick who didn't graduate high school."

"Shut the fuck up." She means it.

We pause.

"I'm sorry," I say.

We pause more.

99

I scoop up the last of my eggs, then drop the fork onto the plate.

"Ah-ight, now I'ma aks you something," she warns me. "You don't gotta answer, but . . . Ah-ight, let's say you stole the car and you really did sell it to someone—"

"OK." This is not someplace I want to go, but we're here.

"—and then they have to register the car, get insurance and shit, right?"

"Yeah?" I see where she's going.

"Well they got computers. Won't the car show up like it's stolen when they try to do that?"

"Yeah, but it would have been long gone by then."

"OK, lemme aks you something else. Your father would have called the police."

"Yeah, but it would have been long gone there, too."

"Yeah, but if the cops seen that nobody tried to break in the house, ain't they gonna go to the only other guy who's got a set of keys to the house? The guy who is you?"

Pause.

"Yeah."

Pause.

She looks at me like she's telling me to add it up.

"We didn't think that one all the way through, OK? Are we done?"

She says, "We done," like she knows something and is not going to share it.

I pull the paper napkin off my lap, wipe my mouth, then ball it up and throw it on the table. I stare at the red streaks and blotches on it as it tries to unfold itself back to life. I see the refrigerator. Hear the hum of it. The picture on it. The paint. Red and white. The magnets. I see white underwear. And I can't help it, but I see bloody pussy.

"Shit!" Stephanie yells.

"What?"

She sinks down on the booth and puts her face under the table.

"You gonna puke again?"

"It's Nelson."

"Where?"

"Across the street waiting for the light."

"Oh, shit."

"He see me?"

"I don't know. Fuck's he doing up this early?"

"Fuckin tonto."

"He just saw *me*."

"Shit."

"He's lookin right at me."

"Shit."

"He's walking this way."

"Shit!" She slips out from under the table, starts to crawl.

"The fuck you doing?"

"Don't look at me, don't look at me."

"OK. But get off the floor, you look deranged."

"Shut up."

Stephanie makes it to her feet and runs hunchbacked low to the floor all the way to the back of the restaurant. A waitress spins out of her way. Everyone watches her until she pushes through the bathroom door. Then all eyes come to me. I take a sip of water, like nothing happened. I look at the people in the booth in front of me. "How you doing?" I ask. They go back to their breakfast.

I look out the window and Nelson is right there. We lock eyes. He looks around the restaurant. Back at me. Now we're having a tough-guy staring contest. He steps away slowly watching me over his shoulder until he's out of sight.

This guy's a monumental fucking problem.

———

From a few buildings away I see someone that looks just like Nokey sitting on my stoop with a six-pack of something next to him. I don't want to believe it's him, but it's hard to argue with my guts when they're churning. He looks at me. Yup, that's him. At the precise moment I think to turn and run he calls out my name and stands up. Fuck. I've been working in what feels like a goddamn oven all fuckin day, now I gotta climb out of the quicksand of this motherfucker's bullshit.

I stand still as he walks toward me. A very clear vision of the kind of heaven it would be for me to personally carry this kid to his grave comes to me. Burying him in the old lady's Upper East Side backyard so deep not even her heirs would find him.

"JT," he says all gentle and shit.

"Hello, Eugene."

"Eugene?"

I look into his face and it brings up clear, deep flashbacks of that night: him driving like a maniac, fucking with people on the road just to inflate the ignorant cowboy in him. The panic coursing through his eyes when he realized what happened. "You look like a bucket of shit," I tell him.

"I can appreciate that."

"How'd you find me?"

"Your dad."

"You went over to my dad's? That's ballsy of you."

"Actually, he kind of came to me."

"*Did he?* Sent you down here to get some dirt on me, huh?"

"It's not like that, man. He's worried about you."

"Too late."

"Says you're really skinny. And he's right."

"Then tell him to send me a quiche." I try to pass him making for my building. He stands in my way.

"He doesn't blame me, Jake. And you neither."

"Yeah, right. Then why doesn't he drop the charges?"

"I'm sorry. JT."

"Oh, please." I get past him, but stop when he yells behind me.

"Jesus fuck, Jake. Can you loosen the fucking hook you got on me already?"

"Oh here it is. I get it now: If I cop to my end of it you feel better, right? Right?"

"It was my stupid fucking idea, OK? But how long could everyone have just done nothing? At least we tried to help her, JT. I'm sorry, OK."

"No, you're pathetic. If you had my head for one fucking night, sorry wouldn't even enter into that shit, You'd fuckin crap out your insides, man. You'd be like: Holy shit, am I hot? Am I cold? Can I speak? How come I can't feel my arms? Am I seeing shit?" I get up in his face; he flinches back a step. "You'd believe there's no way you're making it through the night. And you'd wonder if you should take yourself to hell and be done with it. And we both know that's what you'd do. You're not tough. Take away your looks and you ain't shit. Admit it dick smack, the whole thing was about you and you, not about helping Danielle."

He leans against the building, head to the sky, the beer dangling in his hand, his eyes welling up.

"Bout fuckin time. Now leave."

"It was my fault." Words barely coming out.

"Leave."

He rolls his back against the building, pushes off and walks in the opposite direction from my apartment.

An offering disguised

Summer between junior and senior year me and Noke worked pretty much full-time at his father Ricky's garage on Lockwood Ave. We did simple stuff like oil changes, belt replacements, inspections, and we cleaned the place during downtime. The job let us support our summer, our drinking, and our desire to stay out of our houses—which at times were all excessive.

Ricky never cared about the rough nights I brought to work or personal phone calls, and didn't get bent if I came late or left early—*as long as the job gets done*. He was always civil about reminding me he was in charge and he never snapped at me even if I might have had it coming. He was a patient teacher and never tried to sound like he knew more about cars than I did, even though he did. He ordered lunch from the same deli six times a week. He used to talk to me about girls only if I brought it up, smiled at women customers but didn't flirt. He wasn't big on preaching or asking questions. He seemed to be OK with knowing very little about me and Nokey's lives, and probably knew more than he let on.

As actual bosses went, Ricky was real easy on me, but he and Noke were another story. Nokey said, "Best thing I can say about my dad is that he knows he can't stop us from being seventeen."

104

Why Ricky and Nokey went at it all the time is beyond me. The father and son thing covers a lot, but they drew that line so thin it was nearly invisible. They treated each other more like brothers with bad blood. They worked on cars together like wolves fighting over the last piece of dead cow.

Ricky's hands were covered in what you could call a mechanic's tattoo. Twenty-three years of grease and dirt permanently baked into his skin, like he'd blackened his fingertips over a flame. Whenever I caught him at the sink trying to wipe some of the grime off he'd tell me, "If you don't want your hands to look like this for the rest of your life, stay in school."

Ricky Cervella gave me two things I can't shake: a mechanic's education, and the question of what I want my hands covered in when I'm fifty.

I was under the hood of a Sable when the phone rang. This was early July. An afternoon flash thunderstorm made little rivers against curbs. Nokey was working on the car next to the office and his father picked it up then yelled, "Noke?"

"What?"

"It's for JT."

"What is?"

"The phone."

"The what?"

"The PHONE."

"Huh?"

"What does this look like, a dildo? It's a fucking phone. Clean the potatoes out of your head and tell JT it's for him."

The potato thing always pushed Noke over the line. And Ricky knew it. There was always a silence after that with some kind of injury in it. Nokey looked at me. "JT."

I said, "Yeah, I got it."

"He's coming, Ricky. And Ricky?"

"What?"

"Your mother thinks it's a dildo."

"After having four kids I think she knows the difference, you hopeless degenerate."

"No, I'm not kidding. Smell it."

Ricky said, "Who are you, where did you come from, and why do I let you work here?"

"I'm your wife's kid, I came from her, and I work here because she told you she wanted me out of the house."

"I don't know you," said Ricky.

"It's mutual."

On my way to the phone I said, "Noke, why don't you leave the poor guy alone for once?"

"If I survived him, he can survive me."

I could feel Ricky behind me while I got the news. He wasn't eavesdropping, he just knew something was up and kept watch over me. I guess I looked a little freaked out when I hung up because he asked me if everything was all right.

"My dad hurt his leg on the job. They dropped a piece of sheet metal. He's at the hospital. They said he's got crutches. He can go home, but my mom can't leave her shift so they need someone to go over there and pick him up."

"Yeah, go head, we got you covered. Take my car." And he reached in his drawer for the keys.

What I remember most about that phone call was the sound of my mother's voice. Underneath the words something small and distant was poking its head out. An excited person on their toes waving at me above a crowd, telling me that what was coming for a long time was finally here.

Walking to the entrance, I looked up to a second-floor window and remembered that Lawrence Hospital had been in my family for three generations. I was born there and my grandmother Terri died there. My mother was already working there at the time, and says everyone agreed that Terri was a real pain in the ass patient. Sounds like Terri confused nurses with waitresses, asking them for things like different color sheets. Because she complained about the food so much, and because my mom could sneak her in only so many lunches, she had a nurse bring her a legal pad and a magic marker and made a sign that she put in her window facing the street that read: *THIS FOOD WILL BE THE DEATH OF ME*. Turned out it was her heart. Mom says she still reminisces with the older doctors who knew Terri about all the demands she made that, after the fact, they see as her spirit fighting to survive. If I had to guess, and I do, I'd say it's possible she was like many people—much more charming in retrospect.

Dad sat on the edge of the bed with his leg propped up on a chair, staring through the vertical blinds with something heavier on his mind than the accident. Decay blew through the yellow room in slow motion. Lights threw this grayish-green tint on his face like the first layer of rigor mortis. I said, "You OK?"

He kept looking out the window. "Yeah."

"I guess I'm gonna take you home now."

He turned his head to me and shook off whatever thought was beyond the window. "Let's get on it then." He lifted himself off the bed, grunted and his face squished in pain.

"Should I help you?"

"No, no."

"Didn't they give you crutches?"

"Yeah, but I don't use crutches, thank you very much. They wanted to put me in a chair to get me outta here, too, but I told your mother to nix it. I can do it. They gave me these." He held up a bottle of pills. "Up the dosage a little and they're even better than crutches." He tried to straighten himself and couldn't take more than one step without having to catch his balance on the bed. "I guess these pills don't work without a shoulder. Get over here."

I managed to help him out of the hospital and dump him in the car. The thunderstorm had let up. Bars of light broke through the clouds and pulled steam out of the streets. I kept the windows down so I could smell the wet asphalt, and take my mind off having to schlep my father up the front stairs.

He had one hand on the railing and leaned all the rest of his weight into me. My shoulder was under his armpit and his breath was hitting me in the right side of my face, stagnant as a hospital room. He took each step in an off-balanced hop. His face crumpled up again, but he laughed and said, "We should have built these things more even." I helped him redo those stairs when I was like nine, which meant I occasionally broke rocks with a hammer, carried bags of rubble to the rented dumpster and scratched my initials in the wet cement with a stick. "Yeah," I said, "that woulda come in handy about now."

We made it through the front door and I unloaded him on the couch. He was down and it was done and I wanted to get the hell out of that house before he had me rubbing his feet. I said, "I gotta get Ricky's car back to the garage."

"Yeah, go head."

"Mom'll be home soon. I guess. Or later."

I turned to leave and he said, "Thanks, Jake."

I think I nodded my head or maybe I said *yeah* or *sure* or *no fucking problem, man.* Or some combination of the three.

On my way back to the garage I drove on the highway, parallel to the Bronx River for a stretch, and I so wished it was clean right then, or that the thunderstorm was still hammering down because if you've ever carried one of your parents on your back then you know why right then I could have really used diving into some water.

A week after my dad's accident I was at Ricky's garage adjusting a timing belt on a Buick and Mom called to tell me she had to stay at work late and could I pick up Dani from swimming practice. "No problem," I told her. And that was my first sign that she had something going on, because staying late at work wasn't ever her stride.

"But don't bring her home," she said.

I borrowed Nokey's car and took the fifteen-minute drive to get my sister at the pool. When I pulled up outside Dani and another girl from the swim team were sitting outside waiting. They were straddling the bench with their bathing suits still on and towels wrapped around their waists. Dani had her back to the girl who was combing out her wet hair with a brush.

I didn't know this other girl. She was a few inches shorter than Dani with more muscles, like a gymnast instead of a swimmer. She had lighter hair pulled into a ponytail, a few earrings in each ear, a string of bottle caps as an ankle bracelet, and one on her wrist homemade from colored thread. Dani had her beat with the bracelets: different sizes of silver rings covering her wrists halfway up her forearms, reflecting the sun like disco balls. I don't know if she wore them to swim, and if she'd taken those things off once in the past two years, my back was turned.

While this other girl was brushing out Dani's hair she was telling her a story that seemed to be the funniest thing the two of them had heard in about a year. At one point Dani whipped her head around and opened her mouth wide like she couldn't believe what the girl just said. The girl stopped combing, put her hand on her heart and looked up to the sky swearing to God she was telling the truth. This made them both bend over at the waist in a laughing fit and this girl crashed her forehead into Dani's back. They stayed there convulsing until their faces turned red. I wanted in on it, but if I rolled up the joke would have been shot in the ass, so I pulled the car over before they could see me and watched.

They recovered from the laughing fit, sat up again, and the girl went back to brushing. She held a small section of hair at the roots and, starting at the ends, she pulled at the knots in little jolts, working her way further up with each stroke until finally she ran the brush through the whole section without a snag. And there was something in that free swipe that transformed Dani's hair and then the rest of her into someone else. If I didn't know her, I would have thought she was some girl who drinks beer on the hood of her boyfriend's car. A girl who flirts, goes skinny dipping, and spends a lot of time being cool. For the second it took that girl to swipe that brush down one long section of my sister's hair, Dani was that girl. Or maybe she was always that girl and it took a hair-brushing for me to notice.

I felt like a schmuck for beeping the horn, because as soon as I did she replaced her smile with straight lips, stood up, grabbed her backpack, and waved goodbye to the girl. She walked to me, and got in the car as the quiet uncool thirteen-year-old girl who only swims indoors and lets no one but her teammates touch her hair.

On the ride home I asked, "How come you never got your ears pierced?"

She shrugged and said, "I might. I might get everything pierced. Ears, eyebrows, lips, tongue, bellybutton."

"O . . . K. Think that might hurt?"

"Not even a little," she explained. And was proud of that fact.

I pulled into Ricky's place, got out of the car and made my way back into the garage to the Sable I'd been working on.

Dani stood near the gas pumps with her backpack over one shoulder, tucking her half-brushed damp hair behind her ears. She was teetering on the outside edges of her sneakers, not wanting to come inside the garage, not really wanting to go anywhere else, so I went over to her and said, "What's up?"

"Mom didn't want me to go home after practice, right?"

"Right."

"So I'm here with you instead?"

"Right."

She adjusted her backpack as if it needed it, and looked away from me. "Listen," I said, "we'll be done in like an hour. Probably hit the river later. Is that cool?"

She nodded her head a few times.

I pulled money out of my pocket and handed her ten of it. "Here. If you're hungry or something, go to the deli." She pocketed the ten and walked to the corner.

On my way back inside Ricky waved me in through the glass window of his office. He was standing behind the desk leafing through invoices.

"What's up, Rick?"

"I know this is cutting it close, but I need you to rotate this guy's tires before you leave. Can you swing it?"

"Do you need the belt on the Sable done first thing tomorrow?"

"Afternoon's OK."

"Then yeah, I can do it."

"Good. Normally I'd tell the guy to get in line, but he's a friend of a friend who's calling in a favor."

"I gotcha."

"The barter system's a beautiful thing."

"Yeah, it is."

"Listen, JT, I forgot to ask how your dad was."

"He's, you know . . . hurt. They're not sure how his leg is gonna be. Sheet metal ripped up his ligaments and I guess they don't heal too easy. They said it's too soon to tell, you know?"

"Can he walk?"

"He can get around, but not so well. Has to stay off it for a while."

"Shit. At least he's got comp. Well tell him I was asking for him, all right?"

"I will."

I took another step toward the door when he said, "How about your mom?"

"She's . . . still my mom."

Ricky laughed. "Tell me about it. I got one too." I hung back as he looked out the office window at Dani waiting for the light, so she could cross to the deli. "Your sister need anything?"

"No, she'll be OK till we leave. She's just thirteen, you know, she can't drive yet so she comes for the ride."

"Yeah, thirteen's a rough one. You sure she's OK?" he said with the tone of someone who honestly cared about anything that might come out of my mouth, barring nothing. I'd never really seen him as someone I could talk to about the whole situation, but the time, the place and the me weren't right, so I scratched a fake itch on my forehead, hiding what my face might have shown.

"Yeah. I mean . . . She's cool."

"Um hum," he said with another invitation to go on. But I didn't. I just waited until the pause started to feel a little weird then I said, "I'm gonna get going on the rotation, Rick."

"It's all you. Keys are up there." He pointed to the corkboard where we hung all the keys to the cars we worked on. "The ones with the red tag." I reached up to grab the keys and I knocked off another set by accident. I picked them up and when I tried to hang them back up I knocked off a different set. I crouched down to grab them, but couldn't. I could feel my fingers on them but I couldn't get a grip. Then I realized my hands were shaking. I could see the keys, I could see my hands and I was telling my hands to chill out, pick up the goddamn keys, and put em on the friggin board already, but they wouldn't. Ricky let out a little laugh and said, "You need some help there, tough guy?"

"No, I got it."

I got on my knees and I tried picking them up with my other

112

hand. No good. Then I tried with my pinky, which was stupid. I tried with two pointing fingers. My hands were short-circuiting.

Ricky said, "JT, just leave em already, I'll get em."

What he said set something off in me. Of all the things my hands couldn't do right they had no problem making fists by themselves. I raised them above my head then came down and pounded those keys into the floor. Hard as I could. *Bang*. I did it again. *Bang*. Then my mouth opened and this big sound came out. "Leave them." *Bang*. "I'm not leaving a fucking thing." *Bang*. "Mother fucker." *Bang*. *Bang*. *Bang*. It felt like I was doing it in slow motion and it went on for a long time.

Finally Ricky put his hand on my shoulder and said, "Take it easy. Come on, take it easy." He wasn't saying it like I was fuckin insane. He was saying it like there was nothing wrong with what I was doing, but it was just time to stop. So I did. I stayed on my knees and thought, *did I just do what I fucking think I just did?*

I looked up to the glass of his office door and saw him in reflection nod his head like he understood, like he sees people do what I just did every day on his way to work. He said, "Seventeen's a rough one, too."

I stood up, but I was too embarrassed to look at him. "Sorry, Rick."

He said, "It's all right," like it really was. I kind of believed him, kind of didn't. "Listen, JT, I got no opinions, just a good ear."

"What?"

"If you need one, I got a good ear. I know I got a big mouth, but I got big ears, too. You understand me?"

I said, "Yeah."

"You can take off the rest of the day if you want to."

"No, I wanna keep going. I wanna do the Monte."

"You sure?"

"Yeah, yeah."

"All right." Then he reached over to the board, grabbed the keys and held them out in front of me with no sense of urgency. I didn't want to reach for them so I cupped my hands below his and he dropped them right in my palms. My fingers closed around them. I looked up to him and saw a look on his face I'd never seen before: a sad smile.

Maybe the friend-of-a-friend thing and getting me in the office to tell me about the Monte was bullshit. If I'm right, I don't feel like he was really throwing me a lie. It was only an offering disguised as one.

"It's around the side," he said.

"I'm on it." I looked at the floor when I said thanks. Then I walked out. I never even realized I punctured my hands until I tried to get the keys in the car door and saw blood.

July 20

COUNSELOR: What do you all most desperately want?

The problem with this counselor is she thinks she's dealing with people who can answer that question. One parent should be certified, and the other one should also be certified. The kid should not even be here, and wouldn't be unless a judge told him to.

MOM: I want Jake to come back home and live with me.
COUNSELOR: Jake, have you considered that?
ME: No.
COUNSELOR: Francine, why do you think that would be a good idea?
MOM: Well, don't you? Look at him.
COUNSELOR: Tell me what you see when you look at him.
MOM: I see a kid who made a mistake and the world is treating him as if he's a hardened criminal, and I want to remind him that it's not true. And I want him to know he needs more help right now than he thinks he does.

COUNSELOR: Jake, you want to say anything about that?

ME: Yes. What I most desperately want is to know why I feel like I'm on trial every time I come here? Like I'm the one who you're all trying to figure out, or straighten out, or freak out, or whatever out.

COUNSELOR: We're not trying to figure you out, Jake. I just want to give you all a chance to tell each other what you want to. There's a lot of anger, and that's normal, but it—

ME: Lady, haven't you learned who you're talking to yet?

MOM: Jake, don't talk to her like that.

ME: And there *she* goes, coming to the rescue. She comes to everyone's rescue but who she's supposed to.

COUNSELOR: Who's she supposed to rescue?

ME: (Looking at my father who is getting skinny, has less hair and more of it is gray.) Who do you think?

COUNSELOR: I don't know. Tell me.

ME: My sister.

COUNSELOR: From what?

ME: (Looking in his general direction.)

DAD: (Looking at the ceiling, rolling his tongue around the inside of his lips instead of yelling.)

COUNSELOR: Why your sister?

ME: Because he was messing with her, I thought we already established that.

COUNSELOR: Well, you established that in your written statement, Jake. But your father didn't corroborate it so—

ME: And did he expect you to smell good after he slung that shit on you?

MOM: Jake, please.

ME: (Loosing my shit.) NO.

MOM: (Covering her mouth with one hand.)

DAD: I CAN'T DO ANYTHING ABOUT WHAT HAPPENED.

EVERYONE ELSE: (Startled and confused.)

DAD: (A softness takes over his eyes.) OK? I can't. Look. (Putting his hands out for all to see. The nails are chewed almost to the cuticles, which are also chewed. They are scabby. Destroyed.)

COUNSELOR: (Flinches.)

ME: (Not recognizing or trusting this guy and his new hands.)

DAD: All right? Want me to get all emotional and shit. I mean what the fuck do you think I am? Can't we see what we're doing now, instead of what we were doing then? (To counselor.) Everybody changes, right?

COUNSELOR: It's possible.

DAD: Well look at me. (Spreading his fingers out wide.) You want me to bury myself in the dirt below the wrists? (Making fists.)

ME: You haven't changed. Since when do you change?

DAD: That's your brain talking. Not mine.

ME: Your brain talks? You hearing voices now?

MOM: Jake.

ME: Because *I* am. All night. You know what that's like?

DAD: I do.

ME: Good.

DAD: At least we're in something together.

ME: We ain't in shit together.

DAD: (Shakes his head, puts his hands in his lap.) You wanna keep it that way that's good for me. (Leaning violently back in his chair.)

ME: (Seeing the guy I recognize.) ISN'T IT FUCKED UP AND STUPID TO ANYONE ELSE THAT *I'M* THE ONE WHO MIGHT GO TO JAIL AND THIS

117

FUCKING GUY GETS OFF ON A *TECHNICALITY*? IT'S NOT FAIR. IT'S NOT FUCKING *FAIR*.

EVERYONE ELSE: (Quiet.)

ME: (To him.) THEY LET YOU OFF, BUT YOU'RE NOT FORGIVEN. NOT AFTER ALL THIS TIME AND ALL THIS SHIT. YOU'RE *NOT*. NO ONE FORGIVES YOU. I hope you cry alone.

DAD: I do.

Silence.

COUNSELOR: (Handing me a box of tissues. Speaking calm as fuck all.) Your father's problems with your sister are a separate case that I assure you all will come up. I'm not at liberty to judge it, but we can talk about it. John, would you like to say anything to Jake, about what he said?

DAD: (Shaking his head, eyes almost closed.) No.

ME: (Leaning toward him.) Goddamn you fuckin mutt.

Mom: Jake, stop already.

ME: Yeah sure, I'll stop. (Leaning back in my chair, legs stretched out in front of me, hands clasped behind my head.) No more open exchanges for me. I'm now a closed exchanger.

COUNSELOR: Jake, I know you're in pain.

ME: I'm *not*.

COUNSELOR: And I hate to have to put it this way to you, but understand: the judge gave you the benefit of the doubt.

ME: What doubt?

COUNSELOR: The judge knows you're not a thief. You're a kid in pain and you were driven to do something you wouldn't have done otherwise. Your defender said it and we all believe it because it's obvious. You're still guilty of a crime, but you're not headed for a life of thievery. You're too lousy at it and I think you've learned that by now. If we don't open up—and I say this to all of you—I'll have to end these sessions and Jake will go right to trial with no other plea available but guilty. You will be tried as an adult and you can be looking at a year for grand theft auto. I mean you did do it, Jake. And here's what I'm not supposed to tell you: the only thing that a defender can help you out with is *why* you did it. If we don't get to those reasons then you're probably looking at jail time.

ME and DAD: (Lock eyes in assessment and challenge.)

ME: Give up?

DAD: (Eyes lean toward something compassionate, but shakes his head, no.)

COUNSELOR: As I've said, every family that has ever existed has had wrongdoing in it. Human error is as old as humans. My job is not to get you all to decide whose wrongdoing is worse than the other's. My job is to get you all to talk about the wrongdoings, and see if you can try to understand each other and come to some form of forgiveness.

ME: Like we know what forgiveness is.

COUNSELOR: Well let me offer a possible . . . (choosing her next word like playing pick-up sticks) . . . definition. Forgiveness is giving up all hope of a better past. And, once again, it will not only keep Jake out of jail, but it will—

ME: (Still looking at Dad.) Him dropping the charges would also keep me out of jail.

Pause.

COUNSELOR: John?

DAD: (Slumping forward, putting elbows on knees. Looking at floor.)

COUNSELOR: John?

DAD: (Shaking his head. Offering zero words.)

ME: I think their relationship should have ended before they had kids. That could have put a—

DAD: Learn from my mistakes.

Short silence.

ME: (To counselor.) And for a second there I thought he was about to turn a corner.

August 1

Five forty-five a.m.-ish. I sit at the table writing a letter to Danielle by the pale light of a sun still below the skyline. Behind me Stephanie throws the sheets off her and makes for the bathroom. I snap my notebook closed and when she runs past me I nonchalantly say, "Oh, hi Steph."

While she vomits I say, "Just another happy morning on East 9th Street."

"Damn." She flicks the light on. Shuffles around the medicine cabinet. I lean to my right and through a crack in the curtain I see her washing her mouth out with my toothpaste.

"I promise I won't think less of you if you brought over a toothbrush."

She spits. Pushes the curtain out of her way. "Don't call me Steph. I hate that." She grunts like she's fucking had it already with the whole throwing up thing. "Some mornings I wish I was throwing up in the Dominican Republic." She looks at the notebook.

"But America takes in all the hungry, tired, poor, puking and pregnant. This is the land of hopes and dreams. Amber waves of grain, and shit."

"Waves of green."

"Freedom ain't all about money."

"What else?"

"State of mind."

"That's privilege talking right there. When your mind lives in a studio apartment with six people, the last thing gets free is your mind." She massages the corner of her eyes with her middle fingers until her eye crud falls to the floor.

"I hear you, but I'm not feeling particularly privileged right now."

"I ain't saying there's anything wrong with it. Now that you got me on this shit at the crack of ass in the morning, that's the kind of privilege I want for my kid."

"Good morning, by the way."

"Yeah, sure," she manages.

"So if you want cash and privilege go back to school."

"What are you, a guidance counselor?"

"I'm just—"

"I don't want to give it to my kids by myself. You feelin me?"

"I am. So who you gonna give it with?"

She has no response to that, and appears pained by the thought of who might and might not be helping her bring some kind of liberation to her kid's life.

"That's why you wanna go to the DR?"

"Maybe."

"Then go."

"Yeah, I'ma walk there."

"You'll drown. Ever think of flying? Just a suggestion."

She reaches behind her head to retie her ponytail. "I don't fly."

"Oh, come off it." She stops mid-tie and looks at me like she fuckin means it. "You're serious? You don't fly?"

"Didn't I just say so?" Now she's raising her voice.

"Why not?"

122

"Fuck you care? I just ain't getting on no plane."

"Ever been on one?"

"No."

"Then how do you know you're so scared?"

"You don't have to do things to know they scare you."

"OK, pipe down, it's just a thought—"

"Bad thought." She goes to the refrigerator, gets water.

"Can I ask you something?"

"Again?" At the cabinet she grabs a glass.

"Why've you been sleeping here? I mean, I dig it, but it's going on two weeks now."

She uses the moment it takes to pour the water to find an answer. "Cause it's better than sharing a bed with my little cousins."

"Cause you don't want your uncle seeing you puke every morning?"

"Maybe." She sips.

"That all?"

"Cause I know you won't hit on me."

"No you don't."

"Yes. I do. And even if you did what'll happen? I get pregnant? Oops, can't do that again. At least not now." Another sip.

"That doesn't explain why you're not sleeping at Nelson's."

"You finally said his NAME," she yells.

"Tell me why."

"DON'T TALK TO ME ABOUT NELSON." She slams the water pitcher back in the fridge then slams the door shut even harder.

"Why not?"

"Because Nelson is two guys. One before he got me pregnant, one after, OK?"

She luckily gets cut off by the downstairs neighbor who bangs what sounds like a broomstick on their ceiling a few times.

"You woke them up," she says.

"You're the one getting loud. So what was he before?"

"I'm not getting loud."

"You're right, you're not *getting* loud, you *are* loud."

She looks wounded by that. "No I'm *not*," she yells.

"You wanna notch it down before they kick me out."

She sips her water again and thinks hard. "Am I loud, for real?" she sincerely wants to know.

"Is this one of those questions where no matter how I answer I'm gonna get a lesson on how to talk to women?"

"No."

"You sure?"

"Just tell me."

"You're loud." She slaps her glass on the slate table. For some reason this offends and saddens her. "Take it easy. All I'm saying is that you'd be good at Yankee Stadium. What's the big deal?"

"Because the guys in my family are all so loud . . . my mother is loud . . . *was* loud, or whatever. She couldn't talk to me without yelling. My father couldn't talk to her without yelling."

"Maybe you're not loud because they're loud. Maybe you're loud because you're loud."

"I don't wanna be." And there's something in her face now that is unlike all the other things I've seen. Her fighting mask just melted off and a lonely one replaced it.

"Well, you're not always loud," I say. "I mean you're not loud like a motorcycle is loud. You don't just stand there being loud all the time, or like announce yourself from ten blocks away."

She smirks as if that's a lame consolation.

"You're like a wind chime," I tell her. "The more you're pushed around the louder you get."

She calculates that with the glass paused at her lips. From where I'm sitting it seems she's silently accepting a part of herself that I can't really see and will never really know. "That's funny," she says. Something rises in me that makes my past feel further back than it is.

She looks directly into my eyes. She doesn't blink. "What's wrong?" I ask.

"Nothing."

She comes over, never losing my face, fits herself between me and the stone slab. She looks at me for a couple seconds longer then wraps a hug on me, her palms kind of patting my back, kind of rubbing it. I clasp my hands behind her. I feel her arms loosen, but she keeps holding on. She slides onto the floor, her head now in my chest. I put a hand on the back of her head. My shirt is wet where her nose is.

"What do your aunts and your cousins do in the DR?"

"They live in Santo Domingo, it's the capital. They work together cooking for a big restaurant. You know, like a tourist restaurant. They say they get treated nice and that . . ." She breaks the hug. Stands up. Wipes her nose. "That table was digging into my back."

On the street I pick up two sacks of rocks off the pile. I turn, carry them down eight stairs, into the brownstone. Up eight stairs, into the backyard, drop the sacks. Brian stands in the shade of the trees, his back against the brownstone wall.

"You're making me look bad," he says. It's more than ninety-five degrees and he's having a slow day. I've lapped him twice now.

"It's all I have to live for."

"Then you're wasting your life."

"Actually it's already wasted and it wasn't as bad as people say."

"Oooh, a tongue that can clip a hedge. You get a nut last night?"

125

"Are you high?"

"No, Boss." He army-salutes me.

"Then you should stop drinking."

"I did once, but I became cranky and boring so I had to go back to it. Why you holding out on me?"

"I'm not."

I turn, go down eight stairs into the brownstone. Brian follows me.

"You're bullshitting a bullshit factory."

"So we cancel each other out."

"I don't even get to know what she looks like?"

We go up eight stairs, onto the sidewalk.

"She's just a friend."

"AH HAAAAA. Does she know you don't believe that?"

"I do believe it." I pick up two more sacks.

"If you're straight you don't believe it, and you are straight."

"Any chance of us baggin this conversation?"

"Sure, but first let me tell you something about women, Wedgie."

"Somebody is always trying to tell me something about women."

He pulls off his gloves and slaps them on the pile of rocks. "There's only three kinds of men who can't understand them: young men, old men, and middle-aged men."

"That some kind of Irish proverb?"

"That's a human proverb. Let's take a break, Wedgie."

"I wish you'd stop calling me that."

"I know. Come on, it's break time." He cracks open his orange Gatorade.

"You go ahead. I'm good, I'm gonna keep going."

"Really, stop. It's more than ninety degrees and we got six hours left."

"Really, I'm good."

I go down eight stairs, into the brownstone. Up eight stairs, into the backyard. The sun stings my shoulders. I look at the hundreds of bags of stones lined up on the ground, standing upright like gravestones. They make a path across this back lot like the stones across the Bronx River.

I see my dad.

I see my old bathroom.

I see his face in the mirror. One of his palms is full of shaving cream, the other holds the can. I stand on the edge of the white bathtub, my hands on the sink for balance. From here I'm almost his height and can see my face in the mirror next to him.

"Putting shaving cream on is easy, you just gotta make sure to cover all the black."

"Dad, I got no black. I only got a little fuzz."

"No, I know, this is just to get in some practice for when your beard starts coming in. Here. Watch. I'm covering the black, I'm covering the black . . ." He raises his chin and checks his neck out in the mirror to make sure he has everything whited-out. "There. See? Now you."

He shakes the can of shaving cream up and down, I hold out both my hands.

"You're right-handed, right?"

"Yeah."

"So you put a pile of this in your left hand so you can spread it with your right hand." He fills up my palm. "Go head cover where there's black. Or where you think there's gonna be black."

I rub the cream on my cheeks.

"You got it."

It smells like pine trees and dish-washing detergent.

"Now look—when you're doing the mustache part you can just cover your whole mouth." He watches me do this. "Good. Now just wipe your finger across your lips like this. Got it?"

"That's cool."

"Ain't it? OK, let me see. Look up. You're looking good. Now the shaving part. You gotta shave it all even. You gotta make sure you're putting the same pressure on the razor the whole time because if you don't then you got an uneven shave and you look like what your mother calls a *cavone*. You know what that is? It's a pig. You wanna press hard enough so you get a close shave but you don't want to press too hard that you cut yourself. Watch me."

He drags the razor across his face and the whiskers crackle under the blade. He maneuvers it with the kind of steadiness it takes to decorate a cake. I've never seen him move so slowly or touch anything so gentle. Nothing. Not his wife, not his food, not his kids. And still, he somehow manages to cut himself. Right where his jaw meets his neck he gives himself a nice little slice. The red mixes with the white and this pinkish liquid oozes down his neck. I don't say anything for two reasons. First: I feel, as the apprentice, I should keep quiet until the teacher gets to the how-to-handle-cuts part of the lesson. Second and more honest reason: I want to see just how hard and long he'll bleed.

"If you want a really close shave you go against the grain." I nod like I hear but I'm preoccupied with his cut and when the hell he's gonna notice it. A drop of blood falls into the sink. I hear the plop. How could this guy not even know he was bleeding? How could he just shave around something like it's not even there? The blood keeps falling. How could you ignore it, you son of a bitch? Bleeding is bleeding, it hurts you fuckin asshole. Can't you feel?

"Wedgie."

"What?"

"Slow the fuck down, man."

I'm standing on the sidewalk near the rock pile. "No, I'm good."

"No, stop. Look at your hands."

"What?"

"You're not wearing gloves, genius."

"So what?" I snap at him.

"They're gonna crack if you—"

"LEAVE ME THE FUCK ALONE." Barehanded I grab two more sacks, turn, go down eight stairs into the brownstone. Up eight stairs into the backyard, drop the bags. I replay the sound of my voice in that last exchange and don't feel right about it. Down eight stairs into the brownstone. Up eight stairs, on the sidewalk where Brian is holding his drink and staring at me through squinted eyes.

"All right," I say. "I was being a prick just then."

"It happens." He finishes the last of his Gatorade. "You ready to take a break now?"

"Yeah." We sit on the sidewalk, our backs against the building. Brian cracks open another Gatorade for me. I thank him.

I say, "Fridays?"

"What about them?"

"I pull half days because I go to counseling."

"OK," he says in a way that lets me know he's open to hear more, but is not going to ask.

"Not last week. I played hooky. But I go."

"I hope you don't mind me asking, but why the hell are you doing this job?"

"What's wrong with this job?"

"Nothing's wrong with this job, but you seem like . . . Let's put it this way: if you keep working the way you do you're not long for it."

"What way?"

"Oh, the way of someone who never takes a break and works double-time during one of the hottest days of summer on what looks like no sleep or a deep hangover or both." He lets that much sink in. "Couple guys in my family worked themselves to death. But that's not because they loved working so much. It's because they hated everything else. But fuck me, I could be totally wrong. Am I?"

I shrug.

We sit in the heat for a while. I drink my drink.

"You think Starbucks is hiring?" I say.

"Always."

"You got a pen?" Brian reaches into his back pocket and hands me a pencil. "Piece of paper, too?"

"What for?"

"I'd rather not write my phone number on your hand, because we're not going steady yet. No offense."

"None taken." He looks through his wallet, pulls out a faded receipt that documented the purchase of something old and forgotten.

I write my number on it. "Here."

He takes it back. Looks at me. I say, "In case I leave this job soon."

He nods his head and puts the paper back in his wallet. "You know the one about the five frogs?"

"No."

"Five frogs are sitting on a log—"

"Frogs or toads?"

"Either one."

"Which?"

"It doesn't matter. Five of them are sitting on—"

"I'm just trying to get a visual."

"Frogs then."

"You sure?"

"They're green things with long tongues, OK? You're ruining my timing, now shut the fuck up."

"Go head."

"Five frogs or toads are sitting on a log and four decide to jump off. How many are left?"

"One?"

"Five."

"How you figure?"

"Because there's a difference between deciding to jump and actually jumping."

After the sound

About a week after I punctured my hand in Ricky's office I was laying in my bed and heard my father's car door slam. I checked the clock on my night table: 1.30 a.m. on a Tuesday. Then I heard him trip; the palms of his hands slapped the slate of the front stairs and I heard him yell, "Son of a bitch." My mother creaking down the stairs is what got me out of bed.

When I came downstairs Mom was standing in the kitchen holding her robe closed at her neck. "Please, Jake, go back to sleep." Which is what she always said when my father came home in a drunken or even sober rage, or when they were having a screaming match in the middle of the night and I poked my head out from the staircase and tried to watch: *Go to sleep, Go up to your room, Get scarce, Leave so we can pretend you don't see this* . . . I always listened to her. Pretended to have gone back to sleep and stood with my face against my closed bedroom door recording their words and slaps on some permanent tape in my head. Yelling about bills and credit cards and drinking and dirty clothes and food and bullshit and something else entirely. Like an obedient little dog I'd listen until everything went quiet and my mother came up the stairs.

Then I'd jump under my blankets, knowing the next morning we'd all play dumb about what happened. But that night I'd had it with the good pet routine and when she told me to go to sleep again, I stayed.

He was drunk and pissed off—pissed off because he had to leave his job, pissed off because he couldn't walk straight anymore, pissed off at the side door for not staying still while he was trying to get the key in it—and if you've ever seen a raccoon on the side of the road just before they're about to get squashed by someone's tires, then you know what my mother looked like when he stumbled into the kitchen. She was too petrified to blink, hoping the two tons of drunken metal wasn't going to slam into her.

"Pissin piece of crap door. I raised that thing from a peephole, now it's making pretend it doesn't know my key no more." He teetered around the room, unable to bend his left leg, and grabbed for the oven to keep from toppling over. "And the stairs, they're no better. I built that dumb stack of rocks. Jake, remember we cracked them up with sledgehammers and redid those bastards? You and me." He made this long sweeping motion over his head like he was swinging a hammer. "Bang! Jake, you remember? Sure you do. I know what you remember." He squinted his eyes at me. "And whudda the stairs do? Make advantage of the dark and try to trip me up. Schmuck bastard ingrates." He got his balance on a chair and tried to look at our faces. "These are the jokes people. What's the matter with yous? Did somebody die?"

"Night's young," I said.

Mom said, "Jake, don't."

"Plan on killing someone, Jake?"

I didn't respond.

"Didn't think so. Hey, how come no one left a light on for me? Huh? What? I have a few drinks—which by the way there's nothing wrong with because I don't have to get up in the morning now that I got nowhere to run to—and I'm not worthy to have a light left on for? What gives?" He looked my mother in her eyes. "Let's see what you got in there? Judgment. That's right. Look at you looking at the bad man. Am I a bad man?"

"She didn't say anything to you, Dad."

"Hey. I raised you from a fucking peephole too, so don't wise off to me. I'll rip you off your hinges."

I got the gist of the metaphor. I said, "I'm not wising—"

"Shut it."

My mother looked at me like shutting it was the best thing to do. So I did. She said, "I'm going to go to sleep now," and started to move.

"No, come here, let me look at you." He hobbled over to her and put a hand on each side of her face.

Mom tried to squirm out of his grip. "Let me go to sleep."

He stopped her. "Cut it out. I just wanna look at you."

"Dad, let her go."

"Shut up for a second, Jake. I just want to look at her. Look at me."

Mom kept squirming.

"See that? She can't look at me." He stumbled back, holding onto her face and the rest of her body followed.

"Stop it," she said, and grabbed both his wrists.

"Look at me."

"I want to sleep."

"No one sleeps till you look at me."

"Mom."

"OK, I'm looking at you." She tilted her head up to his eyes that were a foot higher than hers. "See, I'm looking."

He looked back, smiled and said, "I am a bad man." There was silence. "Right?" Mom shook her head. "Yes I am. Come on, say it. Say what I am. Tell me how bad I am."

"I don't know what you are."

"Yes you do." Right then he slid his hands off her face like he was finished with the interrogation. She took one step back from him. He said, "Bad dog," and shook his head.

He threw one short fast jab right in her breastbone below her throat. It made a thud like someone serving a deflated volleyball. Her ribs caved in around his fist like they were made of rubber. She fell back and tried to grab the kitchen table, but her nails just slid off it and she went right to the linoleum. I shoved Dad in his chest and he backpedaled into the counter, bounced off it, then came at me. This time I pushed him in his face. I accidentally squished my thumb in his eye socket and that's what stopped him. "Fuck it." He put his hand over his eye and staggered out of the kitchen toward the basement stairs.

From the floor Mom held a forearm above her head and her eyelids blinked a mile a minute because she thought another hit was coming. I knelt down and grabbed her arm to lift her up, but she swatted my hands away. She stayed down, breathing heavy with one hand on her chest where she'd been hit. We both looked down and at the same time noticed her robe had come undone. She pulled it back together.

"Let me help you up."

"Why didn't you go to sleep?" Like it was my fault.

She crawled on her hands and knees to the sink, then used the counter to pull herself up. She turned the cold water on, collected it in her palms and threw it on her face. She leaned on the edge of the sink with all her weight on her elbows and just hung there for a while, let the water drip off her chin and tried to catch her breath. She walked to the freezer, her posture like a weeping willow tree, and got out some ice, put it in a plastic bag and held it to her chest. When the cold hit her tender ribs she sucked air in fast through clenched teeth.

We heard my dad stumbling down the basement stairs moaning in a language that was slightly left of English.

135

"You OK, Ma?"

"How do I look, Jake?"

She looked bruised, old, underweight, and done.

Silence would be next. Three or more long days of it as she retreated into her bedroom, not even coming out for meals. My father would sleep on the couch and no one would talk to anyone. You couldn't do a thing about the quiet that followed violence. I left her there in the kitchen so she could get on with it, and crept downstairs, to do what, I wasn't sure.

He sat on his workbench. One dim, bare light bulb dangling on a cord over him, a bottle of scotch in one hand and a hammer in the other. I didn't know what I was dealing with—whether he knew what he was doing or saying or if he was in a black-out or what. And I had no idea why he was holding that hammer, so I laid back a little. "That bottle from your private stock?"

"I got em stashed all over the county." He held it up and took a sip. "Go head, Jake, read me the riot act." His words were all glued together.

"I don't know what that is."

"The speech. The one you give to people when they messed you up. Starts off like, 'I'm telling you this for your own good.' Or 'You're a fuck up, here's why you're a fuck up, so from today until always you need to stop fucking up or I'm outta here.' I already know I fucked up, and I already know she's outta here. I'm not stupid on top of everything."

"You're sloshed. You don't know what you're talking about."

"You don't know shit about life. Your ass, your brains, and your dick are all pointing in different directions. She don't look at you like she does me. Judges me. Every day. And for what?"

"Why don't you tell me for what?"

"For nothing."

"No, no. For something. She does it for something. Tell me what for."

He held up his bottle. "For this. Because I turned out like my father. On a lone continent with his homemade wine. Terrifying, aren't I? You think I'm messed up, you should have seen him. Lucky you didn't. So if you gotta know, that's why she's leavin." Then he pointed to his leg with the hammer. "And for this. She's runnin. I can feel it. It's easy to . . ." He coughed, took a huge sip. "It's easy to run from a guy who can't. And I'll fuckin kill the guy who comes near her when she does. I show you what." He put down his hammer and pulled out a box.

"Inside this box, booby boy, is a magic rabbit." He opened it and took it out. "Browning's best. A magic wand that's got a permit to let me legally kill the guy who goes near her when she leaves." It was a small gun, whose handle got a little lost in his hand, but as he held it I could almost feel the weight of the metal that looked like a tarnished green under the bad light. "Fuck do I care though. Go ahead!" he yelled to the upstairs. "Leave!" He took another epic sip. "You know, the first time I saw your mother feeding you, you know . . . from herself, I thought, aah, there might be a God. Now . . . ? Huh. Why do I always feel like I'm about to fall off a roof if there's a God? Ah, fuck this shit." Then the tears came. He curled into himself like a burning spider. I understood that the car wreck of this guy's life started way before he found a wife and kids. And whatever caused the accident was still riding his back.

I said, "That is one sob fucking story." It came out so easily. "You know what a sob story is, right? Starts out like, 'Why does everything bad happen to me?' and ends with, 'No one loves me.' The beginning is bullshit for sure. But I gotta give it to you—the ending might be true."

He wiped his nose with his wrist. "What's true is you don't have no guts to come over here and say what you just said."

I guess he was right, because I stayed put.

137

"OK, I'll put this back. See? Gun's away now. Back in its box. Now come over here."

"I'm right here."

"So say it."

I paused.

"Say what?"

"Say who no one loves."

I paused again.

"Come on. Who's the guy who no one loves." He laughed at me. "That's what I thought. No guts." He stepped over to me and poked me hard in my stomach. "Empty."

"You," I said. "No one loves you."

"There we go, now you're showing some guts. Impressive. Fucked *up*. But impressive." He picked up that hammer again and lifted it over his head like he was trying to break concrete and swung it down aiming for my head. My hands shot up and I caught the wooden part of it on my forearm and knocked it away. I managed to get a hand on each of his temples and yank him down to the floor. His knees and elbows slapped the concrete. I held onto his head and pushed his face into the floor with all my weight until he stopped struggling. "Ouch, you Mary dyke. You fuckin hurt me."

He breathed in hard and let out a big "Ouch" on his exhalation. He did this over and over—deep breath in, let out an "Ouch". Deep breath in, "Ouch." Eventually the ouches turned into grunts and the grunts turned into sloppy exhalations. Finally, he was out cold.

I let go of his head and stood up.

"Hey."

He didn't move so I said, *Hey*, louder. Nothing. I gave him a little kick in his back. His body didn't flinch or anything. All I saw lying there on the basement floor was a drunk who forgot to say when. And I had put him there. I had beaten him and successfully taken "father" out of the equation.

But why—here's the tricky part—why was there no satisfaction in that? Why didn't that make up for him and Danielle in the bathroom on my twelfth birthday? And God knows how many other nights. And why did it take me this long to get him ass-flat on a cold floor? Instead of kicking him again I picked up the hammer. I tried to hit him hard, but it was more like a tap to the ribs. He didn't let out so much as a grunt.

I hit him in the same spot harder.

He wasn't moving for nothing.

Then I whispered, "You son of a bitch," swung the hammer over my head and came down as hard as I could right above his knee on his already messed-up leg. It sounded like pounding meat.

And still . . . Goddamn it—still . . . Not even the next morning when we all woke up to him yelling for help from the basement floor. Not even when I saw him on the same floor, his pants wet with scotch and piss, cursing his goddamn leg, and saying he fell over because of it. Not even when we called an ambulance and the hospital said the ligaments were never going to heal for him to walk right. Not even when he came home with another brace and a cane. And not even when my mom refused to come out of her room and talk to him. Still—I felt no satisfaction.

After I hit his leg I hung the hammer back up in its place.

Walking upstairs I tried to step on the parts that don't creak. I passed the crack of light coming out from under my mother's bedroom door, went to my room, lay on my bed and played over and over the hollow thud his fist made on my mother's chest.

I thought he might have been right, maybe I didn't have too much guts. I mean, how could you hit an already annihilated guy in his most damaged part and feel like you did something ballsy?

A dim orange from the streetlights sliced through my aluminum blinds. All I could hear was air coming in and out of my nose. I tried for a long while to breathe the silence deep inside me but my breaths wouldn't go down.

Three little taps poked through the silence. Dani's fist on

the wall wanting to know what was up. We had no code for: *Just beat up Dad with hammer, having trouble breathing*, so I answered with four quick knocks: *All clear.*

———

Mom only left her room, and that niche in her bed that outlined her body, to go to work. A princess trapped in the second-floor suburban tower who long ago told her prince and his rope ladder to go to hell. At night I could hear her talking to herself—I couldn't make out words, just sounds. We only saw her when we brought her food. By "we" I mean me.

Apparently the last thing my father remembered of that night was hitting my mother and he spent his first week home from the hospital clammed up and on the couch. He wouldn't open his mouth for any kind of help, not for tissues, food, water to swallow his painkillers or for someone to change the TV channel. He knew better. Instead he set up a line of chairs from the living room to the kitchen, little islands he could hop to for access to the refrigerator and bathroom. He held to his no crutches rule. These were some quiet days. I'd pass him in the morning on the way to work and at night when I'd go upstairs to sleep and we didn't even give each other the courtesy of a grunt.

With a bowl of soup in my hand I knocked and heard nothing, which was her way of letting me know it was OK to bring her dinner. She was in the same blue terrycloth bathrobe she'd been in for the past four days. It's not like she was catatonic or all weepy and shit, she was just playing up the rock-hard silent treatment. And she was paying bills. Fucking bills. Had them spread out on her bed with her checkbook next to about a week's worth of newspapers that I had refolded and delivered to her after my father finished with them. I had laid them next to her and on my way out I'd say, "What, no tip?" And she'd give

140

me a dismissive look that didn't have the hint of a smile in it. But when I walked in this time it seemed she was ready for jokes.

"Two things you have to do in this life: pay bills and die."

"In that order?"

She thought about it. "Only God knows."

"Well, you gotta eat too. Keep up your strength to write checks."

"Cute. And true." She probably hadn't washed her hair since she went into hiding, because when she scratched her head little white flakes fell off her scalp.

"Chicken noodle?"

She pushed the papers out of the way. "Put it here." I walked to her and laid the bowl down. "Where's your sister?" she wanted to know.

"Swimming. I'm picking her up in a half hour." Then she gave me this loaded stare and I knew I wasn't going to like one inch of what she was thinking. I thought to just get the hell out of there, but you had to see her in that worn-out bathrobe with the bills, the dry scalp, and the dinner that would probably go cold—she was like a dog locked out in the rain. So against instinct, I bit. "Why? What's up?"

She said, "You really hurt your father."

I fuckin knew it. Here's this chick just got slammed around by her husband, who I, in turn, put in the hospital. You'd think maybe I'da gotten a thanks for balancing out the score a little bit. Nooooo. I got sent to the principal's office. Only a twisted statement like hers could have reached so far down my throat to pull out the line I'd never thought I'd say: "Yeah, well you really hurt my sister."

A tremor of fear flashed over her face, but she didn't back down. "Don't be smart."

"Don't be dumb."

"Don't act tough, I'm still your mother."

"Too bad for all of us."

"Hey. You want me to get the police in here and have you charged with assault?"

It felt like the insults were rolling on their own and we were just following them. This time I put my finger in her face. "You want me to get child services in here and have you charged with neglect?"

"Don't you dare lay a hand on me."

"Do you?"

"Don't be so goddamn dramatic."

And my father, who heard that all the way from the couch, goes, "The hell are you two doing?"

"Mind your business," I yelled down to him. Then so only my mother could hear, "Ya cripple jerk off."

"Why did you beat him like that?"

"Why did you let him mess with your own daughter?"

"What the hell are you talking about? You make no fucking sense."

"BULLSHIT, MOM."

"You wanna be tough?" she said springing off the bed to the door, robe flapping behind her. Holding the door open she said, "Then go downstairs and yell at your father, since you're being so righteous. I'm done with you."

I didn't budge. She called me out and I didn't make a move. Not a fucking inch. I wanted to, man. I wanted to blow the whole thing open. But I just fucking froze. Watching her stand there holding the door open daring me, calling me out, made me even more pissed. So instead of making the scene with my father I grabbed her by her arm and flung her back on the bed.

"You hurt my arm. Damn you."

I got on the bed with her and cuffed my hands around each of her wrists so she couldn't move them. "You watched her childhood go to shit."

"Let go of me."

"You see that picture on your night table."

"LET GO." She kept her eyes locked on me.

"Don't make me turn your head myself." Then she looked. "You remember that fairy outfit? Remember what a riot she was, Mom? She used to perform. Remember? People used to look at her and say, 'What a great kid. Such wide eyes, and such a quick mouth for her age. Way beyond her years.' Have you looked at her lately? She's not so funny anymore. Her eyes are like slits and she's afraid to open her mouth. I mean . . . Did you bury your head so far up his ass all you can see is black? Whudid you get so used to pleasing him that you just lay under him when he tells you to, and shut up when he makes you?"

"Now you have to stop it." She tried to wiggle her wrists free from mine, but couldn't. "You're being disgusting and you're making no sense. Let go of me."

"You chose him over her." Again to the closed door I said, "And you son of a bitch, you let her do it. You're dead. I'll fucking kill you. You're dead, you're dead—" I kept saying that he was dead and every time I did I got less mad and more sad. It got where I started crying. I let go of her hands and slid off the bed, right under her feet. My mom just let me sit there until I got my breathing back together. "Look," she said after I'd come down a bit. "I'll be the first one to admit your father can act like an insane person, especially when he's drunk. But everything is so much worse in your head than it is anywhere else, Jake. You've always been that way." She rubbed her wrists where I had held them. "No one ever cried so hard because their ice cream dripped out of the bottom of their cone. You even yelled at the Good Humor man for it." She shook her head with a little smile and I felt disappointment and acceptance all in one. Like some day I would learn pain is better avoided. "Don't you know happiness isn't in what we have or what we want? It's stuck somewhere between those two." She let out a sigh like there was nothing she could do for me. "Jake, stand up."

"No."

"Come on. Please, just get up."

I stayed on the floor, so she stood up, got me a tissue and laid it on my shoulder. I grabbed it.

"Blow," she said.

I did.

"Always the nurse," I said. "Sometimes for the wrong people."

She slid down the bed and sat next to me. "You know, Jake . . . every dying patient I see at the hospital gets to a point when they're out of the doctors' and nurses' hands. It's right before they go. In those last few minutes they seem completely alone, but they're not. Something is there. To keep them company and give them peace and quiet, because we can't. Yes, it sounds crazy, but trust me, I can see it. Sometimes I think that if I got myself as alone as they are I could know what that kind of company feels like . . ."

"So is that what you wanna do? Cut out and get some peace and quiet?"

"On a nurse's salary?"

"Yes?"

"Jake . . ." She gave my arm a firm squeeze and held it. "You have no idea what alone is."

"I have a pretty good idea."

She let go of my arm. "Maybe you do." Which was one of the smartest, nicest things she ever said to me.

"Mom, are you thinking of leaving?"

Nothing.

"Mom, seriously?"

Nothing felt more like yes than no. But I wasn't sure she had the guts.

"Look," I said, "do whatever you gotta do. And don't stay here cause of me. I can go live with Nokey or someone else. I'm making some money, I'll be fine." She checked my face for whether or not I was serious. "I mean it. Get out. Avoid some pain for yourself and Danielle."

144

Her eyes exploded with shock like remembering she left her oven on and her house was miles away and on fire.

"Jake, do you know what it feels like to try to pray to God every day and the only thing you wind up saying to him is *Are you kidding me?*"

"No, I don't pray to God."

She threw a "Why not" at me.

"I'm only saying this once. If you leave, don't leave Danielle here alone. We all know you don't even want her here for a couple hours with the guy, so don't think about leaving without her." She stayed with her long-distance stare. "You hear me? You got no one to cover your shift on that one. Don't leave her here."

She put a hand over her mouth.

"Did you hear me?"

She nodded.

"Say it. Say you won't leave her here. Ma, say it."

"Your sister . . ." Her eyes turned so red they might as well have been bleeding. I don't know what to do with her. She's in this phase . . . All her black bracelets and her . . . She won't talk to me ever."

A fucking phase? "Say it, ma."

"I won't leave her. OK? I said it. Don't ask me that again."

"All right, take it easy. Come on, you're gonna knock over your soup."

She snapped, "I don't want the soup."

"OK."

It took a few deep breaths for her to get to where she could talk again, and in a high-pitched voice she added, "I want a family."

Since we both knew her family had just been reduced to one can of lukewarm soup, two bruised ribs, a husband on a couch, a daughter she was terrified to mention, a son who could live without her—we figured it was better to stop talking.

145

August 8

In the foyer of an apartment building on Horatio Street I push the 8E button. Stephanie's voice crackles through the intercom. "Who is it?"

"It's me."

"Me who?" she says, playing guard dog.

"JT."

She buzzes me in and I push through double glass doors. They shut behind me and silence the street noise. I walk slowly through the lobby, my boots echo off the marble floor. I come to a mirror with an antique-looking bench at its feet, and take a second to check my look. I really can't wait for my hair to grow back in already. It's in that fuzzy, too-long-for-military-too-short-for-civilian phase. The length doesn't bother me as much as the memories of sleeping in Tompkins Square Park. I try to pat it down, and for a second it submits then pops back into its electric shock routine. OK, I do wish it looked good right about now. There, I said it.

I hit the *up* button in a small mahogany elevator that someone some time ago crafted with painstaking detail. I hear a few clangs in the shaft and the car rises smooth and slow, delicately beeping from L to 8. The doors separate like curtains. I step off and I appear in another mirror, this one flanked by two round tables that hold flower arrangements. A dog that sounds like it's the size of a baseball barks from inside an apartment whose welcome mat asks that people wipe their paws upon entering.

"Papi," I hear from my left. Stephanie stands in the apartment doorway with a dishtowel in her hand next to an empty brass umbrella holder almost as tall as she is. I walk to her. "Nice place."

"Got that right."

She closes the door behind me, the cool air hits my skin, and the living room expands in front of me. Two windows, practically floor-to-ceiling, look south to Tribeca and the Financial District. Between those windows a TV and stereo system with enough CDs to build a small bridge are racked—a couch flanked by two leather chairs faces them. One entire wall has been turned into bookshelves. And a plant, or a tree I guess, reaches almost to what's probably a ten-foot ceiling. Off right a bar with three stools separates the kitchen from the living room. To the left a hallway leads to three other rooms.

I look back to Stephanie who's getting a smile out of how dazed I just got. "What do these people do?" I ask.

"She's some kind of dancer. I don't know what he does, I only met him once. He's on the road a lot." An upright piano with brass pedals stands against a wall and holds pictures of well-dressed, important-looking people with their arms around other important-looking shoulders. "They play?"

"Guess so."

"You play?"

"Someday," she says. And I believe her.

"I feel like I should take off my boots."

"Yeah, you should."

I move back to the door to flip them off and I see a painting

147

of what looks like a fish hanging above a piano. In my socks I step closer to the picture and see it's signed on the bottom right. "Holy shit."

"What?"

"Is this real?"

"It's a real painting."

"No, I mean is it a real Warhol?"

"Who's that?"

"He was a painter."

"Thank you."

"Sorry. He was the guy who designed the Campbell's soup cans, and he did those paintings of Marilyn Monroe that look like cartoons. Someone shot him. I seen a movie about it."

"Don't know him."

"Well, this is him."

We stare into it for a few seconds.

"But check this out," she says like she's about to show me the best thing in the whole place. She leads me down the hallway by my hand. As we walk she flips the dishtowel over her shoulder. It's a movement so natural and habitual—she becomes someone who is used to not worrying about themselves, their marriage, or their money. Like someone who's comfortable wearing a killer dress, a dishtowel, or a kid over their shoulder. Like someone who owns a place and a life like this.

Down the hallway we get to the third of three doors. Stephanie puts her hand on the knob and lets out a smile the size of an eagle's wingspan, holds a finger over her mouth reminding me to keep quiet, and cracks the door open.

A girl sleeps in a white bed. She's got a window that from eight stories lets her scan the tops of brownstones and offers her a small view of the Hudson River. Against a pale purple wall she's got a wooden toy chest that doubles as a bench; it's painted with an underwater theme with a red seahorse as the main character.

Dolls and stuffed animals sit on the window shelf and above her head a corkboard displays her crayon masterpieces. "She sleeps like she trusts everything," Stephanie says like a woman who easily recognizes that kind of trust, but is not sure she'll ever feel it.

Stephanie closes the door, and I hold the picture of this sleeping girl in my mind as we walk back down the hallway. "Veronica," Stephanie whispers. She looks back at me. "She's four." She looks at me again. "You OK?"

"Yeah, why?"

"You look like you're somewheres else."

I shake my head. "No, it's . . . she's just cute."

"No doubt. We gotta make her dinner. She'll be up soon."

We walk into the kitchen. "What does she like?"

"Same thing all kids like. Macaroni and cheese."

"I like that, too."

"Yeah?" she says, all happy and surprised. "Will you eat some with me?"

"Definitely."

"Ah-ight, grab that pot." She points over the stove where the pots and pans hang off the hood by heavy hooks. I reach for it, bring it to the sink and fill it up with water as Stephanie makes for the fridge. She gets out the butter, holds it up, says "Mantequilla," and throws it right at my heart. I catch it. She grabs a hunk of cheese: "Queso," and hits me with another strike.

She holds up an opened carton of milk and I say, "Leche. No throw."

She brings it over to me, looking impressed. "Donde aprendiste hablar el castellano, chico blanco?"

"Um, that was something about me being white."

"That was something about you being white and speaking Spanish."

"Well, you know, I kill a lot of time in coffee shops. Some of the lingo sinks in." I slap her on her ass and she doesn't even blink. Just says, "Pasta." And points to a cabinet. I put the pot of water on the stove; she turns on the fire.

The cabinet is stacked with five different kinds of pasta. "Elbows?" I ask her.

"Claro."

I throw her the box; it shakes like a muffled tambourine when she catches it with two hands.

Cautiously I say, "Um, I don't like macaroni and cheese with breadcrumbs on it."

"What?" She spits that word at me. "What the hell kind of American pussy are you? You got some seriously stupid-ass taste buds, and no cool at all. Get the fuck out this house. I don't want you here." I look for a smirk on her face but she's dead serious. "Now," she adds.

"Whoa." I'm kind of stunned. "Sorry."

She holds a scowl on me. "Naw, I'm just fucking with you," she says. "I don't like that shit neither." She laughs.

I exhale. "Damn that was good. You had me."

"I know, your face was ten years old, like your momma was yellin at you."

"You're scary, man. I don't want to be the guy who fucks you over."

"Then don't."

The kitchen windows steam over. I stick a fork into the pot, spear an elbow, blow on it then feed it to Stephanie. She chews. Assesses. Swallows. Shakes her head. "Another minute."

"Aren't you supposed to throw it against the wall to see if it sticks?"

"That's spaghetti, and that's stupid, and you ain't throwing no food, on no wall of no kind anywhere in this place." She pokes me in the ribs. "Let's set the table."

Stephanie turns the burner off. From the oven I throw her two mitts, she uses them to lift the pot. I put the strainer in the sink, she pours the water and pasta into it, we both grab for the cold water tap at the same time and both let go. "You," I say. She turns the cold knob and I swirl the strainer around.

"Don't call me a stupid American, but I like it kind of soupier."

"Yeah, just mixed. Not baked and sliced."

"Exactly."

"That's how Veronica likes it. Me, too."

At the stove I dump the drained elbows back into the pot and she slices a hunk of butter on top of them and stirs. "I need the—"

"Cheese grater?" I say.

She points to a cabinet with her chin. "Second from the left."

"Got it." As I reach in it feels familiar and unfamiliar. Scary and relieving.

Over a low flame she grates in the cheese while I stir. We watch it melt. Then she pours in milk. She stops, and looks at me for approval. I say, "A little more." She drops in some more. "Perfect." We let it heat till it bubbles and smokes. I kill the flame, blow on another bite and feed it to her. Then I take a bite. We both chew looking at each other. "More salt," I say with a full mouth.

"You right."

Veronica sits at the table like a bobble-head version of herself, eating with her fingers. Stephanie goes through about eight napkins keeping her clean. I now know that Veronica also likes to eat eggs, except the crunchy parts, that she will own two horses when she gets older, that her daddy likes the Yankees and she likes me because I like them too, that one day she'll go to camp, that she likes the taste of stamps, orange (the juice and the color), and the movie *Antz*.

After dinner we all sit on the couch, Veronica in her *Little Mermaid* pajamas, and watch Sharon Stone and Woody Allen, as ants, pontificate on individuality, free will, and the true nature of love, while searching for Insectopia. Veronica falls asleep between me and Stephanie, but Stephanie keeps running her hand through Veronica's long blonde hair.

Stephanie's cell phone rings Gwen Stefani's "Let Me Blow Ya Mind". She whips it out of her back pocket and answers it before it wakes Veronica. She takes it halfway down the hall and in a whisper says, "Hi . . . I'm still here . . . Because she's sleeping . . . Late . . . Me and the kid, who you think? . . . Watching a movie . . . Yes, by myself . . . Yo, I ain't playin that with you. I ain't gonna start yelling and wake up the kid, OK? So, goodbye . . . Goodbye . . . Good. Byyyye." She sings that last word and snaps her phone closed. "Damn."

She comes back to the couch. We're not saying anything about it, but it feels like Nelson is sitting in the chair next to us.

After a while I ask, "Should we put her in bed?"

"No," Stephanie says, petting Veronica's hair. "She's good here."

Nothing left to do

A picture hangs on the refrigerator in the house that until a few weeks ago was mine—it's of Mom and Dad as kids. Eighteen, nineteen maybe. On a date in some cheesy-looking Chinese place in their old neighborhood. They had napkins folded like origami swans and tall bamboo glasses with umbrellas sticking out. In the background was a picture of the Brooklyn Bridge that had miniature lights poking through the holes. The table behind them had two regular chairs and two metal folding chairs that looked like they'd been brought out from the back room and dusted off. Now that I'm thinking about it, this Chinese joint doesn't sound as cheesy as it does heartbreaking. But hey, it was probably fun for them. Exotic, you know? My dad was in a tie, Mom was wearing a low-cut number. They were showing a lot of teeth in this snapshot, probably laughing at the accent coming off the waiter who took the black-and-white picture.

I wonder if my parents ever thought about this picture when it wasn't in front of them. I mean, they'd gone to the refrigerator often enough, they must have thought about it when they were pulling out leftovers or getting something to drink. But I wonder if they thought about it when they weren't fighting and there was nothing left to do except get in bed. When she was reading and slid over to make room for him without looking up from the page and he was setting his alarm clock for four-thirty, thinking about cement, money, or some other girlfriend he had before her. I wonder if they remembered whether or not those kids in the picture ever took the time out to ask themselves what kind of nights they wanted when they grew up.

Here's the thing about this picture that's always been hard for me to admit. I don't actually think they were laughing because of the waiter's accent. I think the date was going really well. I think they were happy.

What the hell happens to people?

Some days I wish I had walked in, told the waiter to put the camera down before he clicked the picture. Dropped enough cash on the table to cover the check, and broke up their date.

Of course, if that worked—if they didn't go to the car together afterward, and my dad decided he wasn't going to slip his hand up my mother's dress, and my mother decided to say no, and they decided to break the whole thing up—I would have been history by the end of the night. Never to be born to them. Cancelled over a dish of lo mein. Some days I think them staying out of that car would have been right.

August 8

After babysitting Veronica we walk through the West Village. It's after midnight, everything is jumping. We come out of an ice-cream place on Bleecker Street licking cones of gelato. "What did you get?" Stephanie asks me.

"Pistachio."

"Eeewww."

"What do you mean 'eeewww'? Pistachio's the best."

"It's green."

"So?"

"Pistachios ain't green."

"I know, but we think of them as green."

"I think of them as red."

"They're definitely not red."

"Yes, they are."

"No, the dye is red, not the nut. Anyway would you be happy if I was eating red-dye-flavored gelato?"

"I'd be happy if you admit pistachios are red."

I look at her gelato. "Wait a second, what the hell did you get?"

"Avocado."

———

We cut through Tompkins Square Park, pass the handball courts and exit on Avenue B and 9th. We get to our stoop and I unlock the door. From behind us we hear Nelson call Stephanie's name. He's walking across the street looking very perturbed. Stephanie's covered in busted. I say, "Go inside. I got this one."

Stephanie says, "No, you go inside."

"You sure?"

"What am I, a child?"

I'm sure she's not. But at the same time you can't step over the line from kid to adult as fast as she has and not leave something behind. "Go inside," she tells me again.

"I'll be right on the other side of this door."

I let the door shut behind me and think it might be a mistake.

Nelson must be staring her down because I can't hear a thing. Finally she says, "What?"

Then there's all kind of screaming in Spanish and English. I can't make it all out, but I had a pretty good idea what it would be about before it started. The "you're a liar" and the "you're a whore" part I hear clearly. When Stephanie says, "Let go of me," that's when I decide to open the door, and just as I get my hands on it, it swings open. Stephanie is trying to get in and Nelson has her by the arm. He and I make eye contact. Stephanie pulls away and squeezes into the lobby. Nelson stands there holding the door open. "What the fuck are you doing?" I say.

"Mind your business, asshole."

Ralphie comes running down the stairs yelling in Nelson's direction. "Thas it. Get out of my building." He gets right in Nelson's face with his attack-dog eyes. "Cierra la puerta." Nelson doesn't budge. "I calling the police," Ralphie says. This makes Nelson step back. "I calling them right now." Nelson lets the door shut in front of him, then kicks it hard. After the echo of it dies down, there's a momentary quiet in the hallway. A very unhappy woman opens her apartment door and looks at

156

us. Ralphie says, "We sorry. Everything's OK." She nods and shuts the door. Ralphie turns to Stephanie and says, "Toma una decisión ya." Then he climbs the stairs.

Me and Stephanie get to the third floor. "You OK?" I ask her.

"Yeah, I'm OK." And she checks the underside of her arm for marks.

"Let me see."

"No," she says, "I'm going home."

"Come upstairs with me."

"No, I'm going home."

"Would you just come up for a second? Please."

"One second." We walk to my floor.

I let us in and slam the door behind us.

"What are you doing with this fuckin guy?"

"You mean with my kid's father?" She stands in the middle of the room, and folds her arms over her chest.

I grab a beer from my fridge. "You should be outta here, you know? Somewhere making an island for yourself."

"Yeah, cause I got so many places where I can do that."

"Then make an island *out of* yourself."

"What's that mean?"

"Just leave."

I pace the fifteen feet of apartment—look out the window but can't see Nelson on the street.

"I'm not leaving my kid without a father."

"Fucking you doesn't make him a father."

"And what does that make me, a ho?"

"I didn't even come close saying that."

"Yeah, you did."

"Stephanie, stop it. You want this kid to be raised by Mike Tyson Junior then stay. But if I have anything to say about it—and I really hope I do—you'll find a better one."

"Why you think you have anything to say about it?"

157

"Because he's a fucking loser." I kill the beer in two swallows then grab another. "And I don't want to have to watch you from the fire escape, and drop ink balloons on him every time he gets out of control."

"Ink balloons?"

"I just made that up, but you know what I mean."

"You'd feel good doing that, right?"

"I'd feel good if you didn't get the shit kicked out of you."

"Throwing ink balloons, or anything else on him don't do shit for me. You're not getting it."

"I get that you don't have to be with a guy who attacks you for Christ's sake."

She shakes her head at me like I'm ignorant.

"What?"

"Forget it."

"Don't shake your head at me then tell me 'forget it'."

"I got an idea. Why don't you steal his gold chains, sell them, and give me the money."

"What the fuck are you saying?"

"Like you did for your sister. Two or three thousand dollars, that should make it all good. Get me out of town."

"Watch your fuckin mouth. You don't know shit about my sister."

"You just like Nelson."

"The fuck I am."

"This is guys. This is what they do. They make it look like it's about their girl but it's about them."

"IT WAS NOT ABOUT ME." She flinches away from me, covering her face like she's about to get hit, and right now it feels good to watch her like that. "YEAH THAT'S RIGHT, IT'S FUCKIN SCARY." I move closer to her, feeling like I hover three feet above her. "And this ain't shit, little girl. You see how mad I am now? YOU TELL ME WHAT THE FUCK WOULD YOU

HAVE DONE. TALK TO A FUCKING DOCTOR?" I throw the beer against the wall behind her and it misses her by two feet. She covers her head with her hands and screams as pieces of glass make tinkling sounds all over the floor, beer sprays the side of Stephanie's head. She crouches down to the edge of the mattress and hugs her knees to her chest. "FUCK OFF, YOU LITTLE SHIT."

I hear the echo of my feet off the stairwell, but can't feel them hitting the stairs. I bust through the front door and almost hit Nelson in the face with it. I jump down the four stairs and he's right behind me. We lock on each other like Roman wrestlers trying to get the other to the ground. He slams my back into a parked car. I have two handfuls of his shirt and he's got two of mine. We spin off the fender and fall onto the street. My right elbow hits asphalt, but I don't feel it. I somehow get his head between my hand and the street and I'm using my weight to keep it there and line up a shot, but he wiggles an arm free and hits me right in the throat with it. I can't breathe. Now I'm on the street in the fetal position just covering up and I'm getting kicked in my back. I see the lights. Hear the siren. I uncover myself and see Nelson hopping the garden fence next to our apartment. A cop breaks for him into the courtyards of the other buildings. My wrists get cuffed and the cop lifts me up by them.

In the back seat with the grate in front of my face, trying to suck air in, an old image replaces what just happened and I can't shake it. I'm maybe five. Our dining-room table is set for company. It's raining. I'm watching from the side window. My mother and sister get out of the car; my sister is holding a paper bag in her right arm as she runs up the driveway, my mom behind her. Danielle slips, falls forward and I hear glass break under her. Blood mixes with the rain, and rushes from underneath her down the driveway. I'm frozen and can't use my voice to yell for my dad. My mom helps Dani stand up. She's wet, but not bleeding at all. Red wine soaks the front of her. Mom pulls the other unbroken bottle out of the bag. She yells, "Shit," because Danielle has trashed her outfit and now Mom has to go back to the liquor store before the guests come. That only registers slightly, because I'm still in the moment before that, when I saw something that was more real than what actually happened. And I feel myself needing to smash through the side door, run down the driveway and break her fall, but I can't move.

The move

Mom rented an apartment without anyone noticing; put down the first and last month's rent way before the bank statements would get to my father, and called Dani and me to her bedside to ask how we'd feel about the three of us living in an apartment if we had to share a room. There she was right in front of us making a carefully plotted run for it. I said, "That sounds great," and Dani nodded with the speed of a panting puppy dog. I guess Mom was just done with the hiding out in her own room in her own head routine. So one day after I went to work at the garage and she dropped Dani at swimming practice, Mom had stuffed the bag she usually took to work, wrote a note, left it on the kitchen table, and walked out without saying a thing. Assuming, I imagine, she'd see my dad in a lawyer's office some day.

The list of stuff we packed for our first night went like this:

Three winter coats
Three towels
One bar of Irish Spring soap
One teapot
A four-roll pack of toilet paper
One package of hot/cold paper cups—fifty I think

Three toothbrushes
One tube of Colgate toothpaste
One change of clothes each
Zero pictures

The coats we slept on, the towels we rolled up and used as pillows and if we'd taken showers they would have served two purposes.

The apartment was a few miles south and west of our house, a few blocks north of the Bronx border and closer to the Hudson River. Interstate traffic ran outside our windows and replaced the river sounds I used to hear at night. We had no curtains or air conditioners so the sun came in early and brought the heat. The windows were open, but highway noises blew through the rooms more often than breezes.

It wasn't the heat or the passing trucks that woke me the first morning. It was the sound of one long steady whistle, like a freight train busting through the door straight into my head. I sat up fast and saw Dani asleep on the other side of the room. Oh right, I'm in a new place. The noise didn't bother Dani, but now that I was awake I could tell it was coming from another room, not my skull. I walked out of there and closed the door without waking up my sister.

In the living room I heard the whistle, but only saw plain white walls covered in decades of paint. The coats on the steam radiator were chipped in a few spots and I could see fifty years of renters trying to make the place homey with custom blues and beiges. I wondered if my mom was going to put a new color on those walls or keep it impersonal and ride out that flat white until Danielle and I got old enough and went off on our own. None of those thoughts stopped this incessant whistle working my nerve.

In the kitchen I saw Mom in her robe, standing in front of the stove, staring into the steam shooting out of the teapot. The gas was still on. She didn't seem to hear it, let alone have plans to turn it off anytime soon. "Mom, what are you doing?"

My voice startled her out of her trance. "What?"

"What are you doing?"

"Nothing. Why?"

"You're gonna burn your water."

"Oh, shit." Then she turned the gas off and the high-pitched whistle wound down. She gave herself a defeated chuckle and stared into the empty paper cup. "Wow, it's quiet in here."

I rubbed some crust out of the corner of my eye. "Is it that kind of quiet?"

"What kind?"

"You know. The last few minutes kind of quiet you told me about. The peace right before the patient goes. Is that like this?"

She thought about it. Then poured the hot water into a cup, held her hand over it and let the steam collect on her palm.

"Do we have a phone?" I asked.

"Not yet." She opened two empty cabinets then looked around at the completely bare kitchen. "And no tea bags either."

"Guess not."

"Jake, I really need you to help me get things from the house. Would you?"

———

Mom rented a moving van with damp plywood covering its floorboards, and brought a roll of garbage bags. Dani opted to stay in the apartment and wait for us to bring the stuff back. On the way we stopped at a deli for bagels—the whiff of toasted sesame seeds countered the soggy wood smell. I sat shotgun as she drove from downtown Yonkers and pulled up at the curb of what was now officially Dad's house. She killed the van's engine. We sat in silence for a little while as the engine ticked down, and the keys clanged against the steering column. Finally I opened the door and before I got one foot on the sidewalk she said, "I called the cops."

I pulled myself back in and shut the door. "The who?"

"You heard me."

"Why?"

"Maybe it's just me, but I thought there was a small possibility this wouldn't go smoothly."

"Good point." I looked up to the windows to check for movement. "So what—are they gonna pack the fine china for us?"

"Please don't joke."

"OK."

There was silence.

I said, "So they're—"

"On their way."

"OK."

I scanned the block and checked the rearview mirror like what the fuck was gonna jump us on a suburban street on a Wednesday morning. We don't even have alleys for someone to hide in. Just front lawns, driveways and garbage cans. Maybe an occasional cat.

Mom sat upright like a good schoolgirl, looking straight ahead, her shaking hands on the wheel. I swear sometimes she looked like an eleven-year-old trembling under the forty-year-old trench coat of herself. I'd seen it plenty of times. Her breaking down in aisle three of Pathmark, paralyzed by a choice between two cereals, flooded by memories of Terri calling her a lousy-rotten kid and making all choices for her, turning her decision process into something debilitating and scary. This one included.

"Are you expecting a spontaneous high-speed chase?" I asked. She let go the wheel, leaned back in her seat, tried to take a deep breath, clenched and unclenched her fingers. "Wanna take your seatbelt off? Stay a while?"

"Are you under the impression that I'm not scared?" she wanted to know.

"No. But I might be under the impression I'm not."

"Well, don't hold onto that fear for too long. Being afraid of your father is like swimming in drying concrete."

"And next thing you know you're asking the lifeguard to throw you a jack hammer?"

"How'd you get to be such a wise ass, Jake?" And we gave each other a sarcastic smirk because we both knew that the answer to that question was lying on the couch with torn ligaments.

More silence.

I grabbed her a bagel and a napkin out of the paper bag and tossed them on her lap.

"Eat."

She looked at it thoughtfully for a while, then her eyes glassed over like she could see through the bagel, through her legs, through the floorboards, through the street. She reached into the bag. "You eat too," she said. And offered me the bagel by holding it in front of me. I took it from her. "Thanks for feeding me last week."

"Yeah."

I unwrapped it.

"I mean it."

"Sure." I took a bite fast, because I really didn't want to talk about last week.

"I guess I kind of lost it for a while."

I nodded. And thought: *For a long while.*

"I guess I didn't have to make you feed me."

"Guess not," I said with a full mouth.

Then she reached over with the napkin and wiped a speck of cream cheese off the side of my mouth. I didn't look at her and I didn't stop her from doing it. That was the forty-year-old doing that. And I think I was glad for it.

Then mostly to herself she said, "Yeah, I probably didn't have to do that."

So we chewed our bagels and waited for SWAT.

A cop car pulled up behind us. Mom looked at me, said, "Hey," and made real wide lips showing me her teeth. I pointed to mine where she had a sesame seed stuck in hers. She slid her pinky nail between two teeth, ran her tongue over it, swallowed, then showed me again. "You're good," I said. Then she finally took off her seatbelt and we both got out of the van.

This cop was out of central casting, only without a swagger or sunglasses. He was slightly graying, and his eyes were pending arrests, dark as asphalt. Probably less than six feet and his neck may have been slightly thinner than my waist. He walked to us taking his steps like a mechanical bull on low speed. His wedding ring that at one point probably fit perfectly now cinched the fat around his finger into a knuckle-length hourglass.

"Are you Savage?" he asked with a voice that followed suit.

"Yes. Hi," my mom said with a cheerful smile trying to charm the law onto her side.

He deflected all that with a stale "What's the problem?"

I said, "Pick a starting place."

"Jake," my mother said in a low voice coming in straight for the block.

"OK." And I put my palms up where everyone could see them.

She switched back to charm. "Officer, my husband and I are getting separated. I mean we are separated, we're getting divorced. Me and my kids are now living in an apartment—"

"Which one was your house?" he asked, as if he knew exactly what was coming.

166

"Oh, that one," she pointed. "And now my son and I—this is Jake." I said hi and he nodded at me. "We came . . . my daughter is at home. Our new home. Apartment. And Jake and I came to get some things out of the house." She stopped and smiled again like she accomplished something.

"OK, and what's the problem with that?" he wanted to know.

That's when Mom took in a deep breath and tried to figure out how to explain. "He—" she started then reverted to scratching her head. "My husband—" Her head started doing its twitching thing from the house to the van to the cop car, which I took as my cue to jump in.

I said, "She had bruises a couple weeks ago."

Mom cringed from the idea that that was said out loud, and in front of a total stranger. I felt embarrassed saying it. But he didn't flinch. I guess cops are like EMTs of domestic squabbles, nothing turns their stomach anymore.

"From what?" he asked just for the record.

"From him. From my dad."

"Do you want to press charges, ma'am?"

Mom kept twitching her head around until it finally came to stillness pointing at the street. "She doesn't want to," I said.

The cop looked at me like I was being cocky. "You know this?"

"I do," I said, trying to convey that this is just how the game goes around here.

"Ma'am, do you want to press charges?"

She managed a no.

"All right." Then he scribbled something on his notepad and shook his head, like something was a shame, a damn disappointment. My mother and I looked at each other surprised that he seemed to care. And I swear somewhere in his headshake I could see his family, and his relief that this wasn't him. When he looked up from his pad he was all business again. "Let's go inside."

167

Mom led the way through the kitchen and into the living room where Dad was on the couch, his leg propped up, his arms spread on the back of the couch, and some kind of courtroom TV show playing in front of him. Judging from the look on his face he had seen the cop car from the window. "How nice. How lovely." He pointed the remote at the TV and clicked it off. The room was quiet for a second. "Hi Jake," Dad said. "You wanna do introductions?"

I turned to the cop. "I'm sorry I didn't get your name."

"Mr Savage," the cop spoke up, "your wife and your son want to take some of their things to their new apartment, OK?"

"Uh huh," Dad said. And he and Mom locked eyes in something that looked like a silent hostage-negotiation. I don't know what the hell was really in that stare. Meals and drink? Emotions that ran in spirals? Things never said that close throats? The fuck should I know. I just saw it paralyze everything else in the room—me and that hulk of a cop included.

A static voice came over the cop's walkie-talkie; he reached down and lowered the volume. "The children can go with their mother until the divorce proceedings, if they're doing so by free will." He looked at me for confirmation.

"Yeah," I said. "I wanna go."

"That's really it." He looked at my parents who still had each other's eyes. My dad looked away from her and to the cop. "That's it?" he asked him.

"Until proceedings. Yes."

My father then looked into a blank TV screen starting to see the beginnings of what an empty six-room house was like.

Mom, who had been holding a roll of black garbage bags the whole time, said, "I'm going to start," and disappeared up the stairs.

Dad said, "So whudda you takin, Jake?"

"I don't know. Clothes. Music."

He stared at me cold. "Make smart picks."

"I will," and I started to walk to the stairs.

"Because that'll be it."

I stopped with my hand on the banister. "Whudda you mean?"

"I mean, that'll be all you'll take from the house for good."

"What, do I owe you something?"

"No, you don't owe me anything. But now's your chance to ask for what you want. Now. This is the big chance."

"I don't want anything."

"No cash, no watch, no car, no gun."

"Is there a gun in this house?" The cop really wanted to know.

"It's OK," my dad said. "I got it on a permit. I'm a part-time security guard. My wallet's in that drawer." Dad pointed, but the cop had no intention of checking. "The gun's not going to anyone."

"Excuse me Dad, but shut up, OK?"

"Consider the subject closed then. It's off the table. We're done," he said to me. "You wanna play pool? Go ask your mother. You wanna play football? Go ask your mother."

"I haven't played football since I was ten."

"You want money? Go ask your mother."

It was some kind of childish strategy. I mean, what, was I gonna stay there with him? Leave Dani alone? And if I did stay, on account of his twisted logic, then I'd be there for what? Money and sports equipment? Like I gave a can of shit about either.

"I'm going to get clothes," I said. And walked up the stairs.

"Take all you can," he said. "Just remember this: I know a little about fathers myself. You're taking me with you, too. Don't ever forget it."

169

August 8

"Hey-yo, this your first time? You scared? Hey, you scared?"
This guy is thrusting his jaw at me trying to get me to talk, but
I don't answer. I'm in a jail on Center Street. They moved me
here from a holding pen at the 9th precinct. I've been mug-shot,
searched, and interviewed. I can't believe I'm going through the
system again. Fuckin Nelson. There's fifteen guys in here and
one bench that I could have sat on if I desired to be shoulder to
shoulder with some guy who's in for shit I don't want to know
about. I sat on the floor instead and now this guy's sitting next
to me, trying to make friends. I'd break away from his company
but where would I go?

"Don't worry, I'll look out for you, I'll look out for you. I'm
Kenny."

This guy's got black and white curly hair shaved close to his
head, and some kind of wire thing in his mouth that I think is
holding a few fake teeth in. He seems like the kind of guy people
wouldn't think to fuck with. He's got to be in his sixties, and
skinny as all hell. Looks like a car horn can knock him over. I
mean why would someone mess with him? But he also seems
like he could handle himself if someone did.

170

"This ain't *my* first time. Hell's no. I been in The Tombs before. You be all right. I can tell you got a righteous look. It's the righteous that inherit the Earth, not the meek."

Great. Bible lessons.

"He have on rings? The guy who hit you?" He holds his fists up near his face like a boxer. "He have rings? Cause you got welts look like they from rings. I seen that shit before." I touch the left side of my face and it fuckin stings. "I mean I'm not saying you was even in a fight or nothing, I wasn't there and shit. I'm just saying whatever."

I don't know how many hours I've been in here. Feels like it might be getting on morning. Just a little while ago I noticed a sharp throb in my elbow where I hit the street. And I must have bit my tongue deep because I've been swallowing blood since the police car.

"This place ain't nothing, don't worry, don't worry," Kenny's telling me. "I been in plenty of times. I know all about this place. I was here back when Malcolm and Dr King was walking around. They was something. They was the most righteous. Even Bobby Kennedy. Bobby Kennedy was the only white guy ever had a crowd around him in Harlem. He was bad. Talking bout equality—das right, das right. But they kill all the righteous ones. Anyone talks about fair gets what's unfair. You wasn't even born yet, but that happened to all of em—John Lennon, come on. All we are saaaaaying is give peace a chaaaance."

I'm too nervous to laugh at his singing, but he laughs a lot—it comes through a throat that has been scraped by many cigarettes and shots from a cheap bottle of something.

"You can't sing that song and espect you gonna survive. Who he kidding? We knew he was gonna get his."

In the middle of the cell, out in front of everyone, there's a toilet. The seat is broken in half. It's got all kinds of human filth on it. One guy, who looks like he's using, stumbles over to it and for the second time this hour throws up his insides. I feel my own guts start to gurgle. I'm not seeing a judge until sometime tomorrow and I can't hold it in much longer.

This Kenny guy watches the puking guy fall to the ground after he throws up. He stands up, goes to the bars and yells, "Hey-yo. Hey, prisoner needs assistance." Again with more emphasis, "Prisoner needs assistance." "Go fuck yourself," is what comes back. "OK, then he'll be waiting for you. Where's he goin, right?"

Kenny turns, looks at the guy—who looks passed out—and the hopelessness of the situation registers on his face. Shaking his head he walks back to where I'm sitting. "Don't worry, don't worry, I'll look out for you." He sits next to me. "I know all about this place. I been in jail, I been in prison, I been in the shelters, I been in protests in the street, but this place, man, this place is . . ." He shakes his head. "You know what happened here?"

I shake my head.

"I'll tell you. This place used to be marshlands, right where you standing. That's right, marshlands. This was like in the sixteen hundreds though. They had—whatchu call it—fur trades. And this one cat was trying to get to Staten Island, what's Staten Island now, trying to unload beaver skins. Everyone wanted skins back then. So, this cat's with his nephew, right? And on this spot where we sittin now, he was supposed to get a boat to cross the river, but while he was waiting they knifed him. Mufucka died. But the nephew gets away, ah-ight? So then, fifteen years later, nephew's all grown, he's running his own trade and what-not and he sees the same guy in the marsh that killed his uncle . . . and what's the nephew do? He kills that guy. I mean, I get it. I get revenge. I've thrown down in my day. Shit, I'd be happy if it was me killed my uncle stead of my father—I'd be damn happy. And I got more reason than beaver skins."

172

This guy was making me feel a little better a second ago, but now he looks like a war vet having a flashback and I don't want to be a stand-in for the enemy.

"I ain't gettin into all that. Anyway this kid done killed that guy and they was even. But there was something in that marsh. I'm sayin it put a spell on itself cause the killing kept goin on and on and on. Listen to this now. A hundred years later, same spot now, *same spot*, right before the Revolutionary War, the British set up gallows. They was hangin people left and right for being traitors and spies and enemies and whatever. But then, check it, after the war *in the same spot* in the eighteen forties, Americans filled up the marsh and built a prison over it. They designed it from this engraving they found of an ancient Egyptian tomb. Right, a tomb?" Kenny looks into my face. "Hey-yo, you can respond to any of this if, you know, you want to."

He says it with such irreverence, like if I don't I'm not righteous anymore and he won't have my back anymore. "I'm just listening to—"

"But wait, wait, wait, this the funny part. Five months after they built it, the shit started to sink. I mean you on top a marsh, you gotta think your jail's gonna leak. Water was comin in through the floors, everything was crackin . . . The architects said, fuck this, start over, let's dig down this time. So they built another prison underground. Four floors deep. It was really two prisons. One building for men, one building for women. And they connected them with a bridge they called the bridge of sighs. That was the bridge prisoners walked over when they was going to get hanged. And if you looked down from the bridge, you could see four floors below to the gallows. They hung over fifty people here. There's been riots here . . . the guy who invented the Colt revolver—his brother killed himself here. No shit. And he burned down the place too." He pauses. "Hey-yo, you feelin me?"

173

I nod my head.

"Yeah I see you feelin me. This shit is true. All one hundred percent true. Been going on and on. And you can feel there's something about this place. You feel it? Something in stones or the bars. All these years and we still callin it The Tombs. Hey-yo, I ain't funnin you. I know you thinking like this guy's crazy he don't know what he's sayin, but it's all for real. I had a lot of time on my hands alone in the cell at night—I started reading history books and I started seeing where the righteousness is. That what Malcolm told us to do. Know where it is, know where it isn't. Know what I sayin?"

This guy smiles a lot like he's used to and somehow happy with his life, even if it keeps bringing him back to places like this.

But I'm not smiling. "I hear you."

———

Hours after eating a breakfast sandwich that might have been baloney, they put me in front of a judge who set bail at $1000. That's because of my prior arrest. Without it I probably would have walked on my employment alone.

They sit me down next to a cop, in front of a phone. I'm stuck on who to call to post bail. I can imagine getting Stephanie on the line saying, yeah, listen, I know I'm in here for beating on your boyfriend, but you got an extra grand lying around? From my end that conversation would be all dial tone. I'm really wishing I had taken Brian's number when I gave him mine. On the cop's desk his late-morning coffee vibrates in a paper cup. Phones ring and cops pass papers all around me. My heart is on mile twenty of a marathon, my tongue is swollen, and I know it's gonna be hard to talk.

I pick up the receiver and hold it to my ear with my shoulder.

I see my finger hit the right numbers on the pad, but in the little screen on the phone the wrong numbers come up. I hang up, get a new dial tone, hit the same numbers and the wrong ones come up again. I hang up, try it once more and the same thing happens.

I put the phone back down, and now I can see my hands are shaking. I make fists then stretch them out, trying to get them under control. I pick up the receiver and it slips out of my hand. Jesus Christ. I make eye contact with the cop sitting next to me. "Yeah," he says like the world has been personally annoying him forever.

"Could I tell you the number, and maybe you can dial it for me?" He looks at me like I'm the most boring stand-up comedian he's ever seen. Pulls the phone to himself, hands me the receiver, holds his fat and annoyed finger over the numbers and says, "Ga head."

The plan

It was almost a month that I told Nokey about the Dad and Dani thing, and it thickened between us as silence. We hung over the wooden rail of the bridge, beers in hand, another four chilling underwater at the end of the rope. Overgrown green surrounded us and hints of autumn blew on our backs. Dani sat on her rock below us and we watched the falls kick up what little white water they could, its sound drowning out our conversation.

"Wait, wait, wait," I said. "Did I tell you?"

"Tell me what?"

Sabrina. She's a minor player. Sort of.

She and I walked down the path next to the river acting like the bumping of each other's hips and brushing of each other's arms was an accident. Talking about what? We didn't care: what parties we'd been to, how her brother was in college. Soon as we got to the bridge we threw a kiss on each other like satisfying a script. I put my hands on her back and pushed her tits into me. I liked feeling her ribcage expand under my hands, and the taste of her tongue. Soon as we broke the kiss we

176

smiled at each other and I said, "You wanna go somewhere?"
She smiled and nodded three fast yeahs.

"Let me get this straight. The whole time you had a plan to
meet?"

"Yeah."

"You set a time?"

"Yes."

"You know you didn't tell me about this, which you're
supposed to do beforehand, but I'm letting that slide for now,
because more important did she know *why* you were meeting?"

"Yeah."

"No chance she thought maybe you were supposed to do
homework or something?"

"That's funny."

"So she was in it for the same thing you were in it for?"

"Well, yeah."

"So everything was on the level and no one was getting fucked
over by anyone else, right?"

"Right."

"Aaaand . . . soooo . . . *why* didn't you like it?"

We walked down a hardly beaten path, which was more like
an indentation in the grass, until trees and bushes became
thick camo. Everything was summer green. I took off her
yellow t-shirt and white bra, then we laid down—which, in
the bushes, isn't exactly comfortable. You got pebbles and
twigs sticking you in the ass, grass itching your skin. She made
a playful ouch sound and rubbed some dirt off her thighs. So
I took off my shirt and put it under her. She laid back down
and on my lips I could feel the little blonde hairs around her

nipples. When I pulled Sabrina's shorts and underwear to her ankles, the smirk on her face said that that was no big deal; it's just what she was gladly going to do. And I believed all of what I was seeing.

"So where I'm still confused," Noke said, as he hoisted the rope up for another beer, "is why you feel bad about a mutually consensual blowjob."

I shrugged my shoulders.

"Because . . ." He shook his head like he couldn't believe. "I mean . . . Did she swallow?"

I didn't answer.

"Did she?"

I still didn't answer.

"I'll put you down for a yes." As he cracked the beer can.

"OK."

"And you didn't think it was any good?"

"It's not like that."

"Well what the hell's it like?"

"It was like . . . She was cool. I was just . . . thinking things."

"Which brings us back to my most burning question: What the fuck were you thinking?"

Sabrina breathed in with a shiver when I put a finger in her. I never felt a girl's insides before and didn't know what direction I'd be headed. I thought my finger would go straight in towards her back, I didn't think I would be going up into her. Up toward her intestines, lungs, heart. The surprise of the direction and of her shivering kind of spooked me, I didn't know if she liked it or not, so I took my finger out fast. She grabbed my wrist, guided me back in and up and she shivered in another breath.

178

Then I figured she did like it. I took my finger out again, and again she breathed normally. I went back in and she shivered in again. I thought I found a spot inside her that controlled her lungs. If I wanted her to shake I slid in. If I wanted her to calm down I pulled out. I did this for a while. It worked every time. After I figured I had that mastered, my other hand made its way up to her face and I put a finger in her mouth. She wrapped her lips around it and breathed through her nose. I moved faster in and out of her and her breathing got heavier. It was weird that I could have such an effect over her with two fingers. Like she could suffocate if I kept going. I don't know if I liked that or not. My mind was going in all different directions—pictures I didn't want kept showing up.

"Wait a minute," Noke said. He turned his back to Dani and leaned on the rail. "You sayin what I think you're sayin?"

"I'm not sayin anything."

Noke rubbed his hand down his chin like he was matting down an invisible goatee. "You ever see Dani and your dad—"

"NO, ya sick fuck. Shut the hell up, and stop talking."

"OK, OK, OK. I'm just trying—"

"Why you gotta say shit like that?"

"Forget it, forget it."

"*You* fuckin forget it."

"I will, I did, I'm just trying to tie some logic onto this. Pipe down. So what did you do after? I mean, you're laying there feeling bad about getting your dolphin waxed and you just say what, 'Sorry, gotta go'?"

"No. I'm not a scumbag. I walked her back to her car. Held her hand too."

"Well that's sweet," he said sarcastically. "And she just left?"

"Yeah."

179

"No 'I'll see you soon'?"

"Nope."

"No 'wanna do this again'?"

"No."

"No 'thanks for the package'?"

"Definitely not."

"Forgive my incredulousness. But for once I'm not feeling like the sick fuck of the conversation."

"It's amazing how horny and unhorny you could feel in such a short amount of time."

Noke took a huge swig then hit himself in the head repeatedly with an open palm. "I'm an idiot, I'm an idiot."

"Keep hitting yourself. I'm done talking."

"Jesus fuck." He shook his head. "You wanna swap problems with me?"

"Since when do you have chick problems?"

"I got problems. Believe me." At the beginning of this summer Nokey started up something with this chick called Lanie. They would disappear like me and Sabrina did from the footbridge into the overgrown greens at dusk while the rest of us made our way home and there was still enough light for them to do whatever it was they wanted to do by. But Lanie stopped coming around, a tough one for Nokey's ego. "Girls are always making like they're into me and then in like a week they cut out on me. Maybe I'm a freak."

"*Maybe* you're a freak?"

"Fuck you."

"Only if Lanie won't."

"This guy's a real dickhead. You know you're a real dickhead?"

"I might be."

"Look, don't beat yourself up about Sabrina, man. It's not worth it. And don't fret, little fella, I'm sure you'll find a meaningful relationship and all that crap."

Which actually got me thinking. "How do you know?"

"Because . . . I don't know. Because you're un-weird. And you got the sensitive routine goin. Chicks dig sensitive, JT."

"Yeah, but you got looks, good looks trump weird."

"Well apparently some girls can't see the good looks through all my layers of weirdness."

"Noke, you're not that weird. I mean you're fuckin weird, but . . ."

"You don't even know the half of it. You wanna hear weird, I'll tell you weird."

"Go head."

"I'm gonna say this, for two reasons. One: I'm drinking and two: who really cares. Ready?"

"Yeah."

"No laughing?"

"No."

"OK. Here goes." He took another gulp and wiped his mouth with the back of his hand. "I like armpits."

"Who?"

"Armpits. It's not who it's what."

"What armpits?"

"Chicks' armpits. I like them."

"Say that last sentence again."

"I like the armpits of the girls."

"You're a fuckin bone-on."

"I know it. But hey, I gotta be me, right? I like pits, so shoot me. I mean, there's weird and then there's *weird*. It's not like I go to grocery store parking lots sticking my dick in tailpipes."

"Yeah, that'd be crossing the line from weird to deranged."

"You think?"

"Definitely." I took a long sip and finished my beer. "Why, you do that too?"

"I'm not even gonna answer that."

"Well, I'm not sure I believe you, but I'm not checking for burn marks."

"I'm not deranged. Don't you smell a girl's pits—not that girls' pits smell as much as guys'—but don't they smell like sex to you?"

"Um . . . *no*."

"Why not?"

"I don't know, when I think of sex smells I think of normal things like breath. Pussy. You don't?"

"Well, kind of. Not so much. Actually, no, not at all."

"Listen man, I don't know what you're into, but whatever it is, it sounds safe. Unless you run into some hard stubble."

"Yeah, that would hurt."

Then I cracked up at how ridiculous this kid could be and how I could still love him for it. "Noke, you're killin me, man."

"Enjoy the trip." He spit over the rail and I watched it float until it mixed in with the rest of the white water. Dani was being quiet, sitting on her rock like usual. It got to the point where she looked like she belonged there as much as the trees and the grass only she was undergrown in comparison. Nokey saw me looking at her. He said, "She's a good kid, you know?"

"I know."

He cracked open another beer for me. "Here."

We drank.

"Your mom's got some pair walking out like that. She doin OK?"

"Fuck knows. She's not saying much. Nobody's saying much. I don't know . . . Am I the only one who thinks that people will tell you everything but what they're really thinking?"

"It ain't just you. Trust me."

"So I don't know what to tell you. It seems like it sucks for her and it's also great for her, but what do I know?"

"You feelin cool with it?"

182

When he hit me with that question I suddenly thought that the reason people don't tell you what they're thinking could be because they have no idea what they're thinking. "Noke, you remember we used to put quarters on the railroad tracks and let the trains run over them?"

"Yeah."

"And when we'd peel them off the track we couldn't tell if there was a face on them anymore or if they were worth anything?"

"Uh huh."

"I feel like one of those quarters."

Nokey looked at me for a second like he was impressed. "See I told you you got the sensitive routine covered. I mean that's poetry, Jake. You should be getting laid like a rabid bunny."

"Thanks. I feel wonderful knowin you think I should."

Then we sipped at our beers for a while and let the sounds of the river take over the conversation.

"JT, I gotta tell you what I been thinking?"

"Go head."

"It's about your dad."

"What about him?"

"About the Dani thing."

I already didn't like where it was going. "Yeah?"

"Well, I got an idea about what we could do?"

"Noke—"

"It doesn't involve telling anyone about it."

"What doesn't?"

"All right. I'll tell you. Your father's Cobra." He looked at me like I should've known what he was going to say next.

"What about it?"

"Well, I was thinking . . . the guy just lost his wife, both his kids, his leg, his job, and is probably gonna have to sell the house. I mean look at him, he's all fucked up. Now is the best time to

183

kick him. And what can we kick him with? What's the thing he gives the most amount of shit about? You following me?"

"Keep going."

"How would you feel about selling the Cobra out from under him and keeping the money?"

Right there is where I could have put the kibosh on it. Considering Nokey is Nokey and has fuck-up tendencies like no one I ever knew, I might have killed it. But sometimes you hold things for so long, you'll unload them at opportunity one. So I didn't say stop. I asked for his whole plan.

"All right . . . We put an ad in the trade. The classics section. '65 Mustang 428 Cobra. It's a muscle car man, those things sell. That's how my dad got rid of his GTO. You don't need ID to take out the ad, and if you pay cash there's no paper trail."

"What are you gonna do, mail them cash?"

"Yeah."

"You're gonna put money in the mail?"

"Listen, everybody says you can't mail cash, but why? What's the big fuckin deal? Would it get lost? It's a letter. It'll get there the same way a check would. You wrap it up so no one knows what it is, they open it and it's done. And we don't have to bullshit on the specs. If there's one thing your dad took good care of it's that car. It's a hot commodity and anyone who's looking to buy will know that."

"Whose number do we put in the ad?"

"I thought we would use my cell phone."

"Come again."

"I'm kidding, prick. We use the payphone at my dad's garage. Nobody ever answers it, and I'll be there every day from now till the end of the summer."

"Who's gonna handle the calls? You?"

"That's right, me." He saw in my face that him taking the calls was almost a dealbreaker for me. "What was that look for?"

184

"I'm not sure if you should be taking the calls."

"Oh, bullshit. Bull*shit*. Look, I know I got a bad fuckin reputation for bein an idiot and that I've been carrying around this stupid friggin nickname since I was six thanks to my father. But let me tell you something, I don't have potatoes for brains. OK? I got brains for brains. And now that we're on the subject of fucking over fathers—fuck mine too. My name is Eugene goddamn Cervella. I'm not as stupid as the chicks and my father think I am. Don't make me have to convince you too, for Christ's sake. I know more about cars than you and my father, so I *should* be handling the calls. Not to mention that I sound older than you. And how many calls we gonna get anyway? That thing'll sell around thirty-five, forty grand. We'll say 'serious inquiries' only in the ad. No one's gonna call unless they mean it. Either that or they don't have any friends. All I have to do is use your father's name over the phone."

"Wait, why?"

"Because his name is on the title, no?"

"Yeah."

"You gettin it now?"

"I'm gettin it."

"So once we get a buyer we fucking steal it. The car and the title. You still got keys to the house, right?"

"Right."

"We go in the middle of the night. Roll the thing down the driveway. He won't know it's gone until his fat ass wakes up in the morning and we're halfway to Mexico."

"Mexico?"

"It's an expression. We're not going to fuckin Mexico for Christ's sake. Now who's bein an idiot?" He backhanded me on my shoulder, and smiled. "JT, do you see how easy this would be?"

"Hold on. Back up. What about showing it? No one's gonna

buy without looking first. How we gonna show it without my father finding out?"

"I'm working on that part. I think we could just wait till we know he's gonna be out some Saturday or Sunday. We'll figure it out. Listen, it'll be a legal sale. If they trace it to the guy who bought it, he's got the title, which is proof it was a legal sale. The cops got nothing on him, he don't get screwed. And the only name he can give them is your dad's. If you're worried about them getting to you, don't, because I'll bring the car over to the buyer. You don't even have to show your face. We just make sure they don't live in the friggin neighborhood."

"You actually thought this through."

"I fuckin did."

"It's a good idea, dude."

"You surprised?"

"No."

"Thank you. So . . . is it a go?"

"I don't know. I need a little while to think about it."

Nokey spit again and I followed it until it hit the rocks near where Dani sat.

I imagine, for my sister, there's something more in this river than rocks, white water, and goose shit. I imagine she believes if she could just get downstream, then, in some way, she wouldn't have to live her life in her head anymore. I want to believe I know what she wants, and that getting what she wants starts with getting even. And fuck it—I have to be right. I have to feel like I'm getting something right. I mean I can't even have sex correctly. What kind of shit is that?

August 9

A cop brings me over to Ricky. He's wearing a weight I've never seen on him before. It's not just an emotional weight: his gut's bigger, his face is all puffed up, and he's got the posture of an unwatered plant. What's even more shocking is his eyes. Sadness is never a word I would have attached to them until now. We look at each other completely incapable of understanding all that's happened in the past year. Of the millions of things wanting to jump out of my mouth, "Thanks for doing this," is what manages.

"Come on," he tells me, waving me out of this stinkhole. "First, I'm taking you home."

I don't ask what he means by "first".

We drive up the FDR, and get off on 14th Street. I tell Ricky to hang a left down Avenue B, and another left on 9th. I stick my arm out the window and point. "That's my apartment. The gray door right there."

Ricky slows to a stop. He ducks down and leans over so he can see more of the building through my window. The stoop is empty. The whole street is unusually quiet. He takes it in for a second then puts the car in park. "Kids still play stoopball off stoops?" he asks.

"No, but sometimes they shoot up on them."

He doesn't laugh. And with his eyes tells me this is a bad time for jokes.

"What's the apartment like?"

"Well, it's kind of small. I don't think you want to see it. I mean you can if you really want."

"No. Is it a railroad?"

"Maybe half a railroad. It's a studio."

He nods and looks at the building, which makes me look at it too, and for the first time I notice its architecture. Cut white stones surround every window. Turn-of-the-century woodwork borders the door and comes to a peak over the entrance. The railings on the fire escape have curlicue designs like something you'd see on a Jack of Hearts. If whoever built this place was trying to make it look like a place someone could be happy I think they succeeded—problem is we've stopped noticing. Except for Ricky. He's still scoping the place out intently, and registers each detail with a small nod. He used to do the same thing for me when I worked for him—point out car parts I didn't know existed and explain their purpose. "What's the biggest difference between this place and where you grew up?" he asks.

"Well, among other things, they call wedges heroes."

He half grins at my sarcasm, and takes his time with his next question.

"You got a girlfriend?"

"Not actually."

He nods at my answer like he's just brushed another detail of my life onto a canvas. "So what do you do? I mean what's a night out? You know people or what?"

"Not really."

"How bout your laundry, where you do that?"

If the guy didn't just bail me out of jail I'd explain that he's sounding a little psychotic, and if I didn't know him better I'd have one hand on the door handle of his car, the other wrapped around a knife. His subdued wisdom and ability to break things down to their core is familiar. But he seems somehow different than I've ever seen him. Darker.

"There's a place on Avenue B that gives you free soap. I just kind of . . . you know, I work and I'm sort of keeping to myself lately." His eyes glaze over and he goes somewhere inside himself. "Is everything OK with you, Ricky?"

He shakes his head no.

"Why not?"

"I can't . . ." His voice cracks up and he stops himself. This sight is on the cusp of shocking.

"You ever notice that Nokey seemed like he was born old? Like he came here knowing something the rest of us didn't?"

Now he's getting even sadder and weirder. Not wanting the conversation to go to Nokey at all I bow out. "Yeah, could be." I make a fast move. "Listen, Rick, I'm gonna go now, OK?"

No response.

I open the door.

"Thank you for the ride and for bailing—"

"Shut the door."

I freeze.

"Shut the door," he repeats.

"Why?"

"I'm taking you to your father's house."

This is nowhere near where I thought this thing was going. "Wait, wait, why you wanna do that?"

"So you can talk to him."

"I see him every week at counseling."

"This week is different."

"No, Ricky, I don't . . . Look, I'm here, let me stay here."

"This isn't the thanks I was looking for."

"I do appreciate you coming down to do this. I do. It's not like we're not gonna talk about it in counseling."

"Not if you don't show up for it like the last two weeks."

"All right, what the hell's going on? How do you know I missed—?"

"Close the door."

I do it slowly. "Look, I'm running on zero sleep here and—"

"Then take a nap on the way."

"Why'd you drive me here if—"

"Jake." With his foot on the brake he puts the car in drive, and throws a look on me that could stop the New York Stock Exchange dead. "As repayment for your bail let's say you won't ask me any questions or try to jump out the car."

The buyer

A week after Noke and I put the ad in the trade Ricky was yelling for him to get off the payphone at the garage. "Now!"

Noke held up one finger to Ricky, the amount of minutes he threatened to be finished in.

"Nokey, hang it up."

He did and ran back into the garage. "Take it easy. I was talking to a girl."

Ricky said, "Well congratulations to you, you're finally a man."

"With no help from you."

"Yeah, right, all I ever gave you was food and a place to eat it."

"And don't forget about the lousy heart."

"How could I?"

Ricky walked away and neither one was sure who just won that little joust. Noke kept smiling though. When Ricky was out of earshot he said, "Get your hand up." I held out my palm to him, he wound up like he was throwing a baseball and landed his hand right in mine with a loud clap. "We got a guy."

"What guy?"

"A buyer."

I put my tools down. "Talk to me."

"He's from Hudson Falls. It's upstate about four hours from here. I checked it out. I been on the phone with this guy three times, he wants it."

Noke looked back to the office where we could be seen from, then he motioned to me to pick my tools up again and keep working, so I did.

"What's his deal?" I asked.

Noke picked up a rag and wiped nothing that needed to be wiped off the engine. "He's been looking for a '65 Cobra. Says he found one a year ago that didn't have original paint, so he turned it down. And here's the best part, he made an offer over the phone."

"You're fucking kidding me."

"Not even a little. He just needs to see it to make sure what I said is legit, which it is, and he's in. We don't even have to show it to him here. It's beautiful. If we want we can ride it up to him this weekend."

"What if he sees it and doesn't like it?"

"Trust me, I sold this guy. I know every part on your dad's car. We got a nice piece of machine on our hands. The guy thinks we live in White Plains. I told him it all sounds good, but that I'd have to think about it. I said, 'She's gonna be hard for me to get rid of. You know what I mean?' Guy's like, 'I understand, you spend enough time with them they start to feel like family.' Yeah, unused and asleep in the fuckin garage. Exactly like family."

"What did he offer?"

"I let him take me down to thirty-two five, and said we'd keep it kind of open so we can negotiate a little on inspection. But I only did that because he said he'd pay in cash. Dude, *cash*. Do you realize a paper trail on this thing won't even exist?"

"Talk me through this. What happens when people ask this guy where he bought the car?"

192

"What's he gonna say? 'From some kid in Yonkers who ripped it off his father'? No, he's gonna say, 'Some schmuck from White Plains. I think his name was Savage something.' End of story. And how would they track this thing? I mean why would the Yonkers police department look for a stolen car in East Asswick, New York?"

We saw Ricky come out of the office so Noke dropped his rag, went to the sink and started washing his hands, which made no sense to anyone. Ricky went over to the sink and loomed behind Nokey waiting for him to turn around. With a bar of Lava soap in his hands he finally turned and said, "What?" more defensively than he probably wanted to.

Rick took his time answering. "Nokey, if only the expertise with which you run-a-muck would compensate for the amount of shit you screw up."

"Wud I screw up?"

"Come over here, Potato Head." Noke moved toward him. "Leave the fuckin soap in the sink." Noke threw it behind him. "You see that Escort that just got towed in?"

"So?"

"That car look familiar to you?"

"Yeah."

"You work on that car?"

"I did. Why?"

"Wud you do on it?"

"Why don't you tell me what I did on it instead of trying to make me look like an idiot in front of everyone."

"The cover of this guy's cam shaft came loose because you didn't tighten the bolts. He was leaking oil and the car died on the road. You took a half a day on the job that should have taken two hours at worst. So now I got a pissed off customer and I gotta put in free hours for him. What were you thinking?"

"All of a sudden I don't know anything about cars?"

193

"It's not all of a sudden."

"Then you've been a lousy teacher."

"Judging from you I'd say you're right."

That's when it went further than I think they wanted it to. Nokey actually welled up.

Ricky said, "Take the rest of the day off, will ya?"

"Gladly." Nokey threw his rag on the floor. "You want me to sweep the floor before I go?" Ricky said nothing. "I know more about cars than you ever will." Then he got right into his car, greasy nasty work clothes and all, and took off.

I swear Ricky looked at me to see how I thought he handled that. I don't think he was feeling good about it. We both reserved comment and went back to work.

I wondered why Ricky was so hard with Nokey and so good to me—even when I threw a fit in his office. He seemed to treat me like a son. Only better.

August 9

Ricky shoots up the FDR Drive and we hug the East River into The Bronx, then north on I-87 where Yankee Stadium rises on our right. We ride with the windows down, wind and traffic sounds covering our silence. Gradually the buildings and projects give way to trees and a familiar suburban drone. We turn on the Bronx River Parkway and the ugly smell of the river and goose shit makes me nauseous. I roll up my window. Ricky looks over to me for the first time since we left Manhattan. "You shaved your head," he says.

"Yeah." I pass my hand over it.

"Why?"

"Maybe because I'm an idiot?"

He nods in acceptance then takes a deep breath in. "You know . . . you're forced to be a functioning human being when you're a parent. No way around that. You're responsible for another life. You gotta wake up on time, renew your driver's license, shovel snow. Seems easy enough, but you're scared crapless. You're not scared of what people tell you they're scared of, not the broken bottle in the grass that'll cut your kid's foot. You're scared because at any given moment you have no idea what the hell you're doing. Ever. That's what keeps you awake at night. And it never changes." He reaches into his shirt pocket for cigarettes, taps one out of the pack and grabs it with his lips. I'd give my work boots to know what's going on in his brain. "And then when you're done being the parent you gotta figure out some other reason to function. No one tells you about the hell that is." He pulls a lighter out of the same pocket and lights up. I don't feel him wanting a response and I don't give him one.

We get off the exit to my dad's house. I haven't seen this block since that night. I thought I had built up a tolerance to my own nerves, but now my guts are making noises that tell me I'm defenseless against them.

We pull up to the curb outside the house. Ricky jams the car in park, kills the engine and looks at me.

"What am I supposed to be talking to him about?"

He has nothing to say to me but, "Let's go."

He gets out of the car, comes around and opens my door for me. When I stand up the nausea builds, like I drank too much. I hope no neighbors see us. Ricky grabs me by the back of the shirt with the impartial strength of a vice.

He leads me halfway up the stairs with his knuckles against my spine. The stairs I helped my father build when I was young: Dad sledgehammered the old stairs and beneath the slate and concrete he hit something harder. He got down to it with a pickax and uncovered white marble. "Frannie, come take a look at this," he yelled. My mother came out, dishtowel in hand. "Why would someone cover such beautiful stairs," she wanted to know. "Can we use them?" she asked Dad. "No," he said. "They're beyond salvaging." He raised his sledgehammer higher and with a more determined face came down harder and kept breaking them up.

My nausea is rising. I feel the heat coming off Ricky's hand. We make it up the rest of the stairs and I stand face to face with the front door.

Called it a game

Streetlights from the interstate shined through the bare windows of my mom's new apartment and knocked on my eyelids. I opened them and saw Dani's empty bed. I rolled off the mattress that— due to the quick getaway—had no frame or box spring, and was still soaked with the smell of the old house. I reached in front of me navigating through the unfamiliar territory. In my old house I knew exactly where the furniture and pictures stood in the living room and dining room. I could easily walk the dark maze of the coffee table, couch, loveseat, television. But without light the walls of that house disappeared and left a deep empty darkness I could have walked into forever. And there was a presence. I could never see or hear it, but it was relentless. I'd try to rile it and say, *Hey,* but I'd get no answer. I'd yell, *Don't fuck with me,* and it wouldn't breathe. Its eyes would follow me like a moon up the stairs. I'd get to my room and they'd feel closer. I would reach in the air and snap on the light, and that thing would vanish into the brightness.

But in the new apartment the walls are close and I didn't feel anyone tracking behind me on the wood floor.

I saw Danielle's outline through the window, sitting on the fire escape.

She was in sweatpants and a t-shirt, a sheet pulled over her shoulders and bunched around her feet. She took in the highway noise like music. I leaned out the window. "Hey."

Her head jumped but her eyes weren't startled. "Hey."

"You sleeping out here?"

"Not really."

I climbed out onto the fire escape and stood next to her. "Too hot inside?"

"No."

I wiped crust out of the corner of my eye. "Weird, ain't it?"

"What is?"

"This place. Moving. The whole thing."

She hinged a few nods, and kept staring out at traffic. I leaned against the rail and she knew that meant I was hanging out for a while and I knew she was cool with it. That's the thing about Dani—spending enough time in her quietness is just as good as talking to her. That is, until you absolutely have to use words. "Can I ask you something?"

She nodded again, highway lights painting her face red then white.

"I don't know if you're gonna remember this, but . . . this was like a while ago . . . there was this picture you drew . . . well, it was a painting really, and Mom put it on the refrigerator—"

"The sunset?"

"Yeah. That one."

"What about it?"

"Well . . . You want to tell me about it?"

She bunched up the sheet into a little nest at her throat and rested her chin in it.

"I mean you don't have to, I was just—"

"What do you want me to tell you about it?"

"Well . . . OK . . . What was it?"

She didn't answer.

198

"Cause I got the feeling it wasn't a sunset?"

She looked at me until it got uncomfortable and then some. "Come here."

I took a half step in her direction. She reached a hand out from behind the sheet, rotated her wrist into the light to face me. She pushed her bracelets back with her other hand showing me about twenty razor-thin lines of slightly raised scars the color of white tattoos on her forearm. Like crooked ladder steps carved from her wrist to the crease of her elbow.

"Jesus Christ, Dani." I wanted to touch the scars. Maybe to see how real they were. Or to see if putting a finger on the evidence of this whole surreal thing might help. Whatever reasons I can come up with now feel weak. I don't know if I took too long making the move or if she didn't want me to touch her, but, because things go this way sometimes, her hand was under the sheet again before I got to it.

"JT, could you sit down?"

"Yeah. Of course I can."

I faced her and settled my butt on the metal grid. "No, I want you to sit the other way. I want you to look at the traffic. Could you do that?"

"Absolutely." I slid my legs through the bars and held two of them with my hands.

"This OK?"

"I want you to look at the road."

"I am."

"I mean when you talk to me could you only look at the road?"

"Yeah."

"Could you not turn around?"

I rested my forehead on the bars in front of me. "I won't."

I heard her fumble around with the sheet behind me. She took her time before she started.

"He asked me if I was asleep." She fumbled more then started

199

again. "He woke me up to ask me if I was asleep. So no I wasn't asleep. He said he couldn't sleep either, said it was OK, that there's nothing wrong with not being able to sleep. And then he said he would rub my hair until I fell asleep again. And he did. He just rubbed my hair. And, it made me fall back asleep. That was it. He did this a lot, came in told me it was all right to be up and that we should help each other fall asleep again. He'd rub my hair and I'd fall asleep. Then once he said I should rub his hand. And I did that. Until I fell asleep. So it was all right touching each other like that. I didn't think anything wrong of it, I swear I didn't. Then one time he just touched me different. Between my legs. Only for a minute. And again he told me there was nothing wrong with us helping each other fall asleep. Said, that's all we were doing was falling asleep. We called it a game to help us go to sleep. Then he rubbed my hair and I pretended to fall asleep. He did it a few other times. But one time he put a towel underneath me and touched me hard. Inside. And there was blood. Just a little. I only saw it on me, because he took the towel with him. And I wanted to see the red on the towel because I wanted to know how much there was. I don't know why, I just wanted to. So I painted it in art class. And everyone called it a sunset. It happened a few times with the towel. Then one time he came in and I said I wanted to help him fall asleep. So I touched him. I swear I only did it because I didn't want him touching me anymore. It felt like something I could do to get him from touching me. And it worked. But when I was doing it he stopped looking at me and stopped talking to me. He closed his eyes and it felt like he was far away from me. And I liked that. I liked that I could keep him quiet and far away. I did it a few times. Then it stopped. I don't know why. But it stopped. It's done. And I don't want to talk about it anymore."

I rubbed more crust out of my eyes.

200

August 9

"Push the button," Ricky says, his palm still on my back. As I lift my hand to ring my dad's doorbell, the nausea hits hardest. I cough and bend over. Ricky lets me lead him to the side of the house and I puke in the neighbor's flower bed. He keeps his hand on my shirt, the way someone would hold back the hair of a retching drunk. I pick the head off a tulip and chew on it to get rid of the taste in my mouth, then make a mental note: Tulips taste like ass.

"You all right?" Ricky wants to know.

"Define all right." As I spit out petals.

He pulls me up straight. "Come on." Back at the front door Ricky finally lets go of my shirt and I tug it straight. Saliva builds in my mouth and I spit it out behind me on the stairs. I stare at the door like it's supposed to do something. I feel Ricky's eyes on me and turn to him. He says, "Ring the friggin bell?"

"Yeah, OK." I just stand there.

"Or you want me to do it?"

"No, I'll do it. What, I can't ring the bell?"

"Not so far."

"I'm doing it, OK? I just—" I spit on the stairs again. "My breath just fuckin reeks."

"JT . . ."

"I said all right."

"Ring. The. Bell."

I knock softly on the door. Once.

"Like he's gonna hear that."

"He'll hear it."

"If he was a safe-cracker he'd hear it."

"That was loud, what are you talking about?"

Ricky pushes his blackened pointing finger into the doorbell. The chime shoots through my head like moonshine. I don't think about spinning around and running down the stairs; I just do it. Ricky runs down after me. I try to jump the last three steps but I catch the edge of the last one and I go prick over elbow, roll once, hustle up and keep running. I cross the street, haul down the block toward the parkway when Ricky's hand lands on my back and knocks me forward. He stands over me, preventing me from getting up. I'm propped on my palms and ass, breathing heavy, wondering if I'm gonna get cracked in the teeth. "Both of you," Ricky says and can barely get the words out.

"Both of who?"

"You cut out as soon as it gets tough. You fuckin wimps." And now water starts to bead in his eyes. "He's gone, JT."

"What? Who's gone?"

"Eugene."

"Whudda you mean gone?"

"Died."

"Fuckin what? What are you talkin about?"

"You know the LaSalles. James and Laura, across the street from you?"

"Yeah."

"She knew him since he was a kid. He didn't want to live with us anymore, after the whole thing, you know? So Laura, she let him sleep out there on the porch when he wanted to. I mean he

202

was basically homeless. I didn't know what to do. I felt like I'd crowded the kid enough with the whole thing, and the papers were calling the house, the lawyers. So I wanted to give him time to do whatever."

"Did you go over there? Talk to him?"

"What could I say? I didn't know what to— But your dad. Your dad went over there a lot. Tried to talk to him. Shit. This was probably stupid, but I wanted him to tell you about it."

"Why?"

"I don't know. I thought like . . . like maybe people can unfuck things. But maybe I'm an idiot."

"What happened?"

Ricky's face shifts from poker game to car crash. "He laid on the train tracks." He turns his back to me, puts his hands on his hips.

He wipes his nose and takes a deep breath. "JT, get off the ground, walk up the street and go inside your house and talk to your father."

"Ricky . . ."

"Do it."

I stand up. "I can't."

"Goddamn, JT, just do it."

I take a slow step away from Ricky toward the parkway.

"JT, come on."

I take another step.

"JT, YOU OWE ME."

Ricky's face tells me that he knows he just fucked up big time. And right now I feel like I just lost two best friends.

"JT, I didn't mean that."

I turn my back on him and walk away slowly.

"JT, come on. I'm sorry." He steps toward me.

"Don't follow me. Can you just get off my fuckin back? Please?"

I lean over the highway overpass; the cars come at me then disappear beneath me. I sink to the ground, my back against the stones of the overpass wall. I can't do this thing of getting out of bed on no sleep and walking into another day that feels like a tar ocean. If I could pray or beg hard enough to get the last year back I would. OK, God, how about I jump off this bridge and you let me fall into last August right in front of Nokey's GTI just before we come off this exit? Let me stand in front of the car and say the thing that will make the three of us turn back home. I'm making deals with fucking God now. My face is soaking wet and I keep tasting snot. I wipe my eyes with my shirt.

I look at the ground through my dripping eyes and see a dime half buried in the dirt.

I walk past the river moving toward the train station. Dry yellow grass looks up at the sun saying: enough, you destroyed me already, let me die in peace. Geese float on the water pecking at their own backs letting the current take them to wherever. That's what I want to do, man, just fuckin sit somewhere and be taken.

It's the middle of the day so the train station is quiet except for a few people going to the city. I walk to the edge of the platform and look north and south—no trains in either direction. I jump down onto the express track, the gravel crunches under my feet. I remember that sound so specifically. I step over the third rail onto the middle of the track. The air is still. I guess we were way out of the normal range of ups and downs, huh Noke? I hear the whistle of the express train, and look down where the track curves out of view. I stand on the rail and feel the distant wheels vibrate through my feet. An old guy on the platform wearing a hat yells a "Hey," down to me. I look up at him, he points in the direction of the train. "Time to get outta there," he says. I look at this guy and remember Ricky's face when he was scoping my apartment building. I see now what I missed then. He wasn't just looking at its architecture, I think he was imagining Nokey living there, piecing together what could have been the rest of his son's life. I pinch the dime between two fingers and hold it up so the guy on the platform can see it. I feel a breeze on the side of my face. "Hurry up," the guy yells. I place the dime on the track. A used napkin tumbles past me. The whistle blows again and I see the train come around the bend. My hair and clothes are blown to one side. I look up to this guy who is yelling louder for me to get up. I imagine the earth under these tracks. Hey Noke, I bet under the gravel and sewers there's a mess of frozen children buried standing up, their arms reaching toward the sun, fingers inches from poking through the surface. Every new patio, apartment, highway, and layer of living we add thickens the separation between us and them. "Hurry up, kid. Get out of there." The whistle blows steady. I look down at the dime, then at the face of the train, and wonder what happened to Noke's insides right about now—now when it's decision time— now when cashing it in feels like the right move. Was it like floating, brother? Like letting a current take you? Wasn't there a single fucking thing that could have made you let go of this? I wish I was here for it. That guy is still yelling for me, now he's terrified, but the whistle drowns him out. The wind of the train is hot on my face. I fall to the gravel, roll under the platform, grab a crossbeam with one hand. The train flies by a few feet in front of me. Metal wheels squeak against metal tracks, the whistle whines, and the sounds knife through my ears. Pebbles and debris pelt my face. I close my eyes. Damn, I wish I had a quarter to put on the track. I hold tight to the crossbeam and hope Nokey will forgive me for short-changing him.

The job

Nokey turned left onto Central Avenue and stopped at the first light right next to a cop. I tried to look everywhere except at him—at Danielle in the back seat, straight ahead to the road, at the glove compartment, and at Noke. I was wanting to be invisible, and Nokey turned the radio louder. I was like, "What the fuck is your story, man?" And he shushed me. I hoped that that night of all nights he wouldn't live up to his Potato Head nickname.

We idled at the light as misty rain beaded on the windshield. The long line of red traffic lights turned green down the main thoroughfare like a lit fuse, but neither us or the cop car moved. "Go," I said to Noke. He shook his head. "Not yet." Finally the cop pulled out ahead of us, and my heart slammed against my ribs. "I fuckin told you to stay on the back roads."

"What difference does it make?" he said.

"Three teenagers cruising after 1 a.m. on a Tuesday sticks out."

"Calm the fuck down. There's no more cops on Central than on a back road, and even—"

"Can you at least lower the radio?"

Nokey laughed at me. "Why?"

"Because it's not calming me the fuck down."

"Jesus, fuck. Sor-*ry*."

So I turned it down.

I still thought his whole idea was a good one. Sometimes all people have to do to get their brains going is tap into their inner vendetta. But I was also wondering hard if we were really gonna pull the job off.

"What?" Nokey asked.

I thought I was wondering out loud. "What, what?"

"You say something?"

"No."

He knew I was freaked. "JT, this is gonna be over in less than twenty-four hours."

I nodded my head.

"So stay with me, man," and he smiled something vindictive.

I checked behind me. Dani was looking small—swimming in that back seat like a toddler in her brother's college sweatshirt. I was scared and she knew it. She smiled at me and her puffy dark eyes almost disappeared. The chipped red nail polish on her stubby fingernails could have fooled people, but she collected guts like dogs collected years. Looking at her made me so friggin sad, and hungry again to make the whole thing work.

I said, "I'm with you, man," then reached over and turned the radio up again. Noke bopped his head, hung a right, and we headed for the Bronx River Parkway, which would lead us to my father's house.

August 9

I walk up the stairs of my apartment in a numb delirium, my legs burning with a lack of sleep that feels like a hangover. When I get to my floor I see Stephanie sitting with her back against my door, crying. "Stephanie, what the hell?"

"Nelson left," she says.

"What happened?"

"He left. That's what happened." Now she's talking about how her kid's not gonna have a father, and what the fuck's she gonna do, she can't fit at her uncle's, where she gonna live? And money? She's breaking my heart right in the hallway. I figured she'd still be hating me for cursing her out and running out of the apartment, but all that seems to be taking a back seat to this highly fucked reality. I go to put my hand on her head like I did that first night I saw her on the stoop, but now she flinches away from me. "No really, you can't touch me right now," she says. So I lay off, and stand here not knowing what to do.

"Do you want to come in?" She shakes her head. So I just stay and watch her.

After a while I sit on the floor too, like right next to her. She kind of calms down a bit and I see her do this weird thing she always seems to be doing—grabbing the back of her ponytail and yanking it. This gets her all pissed off and she stands up and makes for the stairs, wiping her nose on her hands, so I follow her.

We go out of the building, down our street and across Tompkins Square Park where everyone except dogs tries not to stare at her.

She goes all the way to First Avenue and hangs a right. I'm walking with her, but feel more like I'm following. We don't say much—cause what can you say? Not like I got any philosophies that are gonna turn this whole thing around for her. Next thing I know we're passing the United Nations on 45th Street. I'm guessing a walk is the thing she needs.

We pass all these neighborhoods on the East Side, the Queensboro Bridge, Sutton Place, the Tram. Then she cuts left and we go down 65th Street all the way to the Central Park Zoo. There's a guy outside juggling bowling pins and when we walk by he says, "Hey, you going to the Zoo?" Which is a lousy way to gather a crowd. Stephanie doesn't even notice him.

We walk north through the park and come out on 110th Street and Lennox, pass kids playing hoop in Marcus Garvey Park. I say to Stephanie, "Just so you know I have to stop before we get to Yonkers." No response.

At 129th and Lennox she stops in front of a building. "That's where he lived."

"Your father?"

"Uh huh."

She stares at the building like it's gonna change color. She's looking pretty cried out. I can barely see her eyes through all the puffiness. She keeps staring up to the third-floor window. "You ever want to see him?" I ask.

"Why?"

"I don't know. Try to smooth things?"

"Why I wanna do that?"

At 135th Street we pass a hospital and Stephanie tells me she thinks she was born there. She looks in the window of a small storefront on 141st Street. Steam shoots from the trays lining the counter and she says this is the best ropa vieja in Harlem. We keep walking, and hang a left down 145th Street then a right on Saint Nicholas Avenue. I say, "Hey, Saint Nicholas Avenue. That's like Santa Claus Lane, huh?"

She looks at me, deadpan. "Ain't no fat white bitches in red suits around here."

I make a note to myself: Don't joke with Stephanie about *shit* right now.

On 152nd Street Stephanie shoots up a staircase that feels like it leads into an alley. I grab her by the back of her shirt because, you know, who the fuck knows what's going on in this alley. We get to the top of the stairs, I'm still holding her shirt, but she's not struggling. She just very calmly says, "What the fuck you doing?" And now I see no one is pushing anything, nobody is nodding out, no box shelters set up, no garbage has been dumped, there's not even graffiti on the walls. This alley is not really an alley.

This is a goddamn cobblestone street lined with houses. Not apartments. Houses. I ain't kidding. They look like they've been here since the Pilgrims. Definitely before cameras, because the only time I've seen buildings like this they were sketched in our history textbooks. Wooden staircases, with curling handrails. Big doors with iron knockers shaped like lions' heads. Shutters around each window. Ancient oak poking through chipped paint. Glass lanterns hang outside the front doors. I expect a white horse to come hauling around the corner, the rider done up in a long blue coat with brass buttons and a three-pointed hat, right? Tying his horse to the streetlamp that burns oil. And now I got two questions: What the hell is this place? And is it real?

Stephanie says, "Why don't you let go my shirt, yo."

I do, but can't move anything else.

She's not floored by this place like I am. She walks up the street looking like she belongs, like someone in one of the houses is expecting her to show up with dessert.

After a few steps she turns to me, raises her arm and waves her hand like she's saying *follow me.* Her gesture sends a stiff chill through me. That wave did not just come from her. It belongs to a person of another century, not an orphaned high-school girl of present time, but a girl with ruffles on her sleeves, who knows how to wear a corset and carry a parasol. Stephanie waved herself out of the present and into the body of a woman, and somehow all the women in the past few hundred years that have walked down this cobblestone street carrying children, parents, or men on their backs.

She makes the same gesture again, this time firmer, like I'm being dense, and becomes herself again. I follow her up the street and this whole thing gets even weirder.

The cobblestones lead up a hill. On top of this hill is a black iron fence—ten feet tall, arrow-spikes on top of every post—that covers a three-block square and surrounds a mansion. Yes. Right the fuck here in East Harlem. A mansion looking even older than the houses we just passed. Four floors high with octagonal balconies held up by thick white columns. Green grass all around it. In the front yard is a cannon. A Revolutionary War fucking cannon on wheels. Past this house is a cliff that reaches down to the East River. Commuter boats, the Bronx skyline, bridges, traffic, Yankee Stadium . . . The mansion looks down at all this, like it's been standing guard over everything that has come and gone for centuries.

I spin on my heels, and try to take in the whole scene. "What the fuck? Stephanie, what is this place?"

"It's a house," she tells me.

"Whose house?"

"It's the oldest house in Manhattan."

"How do you know?"

She points to a sign on the gate. "Says it right there."

"Damn. How'd you know about this place?"

"That day, the day I tried to visit my father and he wasn't there, I just went walking. I came outta his building and it was like I could have screamed loud as possible and no one would have even looked at me. And I couldn't go home, back into my mom's place and feel even more invisible. I just wanted to go somewhere I never been to before, so I walked and walked and I got here. I went inside, too."

"They let you in?"

"They let all the people in. It's a museum."

"How come it's not open now?"

"I don't know. You got to pay to get in, but that day I was here, for whatever, it didn't matter. I went to the door and told the woman inside I didn't have any money, but that I had to come in. I don't even know why I said that, but I did. After a few seconds she said I could. I guess she seen I was young and whatever else I was. So she put a pin on me and that was that. It's spooky in there. George Washington lived here."

"George Wa— As in the first president of the United States?"

"Yeah."

"I guess it would suck if it was a George Washington who wasn't."

"And some people from France even older than him lived here. And I'll tell you something—you can feel people moving in there. They dead, but if you get quiet, like if you don't breathe too loud, you can feel em in there."

"I think I know what you mean."

"Maybe you can feel them cause all their rooms is the way they left em."

"Their stuff is still in there?"

"Uh huh. Chairs and beds and glasses. Forks, knives. Even their shoes is still there. But you can't go in the rooms, you can only look inside from the hallways. They put these signs up that says you can't touch nothing. The rooms ain't been touched since like hundreds of years ago. No one touches anything."

Now me and Stephanie are real quiet. Like we're sharing a moment of silence for her too-short childhood.

"I feel like I fucked up for real," she says.

"No, you didn't." I can feel guilt coming off her.

"Hey, Stephanie. I'm sorry."

"What for?"

"The other day I called you little. You're not. No Nana. You're bigger than most people I know." She nods. "And I think you might have been right about those things you said." She nods again. "You know a lot of things. Beyond your years."

"Yeah. I know what it's like to be invisible."

"I'm sorry you do. But you're not, you know."

No reaction.

"You know?" I ask again.

"Sometimes I know it."

"And all that shit your parents did. It's not your fault."

She wipes her nose on the back of her hand. "Thanks for following me here."

There's plenty more silence.

She leans against the gate. The bars make an impression on each of her cheeks. She says, "I wanna put a sign outside me, says the same thing. Says: *Hands off.* For like a hundred years, hands off. Keep everyone out in the hallway outta my room. Cause I got stuff no one should be touching, too."

213

"Like what?"

"It's not like something you can say. It's something you just know."

I search my insides for something that can't be touched or spoken about. I'm half expecting an ancestor or Danielle to come out from behind one of those columns and tell me what my thing is. But all I see is a barge getting towed downriver and cars riding both directions on the highway.

The job

We hit a stretch of the parkway that runs parallel to our river and the smell of it muscled through the open windows—fresh water mixed with goose shit and wet grass, and that or something else made me say, "Stop."

Noke turned the radio down a couple notches. "What?"

"I said stop, pull over."

"What the hell for?"

"Just do it."

"Whuddaya gotta pee, Sally?"

"Pull the goddamn car over. Now."

"Where the fuck am I gonna pull over, we got hardly a shoulder here. Forget it."

I reached over, grabbed the wheel and yanked it to the right. Noke slapped my hand off it hard, and pulled the wheel back to the left. The car jerked our bodies around.

"Cut the shit, douche bag." I grabbed for the wheel again, and again he slapped me out of the way. Harder. "OK, I'm pulling over, Tinker Bell."

"Good."

"It's like dealing with a fucking six-year-old," he mumbled.

He slowed down, easing to the right; the passenger-side tires crunched over the gravel of the shoulder and bounced on the grass next to it. We got knocked up and down like wet noodles then came to a stop. Noke said, "You wanna tell me what the hell?"

I opened my door, got out, slammed it behind me, stepped toward the river through the light rain, and took a deep breath. The smell. Of all things, the smell was fucking with my thinking. I heard Noke's door open and shut. He came up behind me.

"Excuse me, but I thought you were with us on this."

"What the fuck are we doing?" I asked.

"Don't even. You know exactly what we're doing."

"Remind me."

"We're killing our dragons, man. We been wantin to do this since we were midgets putting quarters on train tracks. You need me to remind you who's sitting in the back seat?"

I said nothing.

"You better get your fucking game face on, because it's too late." He turned, walked back to the car, and said, "No more shit. Let's go."

I tried to blow the smell out of my nose. I looked at the river. In the dark it seemed like it didn't move. I didn't make up my mind about anything. I just got back in the car and said, "All right, I'm here. I'm here."

Dani reached forward and gave me a little slap in the back of my head. I said, "All right, forget those last few minutes. I'm here."

We pulled out and I rolled up my window trying to keep the smell from going through my nose to my brain. I did my best to keep my eyes off the river so I stuck them on Nokey's dashboard lights. Numbers and dials the color of burning red leaves. They were the same lights on the same dashboard of the same '91 Volkswagen GTI they'd always been. I'd seen them from the

216

driver's seat, the passenger's seat and the back. I'd seen them stoned out of my gourd at three-thirty in the morning on the way to the diner. Their night job is to tell you how fast you're going, what temperature you're riding at, and what radio station you're listening to. Only right then, for some unknown reason, they brought me a vague feeling of peace. It was how I used to feel—before Dani was born—riding home in the back of my dad's car at night. The weight of his cool hand on the wheel, flicking the blinker with his pinky, easing the car from lane to lane, me knowing I'd wake up over his shoulder with his arm wrapped around my legs, while he climbed our front stairs.

If you've ever been undone by some weird shit like the sound of your dishwasher, a dog barking down the street, a train whine, then you know what I'm talking about. You want the feeling to last so badly, but you know as soon as you twitch a muscle or hear the second hand on your watch, it'll be gone. I stared at those lights until the feeling fizzled out, until the dashboard looked like your average speedometer and gas gage, and I felt my rage again. Peace never lasts. Ever.

August 10

In the quarter of a second after I wake up, but before I open my eyes, the memory of the last twelve months doesn't exist. My heart beats normal, my guts don't churn or bark, and I breathe deep. Not all of my reality is in focus yet. And for a cruelly quick moment I can contact the part of me that has been untouched by my collapsing building of a year, the part of me that isn't hurt, that has never been hurt. I feel the August humidity sticking my sheets to my skin, the early sun on my back, smell the dust on the wood floor; I open my eyes and the memory dam opens—my reality rushes back. I remember where I am, what I've been doing, and my insides snap back into fast motion. I turn over in my bed toward the light, and Stephanie comes into focus sitting on my windowsill looking very pensive.

"Qué lo qué?" I ask her.

"Nada. You slept."

"Really? You put a spell on me?"

"Yeah, go check the mirror. You're a frog."

"What time is it?" I yawn.

"Eight something."

"Shit." I scramble out of bed. "I gotta go." I flip some clothes out of the cardboard box and grab clean underwear.

I make for the bathroom and Stephanie says, "I'm sorry about your friend."

I stop and turn to her. "Huh?"

"I didn't say it last night, but I'm sorry your friend died."

"Thanks." Now I stall. "I don't really know what to say about it."

"His parents feel like they messed up?"

That hits me as a weird question. "I don't know."

She nods, still looking out the window. Now her hair registers: it's out of her slicked-back ponytail for the first time, wet and falling down in corkscrews past her shoulders. Her beauty hits me so hard I feel like I should go to the doctor. Daytime has taken all the gray out of her eyes and left only green. Without the gel in her hair I can see highlights coming through, like thin shards of red glass. She's stone-faced, staring at the street, oblivious to the picture she's created in this window frame.

Last night, for the first time, we fell asleep wrapped around each other. We laid there strung out on our own lives and made for each other's bodies. It was just hugging, we didn't swap any spit, but we did exchange some snot. She rocked, like someone who was cold. "Dormir," she kept whispering, "dormir." And it came out of her mouth like a prayer for both of us. It worked.

I walk over to her. She smells like my shampoo, which makes me feel like we're actually living together. I like that. "Your hair looks great. Did you take a shower?"

She nods.

"You know . . . it may not feel like it now, but I think you'll be better off raising your kid without him."

"We'll see. But if I'ma do it right I got to get out of here."

"Out of where?"

"New York."

219

"And go where?"

"I don't know. Dominican Republic? But who the hell goes there from here? Is that stupid?"

"I don't think so. I mean, people always say it takes a village to raise a kid, and I doubt they're talking about the East Village."

Her face looks like she's doing complex equations that have multiple answers.

At some point during the night I wound up losing my shirt, and now she's looking at me standing here with my pants half undone holding a pair of underwear in my hand. I say, "I'm a size 30 in case you're shopping." She doesn't smile. Then I say, "What if I went with you?"

"Shopping?"

"To the DR."

"You're not coming with me." She folds her arms over her chest.

"Why not?"

"Because you don't want to."

"Why you say that?" I try to squeeze next to her on the sill, she stands up.

"What is this, *The Little Mermaid*?"

"I don't know that movie."

"Well it's make-believe, that's all you need to know."

"Is this a racial thing for you?"

"Oh, please." She starts pacing around the apartment. "I meant you're not even right with your own shit and you wanna what—be a family guy now? If you're lucky, you'll wind up in jail again for fighting somebody. If you're unlucky you'll wind up with a knife or a bullet in your neck. Or put one in mine."

"Bull-shit." Now I stand up. "BULL-FUCKIN-SHIT. Where do you come off? Like I fuck up every person I know? I do not. And I definitely wouldn't do it to you."

"I need someone less fucked up."

"Jesus Christ, Stephanie. If you didn't notice, I'm kind of having a rough week here, why you gotta stick it to me?"

She stops pacing, comes closer to me, and slightly softens her voice. "I ain't saying like you're not a good guy, like you'd fuck me over on purpose or shit like that. You been nice to me for real. And thanks, you know. I mean it." She reaches out for my wrist and squeezes it. Her eyes are filled with enough compassion to feed many, and her lips are full enough for one.

"I wish you could see yourself right now."

She snaps her face into something annoyed and drops my wrist. "Don't play games. I don't want you putting your shit on me."

"What shit, I'm not putting any shit."

"You will. And don't say that we can work out our shit together, cause we can't." She's pacing again.

"Then we'll get help."

"You get help."

This damn fight of hers comes out so easily, and anyone standing in her vicinity gets clocked in the head with it. "I know it sucks that he broke up with you, but why are you taking it out on me?"

"I'm not. I'm just being myself."

"This is only one self. This is the self that's had to deal with assholes her whole life. You're not always like this. I've seen other selfs."

"You think cause I slept in a bed all cuddly with you, you know me?"

"I know something of you. Would you stand still and talk to me." She keeps pacing.

"You don't know shit. You don't know that I was the one who couldn't sleep because I was thinking: this is great, now when's this one gonna leave."

"Where the hell am I gonna go?"

221

"I picked a guy who would leave his own kid. And that's it. I'm done."

"So that's it? No more guys for you for the rest of your life?"

"I made myself pregnant and I made my kid fatherless. Some people are cool with that, but I ain't. Good things don't come from people who messed up like I did."

"Stephanie, you're way off. You're only saying that because every person you ever knew was a screw up, but you're different than them."

"Look, you got to sleep with me, and we talked about some stuff, but enough." She stops and takes a little bow like her show is over. "Thank you very much, I'm out." She makes for the door, I cut her off.

"Why you been sleeping here?"

"Get out the way."

"Why did you ask me to come babysit with you?"

"Move."

"Why did you get up, wash yourself in my shower then wait here for me to wake up?"

"Just because you can talk to someone and sleep next to them don't mean you should be raising no kid with them. Like you ever had any girls as friends. Look how you live." She spins around in a full circle presenting my apartment. "You move rocks for money."

"What if I love you?"

"You don't even know why you're saying that."

"What if I'm saying it cause it's true?"

"You wish it was true, but it's not."

I grab her by her shoulders. "No one else cares about you," I yell. I watch my words go right through her heart, shoot up her chest and come out her eyes as tears. She puts her hand over her mouth to try and stop it. I let go of her.

"Tu ta' pasao," she whispers through the crying.

"I'm sorry. That was . . ."

"True?"

"No. It's not true. I'm a dick. Your baby cares about you. Your uncle. Your aunts and your cousins."

"You're right. They are the ones who care."

"Hold on a second. I'm gonna get you a tissue. Don't go anywhere." I go into the bathroom and wad up some toilet paper. Before I come out I hear my apartment door open then shut.

The job

Nokey pulled a one-hitter from his ashtray, stuck it in his mouth, and with his elbows on the steering wheel clicked a flame under it.

"I'm probably the idiot for asking," I said, "but what the hell are you doing?"

"Don't worry," he said sincerely, "I got enough for you."

"I don't want any, you stupid shit."

"Now I'm not allowed to take a hit?"

I gave him a look that desperately asked him to give me a fucking break. He took one more drag, tapped it on the lip of the ashtray and slid it closed again. In a slight cough he let out, "I'm done. That's it. It's away."

Mist turned to light rain on Nokey's windshield. He put his ancient wipers on and they smeared the water around. He squinted his eyes to see through the glass, then like a stoner said, "Whoaaa, the world looks carbonated, man."

The Bronx River Parkway is a curvy four-lane highway you don't fuck around on in any kind of weather. No shoulders, just a cement divider in the middle and occasional guardrails on each side. Nokey was in the right lane doing sixty in a forty, gaining on a green Oldsmobile. At the precise moment the road snaked under the arch of an old stone overpass, Noke accelerated to pass the Olds. He smiled because he loved that shit. For the few seconds it took to go through this little tunnel the road got narrower and left two inches of negotiation between us and the Olds. I grabbed onto the strap over my window and said, "Jesus Christ. You wanna chill out under the tunnel?"

"I'm a foot and a half away from the guy."

The driver in the Olds hit his brakes and we came out from the tunnel one car length ahead of him.

"Happy?" Nokey asked.

The other driver accelerated into the left lane, got his Olds right up our ass and hit his high beams.

"Oh yeah, now I'm real fuckin happy."

Nokey bent his rearview down to get the headlights out of his eyes then hit his brakes; everything behind us went red. The Olds swerved back into the right lane and pulled up next to us. The driver rolled down his window and called me a fucking asshole.

Nokey yelled, "I HOPE YOUR WIFE SUCKS DICK BETTER THAN YOU DRIVE."

"Nokey, let this fucking guy go. This is not the night to get into a fight."

"Fuck him. FUCK YOU ASSHOLE."

I reached over and stepped on the brake myself. We all jerked forward and Nokey grabbed the wheel with both hands. "What the fuck?"

The Olds sped out ahead of us and kept going, apparently no longer interested in our assholeness.

"That was a royal cunthead move. The alignment's fucked on this car, it pulls to the left when you hit the brakes, and you know it. I could have slammed into the divider."

"You done acting like a potato head for the night?"

225

"Watch your mouth."

"You get it all out of your system? Cause I don't need you fucking this thing up."

"You wouldn't be in this thing if not for me. And I'm not a potato head. I'm the best driver in this car and you know it. If anyone ever got into an accident with me behind the wheel raise your hand." No one moves. "Come on, if you ever—"

"Noke, I'll give you eighty percent of what we score tonight if you just grow up for a few hours."

"Starting when?"

"Fifteen years ago."

"Too late."

"If you can't grow up, then shut up. For two minutes, just shut the hell up."

"Starting when?"

"We can't cowboy this one, we've never done this before. And if we fuck it up it's not just my father we're gonna have a problem with. You understand what I'm saying?"

He took this in, nodded. "I hear you. I hear you."

"Good. Now please. For two minutes. Just shut up."

He thought for a few seconds. "All right, the guy in that car was an asshole, but I admit, on a night like this maybe I didn't need to tell him he was. There. I confess. Three Hail Marys, I'm sorry."

I was unimpressed and he knew it.

"Come on, we're cool man." I looked at him like I was waiting for those two minutes of shutting up to start. "Jake, we're cool, right? Jake? Come on, tell me we're cool."

I said nothing.

"Well fuck, I know I'm cool. I'm James Bond cool." He paused. "Humphrey Bogart cool." Pause. "Linus and Lucy. I'm fuckin Snoopy cool."

I hated it when he made me laugh when I didn't want to. He

knew he had me and punched me in the arm. "We cool?" He punched me harder. "We cool?"

"Being cool with you is like being cool with a swamp."

"Ha, ha! That's good, that's good. I like that. Swamp." His stuttering laugh rose then fell. "Oh, man. Fucking swamp. That's funny." Then he got a little serious. "So, *are* we cool?"

"Yes, we're fuckin cool already."

He punched me in the arm and waited for me to hit him back. "Lemme see it."

"Not while you're driving."

"Oh, come on. Lemme see it."

I finally punched him in his arm.

"That's my brother," he said. Then rubbed his arm. "Good shot."

We squeezed under another stone arch; the road got smaller and louder. Noke adjusted his rearview and caught Dani's face in it. "Dani, you cool?"

I looked to the back seat and saw her nod a very loud yes.

August 10

I walk down to Houston Street near Avenue A to my landscaping company's office. I see the hose on the side of the building that I used to shower with and try to drop that image like a riot gate.

The office is a converted warehouse with high ceilings that dwarf everyone, glassed-in offices against the walls, industrial-sized fans in each corner blowing the smell of damp rug and coffee. Phones ring constantly, people yell over other people and grab papers out of each other's hands.

Frank—my and Brian's boss—stands at his desk. Guy never sits, and runs on a speed unattainable by coffee alone. He wears expensive jeans with work boots and cheap plaid button-down shirts with the sleeves rolled up—like an urban lumberjack. I walk toward his desk. I don't have anything rehearsed. He's looking for a piece of paper that is probably buried beneath eight layers of identical papers. He sees someone walking to him, but doesn't know it's me until the second look.

"Jesus, Jake. Get over here. Where you've been for the last two days? Actually I don't care where you been, I'm not firing you, because between you and Brian you guys moved more rock at that Upper East Side patio in the last month than four guys should have. And from what Brian tells me you never even take a break. Which, you know, you should. But you're still in good standing. You want some coffee? You look like hell, where you been?"

"I was in jail."

This stops him from the paper search. "Oh Jesus Christ, you're kidding me? Do I *have* to fire you now? What the hell did you do?"

"I got into a fight."

"A fight with who?"

"Another guy."

"Was he wearing a uniform?"

"No."

"Was he a high church official?"

"No, it—"

"Just some guy?"

"Yeah."

"You hurt him?"

"Not really."

"Break any of his arms? Pop out any eyes?"

"No."

"Then who gives a shit, it's just a fight." He goes back to his mess of papers. "What, were you drunk? I don't need to know, it's no big deal. There a chick involved? Not my business. Sorry. You know if I got arrested for—hold on a second." He picks up the phone, hits a button. "Linda . . . Where are the invoices from Bayonne Cement? . . . What are they doing *on their way*? . . . Would you please? . . . Now would be ideal." He hangs up. "She's adorable. But . . ." He lifts his hand to his forehead telling me he's had it up to his eyebrows with her. Then sips his coffee. "Listen, if I got arrested for every fight I got into when I was your age, I'd have a rap sheet you'd have to unroll from a fifth-floor window. Did you want coffee or no?"

"I'm leaving anyway, Frank."

"What? Whudda you mean leave? Why you gotta leave?"

"I have to—"

"Wudda you want, you wanna raise?"

"No."

"How long you been here, over six months? About eight months, right? You're due for a raise, we'll get you a raise."

"Frank, that's—thank you, but I have to go anyway."

"I know it's hot out there, but the way you guys are going, you're keeping us ahead of schedule. So we'll be done by, you know . . . fall. Just when the weather gets nice. How's that for incentive?" He laughs at his joke.

"It's not the heat."

"What's the problem? Brian? I'll tell him to shake his legs more, I'll get on him, don't worry about it."

"No, I like working with Brian, he's great, it's just that . . . No offense, Frank, I like you, I've liked working for your company, you've been great, but I don't want to carry rocks anymore."

The job

On the Bronx River Parkway we passed the cluster of trees that cover our footbridge—we were close enough to the river to skim stones.

Nokey said, "Now that we're all back in business again I figured it would be a good time to say the thing nobody has said yet. Um, Dani? Do you even know what we're doing?"

She laughed at him.

"What? What's funny?"

I laughed too.

"JT, what's so funny?"

"She knows," I told him.

"How does she know?"

"Ask her."

"You told her?" he said, all offended. "The whole time she's known about it and you didn't tell me?"

"I didn't tell her."

When I left the apartment that night, Dani was waiting for me with her sneakers on. She was leaning against the door with her arms folded like there was no way I was leaving without her. She had even taken the bracelets off her arm so they wouldn't make noise. I mean it was a quarter to one in the morning, so in a whisper I said, "You know where I'm going?" and she nodded. I guess we started to think that because Dani didn't talk much, she didn't listen much, and we said things in front of her we didn't expect her to hear. But she heard. I'm figuring she knew exactly what Nokey and I had been up to the whole time and was just waiting for the right moment to join in. I asked if she was sure she wanted to come with us and she opened the door and walked out in front of me.

"How long has she known?" Nokey needed to know.

"That's a good question," I said.

"This is bullshit. Danielle, what are we doing?" She smiled at him again. This enraged him. "What's with all the cryptic shit? Tell me what we're doing."

To which she said, "Killing my father."

What followed the short, thick, dead moment when no one breathed, was Nokey screaming, "WHOOOAAA. WHAT THE FUCK . . . DID YOU JUST SAY?" And I slammed my ear into the headrest because I snapped a look back at her so fast.

"Danielle," I said. And then I said nothing because my mouth stopped working. I looked in her eyes to see if she actually held that thought somewhere behind them.

"Settle down, guys," she finally said. "We're just stealing his car."

Noke slapped himself in his face like he had just passed out and said, "OK, Dani, just for the record, that was really fuckin whacked of you. All right? But it doesn't change the fact that she knows, and that you told her, JT. This is real bullshit. The next time you two are thinking about going behind my back tell me first. OK? You know I hate people talking behind my back. It's fucked up."

"We weren't—"

"This was my frickin plan, my idea from the beginning and you guys were—"

232

"Noke, don't get bent."

"NO. You guys were changing the plan without telling me?"

"We didn't change—"

"Stop it, OK. Just don't do it again. See now I'm pissed off."

"And the difference between now and the last ten years is . . .?"

"Just leave me be."

"OK. But nobody was—"

"Just end it."

About a half mile after the footbridge Nokey pulled off at the Crestwood Train Station exit. He cut the lights and drove the last few blocks by streetlamps. As our old house came into view I played over what Dani said. Maybe she wasn't just fucking with us. Maybe she was trying to make a point. Maybe what we were about to steal wasn't even going to come close to being enough.

August 15

I climb the stairs to the third floor and knock on Ralphie's door. I hear someone open the peephole, so I wave at it. Ralphie talks to me through the chained door. "Qué pasa?"

"I'm sorry, Ralphie, I know it's late, but is Stephanie home?"

He takes his time deciding whether he'll help me out on this one. He closes the door and I hear him say, "Estephanie."

The door cracks open enough to show the left side of Stephanie's face. Behind her I hear a low TV and window fan. Her hair is down, she wears sweatpants and a tank top. She squints at the rude fluorescent hall light.

"What?" she asks, unsure if she's in the mood for any more of me.

"You got a second?"

"Everyone's asleep."

"That's OK, I just want you."

She shuts the door and behind it I faintly hear her voice, "Un momento." Then I hear her undo the chain. She comes out with a set of keys in her hand and flip-flops on her feet. She closes the door softly and with one finger points me up the stairs. I'm behind her and can see she's not wearing a bra. When she makes the turn around the stairs her boobs shake, they're getting bigger, and for the first time I see her body as pregnant.

We climb to the roof, prop open the emergency door with a brick and step out into the brightness of the New York night.

I look into strangers' windows because I don't want to look at her yet. "Front row seat to their lives, huh?"

No response. So I look to her. "Stephanie?"

She turns to me. "Yeah." She shakes her hair out of her face and I see the muscles flex in her neck; I see her nipples through her tank top, her slightly swollen belly over her sweatpants, and a hardness in her eyes I could imagine turning soft in the presence of her kid.

"There's probably so much stuff about you I'll never know, huh?" I tell her.

"What do you want?"

"I just want to know something . . ."

"I'm five feet two inches. That's my story and I'm sticking to it."

I laugh but she doesn't. "You're really kind of amazing."

"Kind of? This would be a good time to give it all up."

"OK, you're more than—"

"No, no, no, no, forget that. Tell me *why* I am. Tell me what's so amazing about me. And I don't wanna hear no more wind-chime shit."

"OK, I had that coming."

"Go ahead. Tell me."

"You know what? I don't know. I don't know what's so amazing about you. I don't know what you think. I don't know what you do or why you do it. I don't even know what you look like. I don't have the first clue about you."

"Finally." She jabs me in the shoulder hard. "The boy is talking sense."

"Ouch."

"Come on now, that was a love tap."

"Thanks. My shoulder feels big time loved."

"It should," she says sincerely.

"I don't know why you're not wanting to stay with me no more. And that's OK, I don't have to, but just tell me one thing." Now I'm losing my nerve. "Shit."

"What thing?"

"Ah fuck me, man. Just tell me you believe I give a shit about you. Tell me that whatever else you think about me, you think I can give a shit about a person."

"I do think that."

There's something thick floating between us now. And because I have to guess what it is, I say it's respect.

"That's it?" she asks. "That's all you wanted from me?"

"No, not really."

"Here it comes."

"It's not like that."

"What's it like then?"

"I want to know what you want."

She stops as if she's translating what I said into another language. "What do you mean?"

"I'm just asking what you want. Because these people who been all up in your face and shit, treating you like ass—and I'm sorry for saying it like this, but your mom, your dad, Nelson; I'm thinking they may never have asked you this. I seen the same shit with my sister. It's something I could have asked like a while back and it might have made things—I don't know . . . I just want to do something that's actually going to help. So what is it that you want? Like in general and specifically."

The job

Nokey hung a Louie onto my father's block. He swung a U-turn and backed up the driveway pointing downhill towards the parkway. He killed the engine and we all sat there boiling in our own nerves.

"You ready?" Nokey asked.

Dani opened her door.

"Whoa," I said. "Shut that, shut that." She closed it. I said, "Where you going?"

She gave me a defiant look. "With you."

Nokey said, "I don't think that's gonna work."

"Dani, you have to wait in the car."

"Why?"

"Come on, I took you this far but there's no way you're coming into that house with me."

"Yeah," Nokey said. "That wasn't part of the plan."

"There's no reason to step foot in there again," I said.

"And she's not coming in that garage with me. I'm doing this myself. I don't want or need help."

"Dani, Noke is gonna roll the Cobra down and I'm gonna drive this car. So just hang tight."

She nodded unhappily and looked through her open window at the second story and my father's bedroom.

Me and Nokey got out of the car and shut the door with the least amount of noise we could. I looked down the street. Light rain danced in the cone of light under the streetlamps. A few porch lights were on. It was silent except for the blood pushing through my head. I looked up to the driveway and said, "Listen, all you have to do is take off the emergency brake."

"I know." He was all amped.

"You gotta give it a little brake when you come to the end of the driveway or it'll bottom out. But past that you're good until the parkway without gas."

"This is cake."

"The slower you open the garage door the quieter it is."

"I remember. Let's go," he said.

"Your cell off?"

"Yeah it's off. Let's go already." And he walked slowly up the driveway, his eyes on the second-floor windows.

I tried to take each front stair like I weighed forty pounds. I walked around to the side door, the quietest one. I was shaking so much I had to grab the keys with both hands to guide them into the lock. I got it open, stepped inside and closed it.

I held still, waiting for my eyes to adjust to the dark. I heard nothing except that rush in my head. I sucked in some air and got hit with a recipe of familiar smells: carpet dust, refrigerator exhaust, fireplace. *Fuck this place.*

Darkness peeled off the edges of the dining-room table and chairs. With my hands reaching in front of me I maneuvered around them and into the living room. By the overflow of the streetlights I could see the lamp table. I kneeled down in front and slid the little wooden drawer open and felt for the keys. I couldn't make out the details of the pictures on this table, but I felt them inches from my face, breathing on me.

238

There was one of Dani taken the first day she came into this house.

She was a brand new kid.

Her eyes were closed.

The two days before the picture was taken my dad and I spent alone in this house. Mom was away and all I knew was her trip had something to do with my new sister. For months they kept telling me, *The baby is coming, the baby is coming*, but were real vague about how and when. The day Mom got out of the hospital my dad picked me up from kindergarten and Mom stood on the front steps, gave me a big hug. She had a peanut-butter sandwich waiting for me in the kitchen. While I ate my mother and father sat at the table staring at me like I was gonna do tricks. I pushed the peanut butter off the roof of my mouth with my tongue.

"How was school, Jake?"

"Good."

"That's good."

Then they started grinning.

"Are you laughing at me?"

"No, silly. We're not laughing at you. What did you do in school?"

"We had clay and I made a tall face pole, and Mrs Jaffe said it was a total pole."

"Totem pole."

"Yeah."

"Oooh, that sounds fun."

"Yeah."

I ate my sandwich for about another two minutes with them smiling at me the whole time. I dropped the last piece of crust in my dish, picked up my bookbag and made for my room. In the living room I passed by a big wicker basket next to the couch that at first glance looked like it was filled with a blanket. But when

239

I stopped to check it out, I saw there was a baby wrapped in the blanket. I could only see her face. I felt so victorious because I found the thing everyone had been looking for for nine months. I kneeled down next to her. She smelled like bubble bath and was sleeping so quietly that even when I put my head closer to her, I could barely hear her breathe. I stayed there for a while, alone in the room with her.

Finally, I stood up and called to the kitchen, "Mom, Dad, come here. Come here." My voice woke Dani up, she started twitching around. Dad came in the room and Mom poked her head around the corner to watch. "Look, she's here. I found her."

Then Dani cried the first sound I ever heard her make. I looked for validation from my mom that she was supposed to sound like that, that she was working OK. And Mom smiled.

My dad reached into the basket, lifted her out of there, and jiggled her up and down like he was trying to jostle the crying out of her. I got on my toes and looked up at the new life I thought I had discovered and tried to touch her, but Dad pulled her out of my reach and said, "She's mine."

What can I tell you?

I was five.

I believed him.

The keys were in my hand. There were a few papers in the drawer. I couldn't make out which one was the title, so I took them all out, folded them, and eased them into my back pocket—and that was the final move that proved intent to sell.

From behind my head I heard a car engine turning over. It stopped. Then I heard it again. Stuttering, trying to catch. It was coming from the garage. The loud familiar sound pumped sweat out of my body like a nightmare. It was my dad's car. It did another false start before it caught. Then it revved right through my guts. I thought, *Nokey, what the fuck did you just do?*

Through the ceiling above me I heard my father roll out of bed and hit the floor. I'd never been so glad for his messed-up leg than I was right then. I thought my beating did some good after all. I knew there was no way he could have caught us, but I wanted to disappear before he knew who it was. I threw the keys back in the drawer, turned around and ran. I hit my knee hard against the coffee table and sent it sliding across the floor. I broke out the side door and ran to the driveway. The garage was open and Nokey was in the Cobra waving me out of the way.

We both heard a gunshot.

His face exploded with fear, my forearms snapped over my head for protection, I fell forward and sprawled on the blacktop. Noke jumped out of the Cobra and bolted down the driveway toward his car. I hopped up and followed him staying low as I could. My hand was on the passenger-door handle and we heard another shot. I swear I felt the wind of it pass my ear. I jumped in the passenger's seat and slammed the door. Nokey landed behind the wheel. My dad must have been sleeping with his gun next to his bed those days because for the second I took to turn around I could see him aiming it from his bedroom window. Noke fumbled with the ignition then finally turned it, jammed it into drive, and floored it until we were out of range.

I said, "Holy fucking Jesus Christ."

He said, "Fuckin hell. Oh my fucking God. That did not just happen."

Then we didn't say another word.

Noke got on the parkway and drove about a mile before he thought to put the headlights on.

I saw no police lights in the rearview mirror and barely a car

241

on the road, only the occasional pair of headlights hit my eyes from the other side of the parkway. I realized we were safe. Noke slowed down to the speed limit. Rain built up on the windshield. I reached over and turned on the useless wipers, they squeaked to the left.

And then I was fucking enraged.

"What did you just do?" Nokey wasn't talking. "You motherfucker, you fucking answer me. Why the fuck did you start that fucking car?"

"I don't—"

"You stupid shit, you fucked it up. I fuckin knew it." I pounded a couple times on the dash. "How did you even start it?"

"I hotwired it."

"You *what*? What the fuckin Christ for?"

"Cause I knew I could. It's a '65. There's no computerized security and I knew that . . . It worked, didn't it?"

"I had the fucking keys IN MY HAND, you idiot asshole."

"You didn't tell me your dad had a gun."

"What difference—"

I heard something from the back seat.

"Shut the fuck up, Nokey. What, Dani?"

No sounds.

"Dani, what?"

In that kind of whisper that she talks in she said, "Something pinched me in the neck."

I looked back. Her entire right shoulder was covered in blood.

"Oh God," Noke said, "oh God, oh fuck."

My intestines went numb.

"We gotta get her to the hospital," Nokey said. His hands seizured on the steering wheel.

I remember saying, *Fix this*. I didn't say it out loud. I thought I was asking someone—who some people might call God—to fix what just happened.

"Jake, I'm going to the hospital, now."

"Dani, just don't move. Noke's gonna drive to the hospital. They can fix it."

She shook her head at me. There was rage in her eyes, she was saying no.

"I know you hate hospitals but that's where we're going."

She shook her head again.

"Dani, you have to go."

And then she opened the car door.

She was bleeding from the fuckin neck, we were flying down the parkway, and she actually opened the door like she was gonna jump out.

I reached over the seat and grabbed her by the shirt. I climbed into the back seat, slammed the door shut and held my shirt tail up to her neck.

"She has to go to the hospital, man. If she got hit in the jugular vein, which she might have, they say she could die in like seven minutes."

"Shut up Nokey, you don't know what the fuck you're saying."

"It's true, that's what they say."

"You don't know shit. You fuck up everything, you're a fuckin idiot, you always were a fuckin idiot and you're gonna die a fuckin idiot. I hate every piece of you."

Danielle fought against me and tried to open the door again. I grabbed her hands. She screamed to be let go. I said, "Dani, stay in the car. Stop moving. You're gonna be OK."

She shook her head at me, "I'm not going."

"JT, she has to go to the hospital."

"Nokey, if you say another fucking word I'm gonna throw you out of your own car and leave you dead on the highway."

Again she reached for the door handle.

"Goddamnit, Dani, would you fuckin hold still already."

Danielle looked at me and held a firm pointing finger over her lips, telling me to be quiet. She was thirteen, bleeding from the neck, pulling against me, and inside her there was something steady. Like she'd been expecting it.

"The river," she said.

"No way," Noke said. "No fuckin way."

"Noke, gun it to the fuckin hospital."

He accelerated, and I pulled Dani's back to my chest and pushed the shirt into her neck. She tried to push me off her with her feet. The car swerved and debris from the shoulder rattled under the floorboards. Noke jerked the car back into the right lane; my hands slipped off Dani's neck, she screamed.

"What the fuck are you doing, Noke?"

"I'm sorry," he said.

"Stay on the goddamn road and get us the fuck there now."

"I got it, I got it."

Dani stopped struggling against me. She was looking up. Not at me, or the roof of the car, but at something else. Her breath came in and out in little tremors. Her eyes were wide open. "I'm sorry," I said to her. "I'm so sorry."

I felt like I could have easily killed my father. And myself while I was at it. I could have rammed my head into a brick wall for about an hour. I could have dove off the bridge and landed face down in the rocks. I hated myself. I wasn't ten. I was seventeen. I could have beat him sober body to sober body instead of trying to get even with a stolen car. I could have done it. Fuck. I know I could have. "Why did he do this to you, Dani?"

I wanted to believe that it was going to be OK, that it was gonna get fixed, that no one would find out what happened. I wanted to think her blood wasn't covering Nokey's back seat, that it was staying in her body.

I felt the motion of the car, but it was like we weren't moving. I didn't know when Dani stopped breathing. I didn't know if

I was cold, hot, if I was there, or if I was even me. We passed highway lights that brightened then darkened Dani's face. Her eyes were still open. I touched one and it didn't blink. Her face was different. It wasn't twisted or fighting or mad or anything. Really, it looked just like sleep.

August 16

August trees, green plants, and tall grass overflow on the banks of the Bronx River giving frogs and birds more places to hide, squirrels more food to scavenge, boyfriends and girlfriends more cover to melt into. Summer seems to know it's the strongest season this river's got. The foliage grows so bold, spreading like peacock feathers. Each leaf and blade sticks its tongue out at autumn daring it to take over. Of course summer plants know they'll be dead soon. If autumn doesn't do the job, winter will bury them with twenty degrees tied behind its back. And in spite of that they look in the eye of their murderer and say, I know you're gonna end my life, but this is my time to shine and there's nothing you can do about it. Their short life really makes them pick their brave moments.

————

The train stops at the Crestwood Station and I step off. I don't want to do this. I'd rather hijack this motherfucker, run it full speed past the last stop into the train yard where cartoon-style it smashes the parked trains out of its way, skips off the track and crash-stops in a trench and the cars accordion behind it into a steaming pile of scrap metal. Then I'd get out. And walk north. Until it got too cold and I'd knock on some Canadian's door and sit in front of their fireplace, sip on their moose soup or whatever they eat, and sleep on their couch until I get a job in their quaint town washing dishes under a fake name. Instead of all that, I'm walking in the direction of my father's house.

I ring the bell. In the glass window of the door my face reflects back to me until my dad's imposes itself over mine. He opens the door, leaning some weight on a cane. We stare at each other. We don't know what the fuck to say for ourselves.

"What happened to your face?" he wants to know.

"Nothing."

"Are you coming in?"

"I guess so."

He hobbles back inside leaving the door open for me.

In the kitchen we stand on opposite sides of the table facing each other.

"Love what you did to the place," I say.

"Don't rile me up, Jake," he says as more of a warning than a request.

"Look, I need some cash. So if you hit me with a few large then I'll get outta here."

We stand in silence for a while.

"Don't you think you owe me at least some greenbacks?"

He turns around and leaves the kitchen. I hear him go through the living room and up the stairs; his labored leg creaking the steps. White lace curtains hold still in front of the closed window. The air is thick as soup. That spice-rack radio stands in the corner ready to fall. The steps creak again in a patchy rhythm. He comes back into the kitchen holding a piece of folded clothing in front of him.

247

"What's that?" I ask.

He holds it out further.

It's red. A zipper. It's her sweatshirt. Now I talk through a jaw that's stiff with eighteen years of rage. "Why you giving this to me?"

"Because."

"*Because?* Oh that's brilliant. You're so—"

"Because I'm not the only one around here who fucked up."

I shake back a huge urge to kick him in his throat. "Have you dropped your fuckin nut sack?"

"Take the sweatshirt."

"Give me some fuckin money."

He holds it out with more emphasis, his arm steady, pointing the sweatshirt at my chest, his eyes at my eyes.

"Fuck you," I tell him.

He shoves it right up to my face.

"I said, fuck off," as I slap his hand away; the sweatshirt falls.

"Oh it's like that." He slaps his cane down on the linoleum. "That's what you want, huh? That what you really want? You wanna smack me?"

"I want you to get smacked in prison."

"There was a robbery happening ON MY PROPERTY. My gun was LEGAL. They have explained it to you and to all of us more than once. You have nothing, you have no course of action. You are the only thief around here."

"So you're legally an asshole. Agreed."

"But whose fault does it sould like?"

He pauses as if I'm supposed to answer.

"Huh? Whose fault? If there was no robbery . . ." He shoves me in he chest.

"We doin this again?"

"I'm standing right here. Now's your big chance. Let's get it going. There's no one here. No cops, no judge." He shoves me

248

again. "I just hit you. Now you can come back at me legally." Another shove. "Self defense. I'll even back your story." He shoves me harder in the chest and my heart thumps like a squirrel. "You're so fuckin righteous. You think you're untouchable now you're out of the house. You're little, and you don't know shit. I seen you balls ass naked when you was just born. I seen you puke." He smiles. "And I know how big your dick is."

On top of the rage I am an original kind of disturbed and disgusted. It's fucking gross that he possesses that image, and it's pathetic that he thinks this hypothetical piece of information makes him smarter than me. "Why do you make it so easy to think you're an asshole?"

"That's your opinion," and he pounds himself in the chest twice like he wants me to aim for his heart. "Come on. Come on, you little fuck up."

I'm done talking.

I split-second strategize. I spread my arms out in a cross, like I don't want any part of him, and try to pacify my face, playing the *you wouldn't hit a guy with glasses* routine. Without the glasses. He could give a shit and shoves me once more hard in the chest. You gotta be pretty cranked up to want to hit a guy who's posing like a target. From the crucifix position I take one step toward him, ball up my right fist and catch him square on his left temple. Oh, man, the timing and placement are perfect— like hitting a fastball on the fat part of the bat. His head whips to one side and his whole body follows. He staggers back and to my left, down on one knee, leaving his ribs wide open for a kick.

I haven't been in enough fights to know if the first punch is the most important like they say, but looking at him trying to get his footing I already feel like I own this guy. I see the spot on his side where I could easily land the steel tip of my boot. I can already feel the snaps, one rib for me, one for my mom, and two for Danielle. I love it. I love the thud of all three kicks, the fetal position he would roll into, the cringe of pain on his face, and my feeling of satisfaction.

And I actually hate that I love it.

A feeling comes over me that immediately sucks out my adrenaline and makes me not want to kick him.

My father lunges at me belt-high and throws a combination of punches to my guts. The guy can hit. But as much as it hurts, and it fuckin hurts, I don't go back at him. I bend over and cover my stomach with my forearms. His knuckles connect with my wrist bones a few times.

He stands up, reaches over my head, wraps his arms around my neck and tries to pull my face to the ground. I grab his shirt and sprawl my legs behind me stiffening like a plank. My weight brings him down; his knees hit the kitchen floor like cracking coconuts.

The sound is meticulous.

It rings like a tuning fork, and brings all the noises around us to a perfectly clear pitch: Dad's breathing, his teeth crunching, his shirt ripping, the toes of my boots scraping on the floor. I also hear a car coming down our street, a neighbor's lawnmower, and a dog barking. Each one an unmistakable marker that—while we're here in this limb-cluster like two birds going ballistic over the final crumb—everyone else is routinely doing what they need to do, driving to where they need to drive, cutting what they need to cut.

Dad stands.

I take a hit to the mouth.

I take a hit to the chest.

I take a slap to the side of the face.

I block the next couple punches with my forearms.

I grab him around his waist in a bear hug.

His arms are stuck behind me, he can't swing anymore. He thrashes around against my hold, but can't break it. He tries to punch me in the back of the head, but he has no leverage. He reaches behind him trying to pry my arms apart, but I hold on tighter. He gets a hold of my fingers, but can't separate them. The dog barks again; another car passes. I lift him off the floor. He's fuckin heavy; we swing around the kitchen like a couple of palsied dancers. I suck air. He has waves of struggle and rests, until he finally goes limp. My arms are deadlocked around his waist and I hope I can hold him longer than he can fight.

Now he says, "Get off." It doesn't feel like time to let go. There's more fight left in him, and I let him know I've got plenty of strength left by squeezing tighter and keeping his feet off the floor.

The sounds around us get louder; the refrigerator, the lawnmower, the dog. I hear Dad's breathing now. I hear his knees and elbows slapping on the concrete of our basement floor that drunken night. I hear him yelling *Ouch*, breathing heavy. I'm standing in that damp basement holding that hammer over his mostly passed-out body. I remember lifting it up, and how quiet everything was after I hit him. But I can't remember what was so loud before all that; which noises shook the family so hard that they broke us. I hear the sound of the pool stick—on my twelfth birthday—sliding across the skin of my hand and hitting the cue ball, the cue ball hitting the fourteen ball, the fourteen ball rolling across the felt. I hear my father let out a scream—at my mother, at me, at things I'll never really know. I hear another scream of his as he loudly celebrates my twelfth birthday in that bar; it's mixed with the liberating noises of Van Morrison's "Caravan" delivered from that dirty jukebox. Two beautiful sounds that I cannot separate.

I swing Dad to my left and let go of his waist. He tumbles to the floor and shoots right back up expecting more, favoring his leg. We hold each other's eyes until we're sure it's over. We stare each other down until the moment fades, and he's out of pouncing mode. He backs up way out of swinging distance, reaches for a chair behind him and falls into it.

251

I still feel people moving through their day, uninterrupted by the beating me and this guy put or didn't put on each other.

Him on the chair and me in the middle of the room, we make our breathing sound louder than it needs to, probably because we can't talk or deal with quiet.

For whatever amount of time that feels longer than it is, we don't move too much or say anything. Dad looks at me with his head tilted, interested and confused, studying me out the sides of his eyes. I feel like a fish in a tank that just figured out what a hook is.

After all the breathing and staring he says, "They'll be calling you soon." He reaches for his back and his face bursts in pain.

"Who?"

"The court, your defender?"

"Why?"

"I'm gonna drop the charges."

"What?"

"I'm gonna drop the charges on you. Your case will be closed."

"You will?"

"Yeah."

"So that's it then?" I ask. "We're done with the sessions, the case?"

"We don't have to sit in that room anymore. Not if we don't want to."

I lean against the hard counter. Run my hand over the fuzz of my hair. And take the reality of us being legally off each other's backs.

Silence.

"I don't sleep, Dad."

"Neither do I, kid."

"Sucks for us."

"It sucks bad."

Long silence.

"I tried to talk to Nokey. I did. The whole thing was doing number on him. He just— I'm sorry about that."

I say nothing.

"I mean that. I'm sorry."

"I know."

"Listen, can you give me some money or what? I got a friend in need."

"A friend in need? Where I come from that means you either knocked up a chick or you're doing drugs. And I can tell by your arms you're not using, so who is she?"

"Just don't ask me any questions."

"How much you need? Never mind, I'll use my imagination." He lifts himself out of the chair and grabs his back like it spasms. He tries to bend over for his cane but has to straighten up quick from pain. I reach for it and hand it to him.

"Four digits," I tell him.

The stairs moan under his feet and he comes back with a wad of cash. "This," he holds the cash up in front of my face, "is easy for me." I grab it. "Just remember . . ." he takes a pause like it's rehearsed, "when you get to where you're going it's still gonna be you and you, so . . ." he shakes his head. "Ah, fuck it, just go."

I grab the sweatshirt off the floor. And go.

I walk the few miles to Lockwood Avenue. I get within a block and hear service bells ringing, tools clanging, voices yelling, a radio playing classic rock. The pumps come into view, then the garage itself. Then the office. Ricky catches my eye through the glass. At

253

first he freezes. I lift my hand up as a small announcement of my presence. He drops his pen on his desk, stands up, walks across his office, pushes the door the hell out of his way, and walks fast right in my direction. I can feel the mass of the guy about to collide into me so I stop. He keeps coming until his chest crashes right into mine and we throw a hug on each other.

I feel him breathe heavy. "I'm sorry," I say. "I'm sorry, Ricky. I fucked it all up." I grab him hard.

He breaks the hug to look me square in the eyes. "That's the last time you're gonna say that. Absolute last time. You understand me?"

I say, "OK," and don't believe either syllable.

"I'm not fucking around." He tightens his arm around the back of my neck and gives me a shake.

"I know."

"I mean it," he says right into my ear.

"I know you do."

He eases up with his arm; one of his huge hands cups the back of my head. "It's OK," he's going. "It's OK." I nod. Again he says, "It's OK."

We let each other go. Ricky runs his thumb under his nose like a boxer. We stand facing each other for a bit, letting the familiar sounds of the garage take us down a level. Ricky sucks an epic breath in then out. "Your dad?" he asks.

"I saw him."

September 1

Stephanie and I sit in the back of a cab headed up the FDR Drive. I hold a brown paper bag; she's got a pocketbook in her lap. Today the city looks at us with the eyes of someone about to take a nap. Streets are wet from the early morning rain. Clouds and fog hold a low ceiling over the city that our tallest buildings disappear into. Streetlights and headlights glare through the mist on the highway, and tires spit up water from the asphalt sounding like long ripping sheets of paper. The East River and the sky are the same gray. A red halo frames the giant Pepsi-Cola sign; water taxis' lights disappear midway across the river. It's the kind of September day that feels like it never really broke.

It's somewhere in the upper sixties. People on the path that separates the river from the highway wear shorts and t-shirts, but keep their hands in their pockets and turn their heads to the wind. Soon we'll be wearing sweatshirts and sweaters, leaving sunglasses at home. We'll drink hot things, look for restaurants with fireplaces, and put outdoor café tables inside. The homeless will go back to sleeping near subway grates and exhaust fans. Women will start carrying more hand cream. Streets lucky enough to have trees will be lined in yellow and orange. The weather will bring us a feeling of accomplishment for having made it through another summer.

I lean my shoulder into Stephanie's. "What time you got?"

"Twelve."

"Why did we leave three hours early?"

She shrugs.

"Damn," Stephanie says, "my ankles are already swollen. That shit ain't supposed to happen yet."

"Yeah, but just think of all the amazing things that'll happen to your boobs."

"I'm really looking forward to stretch marks."

"You're young, you'll bounce back."

On the bike path a kid with pants sagging six inches below the band of his underwear stands on the wheel pegs of his friend's bike and holds onto his shoulders. Parents ride behind their kids yelling for them to keep their eyes on the road.

"You nervous?" I ask Stephanie.

She looks at me with a low-level panic. "Ask me about something else."

"Can I see the pictures again?"

She unzips her pocketbook and pulls them out.

Lunie and Odalis. Odalis: curly black hair to her shoulders, blue eyes, hefty in the right places. She holds her daughter's hand and stands in front of a rough but warm-looking house. "Not for nothing, but your Aunt Odalis is hot."

She backhands me on the thigh. "Pig."

"I'm not saying it like that. I'm just saying."

"I'm just saying give me back my pictures."

"She's not as hot as you."

"You're learning."

The driver yells back to us, "Which terminal?"

"Delta," I tell him.

We get off at the 34th Street exit and file through traffic until we dip into the Midtown Tunnel and its yellow lights that form a path under the river.

"You gonna pay him back for the ticket?" Stephanie asks.

"No."

"You gonna see him again?"

"I don't know. I guess. Maybe."

"How about your mother?"

"I think I have to at some point. And want to. But Jesus, one at a time, you know?"

At Kennedy Airport some people get dropped off in Lincoln Town Cars, some pull suitcases from the trunks of cabs and slip their driver a little extra for the help. Some are left by family members who hug and kiss them then wave through their window when they pull away.

I hand the driver a small fortune, tell him to keep it, and turn to Stephanie who stares out the window with a face slapped by fear. I tap her leg, which startles her. "It's safer than a car. And much safer than a New York City cab ride. You ready?"

After she gets her boarding pass we find a metal bench.

"It's not too late to swim there."

"Stop giving me shit."

"I'm sorry. Truth is I'm really impressed."

"Great. Listen, you a good letter-writer?"

"Um, why do you ask?" I say looking at the paper bag.

"Cause if your letters suck then you ain't coming to visit."

"Since when am I coming to visit?"

"Since I'm sayin you should. We got good beaches."

"Yeah, with barracuda, man. You better stay out of the water cause the barracudas'll starve trying to eat your skinny ass. For the love of the barracudas let the fat people swim."

"It ain't gonna be skinny for too long." She puts a hand on her stomach. We hold each other's eyes like we've been doing for the past two days, trying to say and understand things with a look.

257

"I got some things for you," I say.

"I was wondering when you were gonna show me what you got in that bag."

I reach into the paper bag. "Here. On the off chance it gets cold down there."

"That's . . ." She unfolds it and holds it over her chest. "Thank you. It's my size."

"I kind of figured. I don't think it'll puff out at the waist, either."

She folds it again, puts it on her lap and pets it flat with both her palms. "She loved you, JT."

I nod. And feel Stephanie looking at me when I do. My hand is in the paper bag holding my notebook hard. "What time you got?" I ask.

She checks her watch. "I got time to go."

"OK." I decide to loosen my grip. I slip my empty hand out and fold the brown paper over the notebook. We stand up, I grab the handle of Stephanie's luggage and we walk toward the checkpoint.

I've come as far as I can. She takes the suitcase handle from my hand. It's done except for goodbye.

"JT, would you do something for me?"

"Name it."

"Don't ever shave your head again."

I laugh a little. Then a lot.

"Done," I tell her.

She smiles something knowing at me. An expression I hope will never fade from her face or my head.

She walks through the metal detectors, gets nodded through by security and doesn't turn around.

I walk to a window and watch planes line up on the tarmac waiting for their turn. Behind them is fog. On their sides: fog. In front of them there's more. I drop the wrapped notebook in

258

a garbage can to my left. It hits the rest of the trash without much of a sound. The first plane in line looks like it's struggling to gain speed, but is moving incredibly fast for something so monumentally big. It finally lifts off the ground, getting small but staying in focus. Waves of heat roll out behind it. It gets fainter the deeper it goes into the fog, but I trust it knows its course.

Throughout the years it took me to write this book, many people gave me their help and encouragement in different ways. You all sustain me. And make me feel so friggin lucky. I'd like to return your favors with the best food I can manage, but that would be a logistical nightmare. So allow me to unpack my heart with words.

THE HOME TEAM:

Sarah Chalfant, for believing my instincts are worthy.

Jin Auh, for always seeming happy when I call. And passionate when we talk.

Mark Richards, for keenly helping to shape and maintain my voice. No insignificant task.

THE READERS:

Alex Lyras, you read and read again. You're so smart and ballsy that I'd rob a bank with you.

Brian Prager, us being born hours apart was no mistake.

Cathy Day, you're a great teacher, reader and friend. You have a way of making me forget that so much bullshit exists. (Trust me, that's a high compliment.)

Floyd Skloot, you read, you encourage, you share fine port, and you've donated your sperm to a great cause.

Heather Nolan, a careful reader and strong friend.

Kathy Chetkovich, #2, you're so damn insightful, cute, and kind, that someone should name an ice cream flavor after you.

Shannon Kemly Riccio, you're a great reader and friend. It's a joy to have made it past intermission with you.

Alane Mason and Denise Scarfi for invaluable feedback on the early drafts.

THE SPACE-GIVERS:

Betsy and Michael Hurley, you gave me your house where much of this book was written, because you never doubt, and always support, what writers do. I never told you this, but I broke one of your wine glasses. Sorry.

The fine folk of New Martinsville. First Jill (because you're my favorite. Don't tell anyone I said that). Then in no particular order: Jeff, Soren, Lou, Joe, Carla, Swen, Jacob, Donna, and Gary. Thanks for all the open doors, borrowed cars, washing machines, showers, ATVs, copperhead slayings, cook-outs, falling trees, falling trees, Wiffle ball games, mowed lawns, mailboxes, hot tubs, garden vegetables, and chainsaws. It wouldn't have been a real writing retreat without them.

Eileen, Mark, and Joe Roland, your hospitality at the Manasquan Writers' Colony was invaluable.

THE RESEARCH TEAM:

Alan Gompers, you decided to talk to me before you were sure who I was, and you shared your experiences so freely. I mean, who does that?

Paul Ostensen, Scott Klein, and Deirdre Van Dornem, you all gave great legal counsel.

THE HEAVIES:

Gurumayi Chidvilasananda, the idea for this book came while I was living in your house. I hope to have honored that genesis with this story.

Swami Umeshananda, of the all wise things you've said that have made a huge difference to my mind and heart—and there have been many—what you said about my writing remains a classic: "I never tell people what to do, but you have to do this."

Swami Vasudevananda, you've used the words "writing" and "destiny" in the same sentence and have made them utterly believable. You validate my light. Thanks for staying so close. You're the best kind of brother.

Goose, let me start my gratitude by thanking you for not getting bent when I threw my first manuscript against the wall and scared the dog. And let me finish my gratitude never.